MISS BUSBY INVESTIGATES

Murder at Little Minton

KAREN BAUGH MENUHIN
& ZOE MARKHAM

For Mum,
who's going to love Barnaby.
From Zoe.

CHAPTER 1

Cotswolds: Christmas 1921

'And he was dead,' Mrs Adeline Fanshawe said with unnecessary drama.

'I imagine he was, if he were floating face down in the lake at Little Minton.' Miss Isabelle Busby's response was dry.

Christmas was fast approaching, a heavy frost had settled on the surrounding trees and meadows, glazing winter gardens and thatch in seasonal white. The ladies were seated either side of a blazing fire in Miss Busby's comfortable cottage.

'But what was he doing there?' Adeline speculated.

'Nothing at all, if he were dead.' Miss Busby wasn't the sort for idle conjecture. 'Was he married?'

'I don't believe so, but he had a following,' Adeline replied. Bright sunlight falling through the window highlighted silver strands in her hair. A mature lady of comfortable proportions, she had dressed for the weather in a russet-coloured frock, matching cardigan, paisley scarf and a fur-trimmed coat, which she'd left hanging in Miss Busby's small hallway.

Lavender Cottage was her first port of call that morning and she'd just informed Miss Busby of the astonishing news currently speeding through the village of Bloxford.

'What sort of following?' Miss Busby leaned forward to pour more tea from a rose painted teapot into matching cups. 'The romantic type?'

'Well, according to gossip, he was known to visit at least five ladies in Little Minton on a regular basis,' Adeline replied.

'Five, good heavens! He was a busy chap.' Miss Busby feigned shock, although she felt nothing of the sort. A lady of around seventy years, rather short but still as slim and lively as the young girl she'd once been. Neatly attired in a lilac twin set, a string of modest pearls, and a rather old-fashioned tweed skirt, she was acutely clever, having taught at the local school, where all life could be observed for those who cared to look.

'Actually, he was a life insurance salesman for the Prudential, so I suspect the gossip has been embellished.' Adeline sipped her tea and eyed the cake dish.

'Another lemon melt?' Miss Busby was quick to spot her friend's focus. She'd made the shortbread roundels only that morning, before creaming icing sugar, butter, and lemon for the sharply sweet filling just moments before Adeline's unexpected arrival.

'Oh, Isabelle, you know I adore shortbread.' Adeline's plump face creased into a smile as she delicately picked a roundel from the dish. 'And where did you find lemons at this time of year?'

'I pickled them in gin last September,' Miss Busby replied. 'Now, this man who died – who was he and why was he floating in the lake at Little Minton?'

'He was Mr Vernon Potter, and I've no idea why he was there; perhaps he'd been meeting a client and some accident befell him.'

'But why didn't the client help?'

'Oh, good question, Isabelle, I always said you were clever,' Adeline paused mid biscuit. 'Perhaps the client was too frail, or some such. It's said that his customers were mostly spinsters and widows.'

'Spinsters and widows?' Miss Busby tilted her head in a bird-like gesture. 'Surely they would need money when alive, it's no use to them once they're dead.'

'I suppose it depends on one's circumstances,' Adeline replied, content in the knowledge that her late husband, who'd been a highly respected surgeon, had left her very comfortably off.

'But it doesn't make sense.' Miss Busby's eyes fixed for an instant while her mind raced through the puzzle. 'What do the police have to say about it?'

'I've no idea, you could ask your nephew.' Adeline put her hand to her mouth to prevent crumbs escaping.

Miss Busby's nephew had been the local police Inspector until recently. 'They've moved him to Nottingham.

He's quite useless, and it's better he be useless in Nottingham than in Bloxford.'

'Bloxford is hardly a hotbed of crime, Isabelle.'

'Apart from the terrible murders earlier this year,' Miss Busby reminded her.

'Yes, at the Hall,' Adeline recalled. 'But that's best forgotten, and it's not at all likely to be repeated, is it?'

'No.' Miss Busby's blue eyes darkened at the memory. 'The death of this Vernon Potter fellow sounds most peculiar, though.'

'I agree, and it could cause considerable hardship, from what I understand.'

'I imagine it could.' Miss Busby placed her empty cup back on its saucer and leaned forward. 'Do you know who has been affected?'

'I heard the sister of the vicar at Little Minton was one of the ladies concerned,' Adeline said, and bit into the last lemon melt.

Miss Busby paused for a moment. 'But how...and what is being done about it?'

'I don't know,' Adeline replied. 'But I sincerely hope something is!'

Shortly after Adeline had departed – eager, no doubt, to spread the news further through the close-knit village – Miss Busby once more picked up her latest novel and settled back into her armchair beside the fire.

With the cottage now quiet, there soon came a soft padding of paws down the stairs; Pudding, her ginger tom, appeared in the doorway with an indignant *mew*, as if berating her for taking quite so long to attend to the important business of the day. Or rather, *his* important business of the day.

Miss Busby shifted in the chair to offer the maximum amount of lap space – Pudding being rather on the large side. 'Still not keen on visitors, Pud? Well, we can't leave them out on the doorstep, can we?'

He was the sort of cat who probably would, being entirely concerned with his own comfort, as is the way of cats.

She ruffled his ears, setting off his engine-like purr, and turned the page, settling deeper into the chintz cushions, the crackle of flames soothing in the background.

Lavender cottage was neither small nor large, being a typical thatched type of cotswold stone with lead paned windows and a porch over the front door. This led into a panelled hallway, where stairs climbed to two cosy bedrooms, a washroom and closet, all wallpapered in lilacs and roses. The living room was comfortably spacious, the fireplace dominated, with two armchairs and an upright sofa set before it. Miss Busby's davenport desk stood in the front window and a formal table with high-backed chairs took up the area leading to the kitchen. There was little of note to be found there, it being laid out in the usual style with a black iron stove, pantry, enamel sink and a scrubbed pine table.

Miss Busby turned another page of her book. She had left her favourite character in something of a predicament, and Adeline had arrived just as she was about to discover how the ingenious protagonist would extricate himself. But with each page she read, no matter how focused her concentration, the image of a different character would persist in creeping into her mind: a dark figure, face-down in the lake, with tearful faces swirling about him. She attempted to dismiss them with a shake of her head and lifted her book in determination.

Sometime later she was gazing into space with Pud's paws on the open pages of the novel in her lap, the intricate plot forgotten. The sound of tyres slowly crunching over roadside gravel broke into her reverie.

She straightened up, her mind beginning to turn. Now that her nephew had been sent elsewhere, there weren't any senior policemen left in the locality. Who would help these poor ladies? She thought of Major Lennox. She'd received a letter from him recently, he'd just returned from Damascus, which sounded terribly exotic, and was leaving to join his uncle at Melrose Court. Inspector Swift was now in the far distant Highlands, but he had praised her when she'd helped with the awful murders at Bloxford Hall.

Should she look into things on behalf of the poor victims? Perhaps she could just ask a few questions – it wouldn't do any harm, after all, and she was acquainted with most people in the neighbouring villages. And if she discovered anything of use, she could offer her findings to any Inspector that eventually turned up.

She rose to her feet. The book, she decided, could wait, because Mr Potter, it seemed, would not be quite so obliging. Nor would the women to whom he'd apparently sold surely spurious services. She would act!

Congratulating herself on the wisdom of not using up all her store of lemons whilst making the shortbread filling, she went to the kitchen and took a small kilner jar from the pantry and popped it into her handbag. Then, after pulling on her thick woollen coat, warm gloves, favourite hat and sturdiest boots, she headed out into the crisp fresh air.

The crunch of frozen grass beneath her feet was deliciously satisfying – an audible expression of her sudden resolve as she closed the front gate behind her.

Glancing down the narrow lane, she saw that the red post van had not gone far. Young Dennis tended to be as late with the post as he'd been late to class as a boy, but his tardiness on this occasion was most welcome. Miss Busby felt herself grateful, as the walk to Little Minton would have been decidedly chilly, even in the sparkling sunshine.

The van idled just two doors down. Miss Busby walked to its side, then waited as Dennis Ogden ran down Mrs Mary Fellows' path, chased by Barnaby, an almost spherical long-haired Jack Russell terrier. Barnaby had a determined dislike of men – and postmen in particular.

Dennis shouted something quite inappropriate as he shut the gate firmly on the yapping animal. Miss Busby cleared her throat loudly enough to alert him to her presence.

'Oh. Sorry, Miss. Didn't see you.' Dennis had the good grace to blush. 'Was you waiting for the post? Only there 'int none for you this morning.'

'Good morning, Dennis. Actually, I was waiting for you,' she replied. 'I would very much appreciate a lift into Little Minton, if you have the time?' She had always been fond of Dennis, as indeed she had been fond of most of her young charges over her years of teaching.

'Oh.' Dennis lifted his cap to scratch his curly brown hair. 'Well, I s'posse I could, and there's another sack to pick up from the post office there. I'm runnin' a bit late, it bein' so near to Christmas an' all.'

Miss Busby delicately pushed a glove aside and glanced at her wristwatch. 'Very good. Come along, then.'

Moments later she watched from the side window of the van as they passed Bloxford's cluster of pretty cottages, ancient church and small farms to join the meandering lanes leading to the neighbouring town. Dennis had a tendency to grumble over the most trivial matters, and she turned an experienced deaf ear to his latest complaints.

'Just here is fine, thank you, Dennis,' Miss Busby announced as they turned onto Little Minton's High Street some ten minutes later. Although bigger and livelier than Bloxford, with many more amenities, the town of Little Minton was nevertheless compact. One could walk from one end to the other in a little under half an hour, assuming one didn't dawdle. 'I shall enjoy the fresh air.'

'Right you are, Miss,' Dennis replied glumly. 'I s'pose you want…I mean 'ter say…would you like me to take you back an 'all, later on, like?'

The bright, inviting glow from Lily's Tea Rooms opposite caught her eye. 'Thank you, Dennis. What a thoughtful offer. I think I shall take lunch here once my business is concluded, and then I should very much appreciate a lift home around…shall we say two o'clock?'

'No trouble, Miss,' Dennis said, his tone indicating that the opposite were actually true, but he dare not say so. Miss Busby resolved to buy him a slice of cake as recompense. It couldn't be easy, she conceded, being hounded by small dogs and determined old ladies. She might even buy him two slices.

The vicarage wasn't too far distant from the high street. She passed the grocer's, butcher's, florist and bookshop, and followed the road uphill. Stores gave way to rows of honey-coloured houses, their gardens and roofs still dusted with frost, their windows glinting reflected sunshine. Many of the doors had holly wreathes attached, adorned with bunches of red berries and tied with tartan ribbons.

Miss Busby walked briskly toward Church Way trying not to think of the Potter fellow meeting his end in the icy lake – turning her mind instead to the ladies he'd purportedly sold insurance to. Would they struggle, now, to keep as warm as they ought? They would have been meting out small monthly stipends, rather than any significant lump sum, but it all added up. It must have been lucrative for this Potter fellow, she thought, as he would have received commission on every penny paid to the insurance company. What had he done with their money? Had he passed it on, as he was supposed to? Or had he kept it?

Why spinsters and widows? The question nipped at her mind in much the same way as the frost nipped at her toes. Why take out life insurance if you weren't supporting a family who'd have need of it after you'd gone? Something refused to add up, no matter how she looked at it.

Of course, she only had Adeline's word for the circumstances, but her friend, while no stranger to gossip, was no sensationalist. *'No smoke without fire, Isabelle,'* she imagined Adeline confirming with a nod, as if she were walking beside her – before she realised that there was indeed smoke in the air, and she'd reached the gateway to the vicarage.

CHAPTER 2

'Yes?' A nasal whine greeted her as the vicar opened the door, allowing a welcome waft of warm air to rush out.

'Reverend Simpson.' Miss Busby greeted him with a smile.

'Yes?' he repeated in the same vein.

'My goodness, such a chill in the air today,' she continued.

'Yes,' he replied again, as if it were the only word in his vocabulary.

'Miss Busby, from Bloxford. We have met at garden fetes, and the school,' she reminded him. 'And I'm a member of our local choir – we have sung in your church occasionally.'

'Ah, yes, erm…of course.' He peered more closely at her. 'You were the teacher…'

Miss Busby nodded, and gave a rather exaggerated shiver.

'Oh…would you like to come in?' he asked, then moved aside to let her through. 'Perhaps my wife…' he trailed off in distraction, before clearing his throat.

She stepped across the threshold, noting his long nose and hangdog eyes. His thin grey hair was in need of a trim, and his cassock a hot iron.

An awkward pause ensued.

However did the man manage a congregation?

'Shall I go through?' Miss Busby suggested. Leaving him no time to respond, she followed the warmth and light to the drawing room – where loud sobbing came from a woman hunched on the sofa.

'Goodness!' Miss Busby exclaimed.

The figure continued crying, oblivious to her presence.

'I'm afraid you find us in poor position to receive.' Reverend Simpson had trailed behind her. 'There has been…' He gave a desperate glance towards the shabby hallway and stairs. 'I'll just… I shan't be a moment.'

Miss Busby approached the distraught figure beside the fire. She was obviously in need of comfort, and Miss Busby was about to attempt consolation when the commanding presence of the vicar's wife, Mrs Evelyn Simpson, swept into the room.

'Miss Busby, good day,' she said in business-like manner; a large lady with chestnut-coloured hair fashioned in tight curls about a round face. 'You must excuse Harold, he's had a traumatic morning. As have we all.'

'Oh, goodness. I do apologise, Mrs Simpson.' Miss Busby feigned ignorance of the situation. 'Whatever has happened?'

'Have you not heard? Heavens, I would have thought the news would have galloped through the district by now.' Evelyn sniffed, then shot her a look of suspicion. Miss Busby gave a small blush, before rallying. She delved into her handbag and produced the kilner jar of lemons.

'I was on my way into town, it's such a beautiful morning and I felt in need of an outing,' she effused in an effort to cover her guilt. 'And I thought you might have a use for these… But I had no idea that there had been a… well…?' She gave a delicate shrug.

'There has been a tragedy, Miss Busby!' Evelyn replied with an edge of exasperation to her voice.

'Apparently so.' Miss Busby glanced again at the sobbing figure by the fire. 'Can I do anything to assist? I'm trained in emergency medical aid.' That was a slight exaggeration – the training she'd received while nursing injured soldiers during the war had been basic at best, but it wasn't quite a lie.

'We are a little beyond that,' Evelyn retorted. She took the jar with a curt nod and placed it on the sideboard, then turned to call sharply, 'Harold!'

With a rustle of cassock, the vicar reappeared. 'Yes, Evelyn?'

'Take your sister through to the church,' she ordered, then marched across the room to place a hand on the sobbing woman's shoulder. 'Harold will take you now, Frances,' she said loudly, as if the tears were somehow rendering the poor woman deaf. 'And perhaps he can take a look at that paperwork again, it will set your mind at rest.'

Miss Busby looked closer. The distraught woman

had documents of some sort clutched in her hands, her face swollen and almost unrecognisable. Miss Busby moved forward in instinctive sympathy, but was stopped by a hissed warning from Mrs Simpson.

The vicar darted forward and helped his sister to her feet. 'Come along now Frances, dear girl…'

Frances Simpson clasped his hand as he helped her to her feet. She pushed a length of long, grey hair aside, and tried to focus on Miss Busby.

'It's just so awful… why him? Why?' Her voice trembled, before her brother's gentle manoeuvring helped her from the room.

Miss Busby felt a twinge of unease. Perhaps this wasn't her best idea. It hadn't occurred to her that the vicar's sister would have been quite so upset.

'Now then.' Evelyn waited until they left, then picked up the jar of lemons. 'What a pleasant little gift, Miss Busby. So thoughtful. Do you need to sit a while and warm yourself, or will you be straight off?'

Miss Busby bristled. This was not how she'd imagined matters proceeding. And it was too early for lunch at the tea rooms. Quick thinking was required. She remembered hearing that one of the banes of Mrs Simpson's existence (and there were several) was the lack of help she received in the church.

'I've been finding myself at something of a loss lately, and was thinking of extending my efforts in the garden. Would you like any more flowers for the church arrangements, I wonder?'

This apparently was exactly the right thing to say, and a pot of tea later, the woman's froideur had thawed.

'*So* thoughtful of you. You simply cannot imagine how many parishioners flinch at the merest suggestion of support.'

'Not at all, I try to help where I can. Speaking of which, I do hope the vicar is managing to comfort his poor sister.'

'Yes.' Evelyn stirred another spoon of sugar into her tea. 'I'm in need of sweetness, for the shock, you see,' she explained by way of excuse. 'And what a shock it was. An acquaintance of hers, Mr Potter, was found dead just yesterday.'

'Good lord.' Miss Busby clutched her modest pearls in best amateur dramatic manner. 'I assume it was unexpected?'

'It was entirely unexpected. The man was discovered drowned in Little Minton lake. Can you imagine?'

'Potter... not Vernon Potter, the man from the Prudential?' Miss Busby feigned incredulity.

'The very same.' Evelyn nodded, her carefully arranged curls bobbing with the movement.

'Was it some sort of accident?'

'I should imagine it must have been.' Evelyn raised arched brows. 'One may wonder how a grown man manages to fall into a lake, of course, but I shouldn't be surprised if drink was involved.' She paused to pick at an imaginary speck on the mauve velveteen skirt she'd paired with a purple floral blouse. Her colourful outfit looked strangely out of place in the antiquated vicarage. 'You'd think he'd know better, but he can't have been as clever as supposed.'

'Really? But he must have had a good head for facts and figures, given his profession?' Miss Busby asked, then changed tack when she saw a sharp look dart across Evelyn's small brown eyes. 'But of course, if it wasn't an accident, the alternative would be quite preposterous…'

'Of course it would.' She waved a dismissive hand. 'Although Harold and I have been debating that very point. As have the police. *What* a morning it's been. They've only just left, hence Miss Simpson's state – not that it takes much, the woman was *born* to hysterics.' She gave a long sigh, quite full to the brim with her own suffering. 'It's been so horribly intrusive, you simply cannot imagine. Frances, Miss Simpson, I mean, has never once brought anything but distress to our door. The woman is a constant thorn, but when it's family, what can one do?'

Miss Busby gave a nod. No stranger to family thorns, she tended to have little truck with them herself.

'But yes,' Evelyn continued. 'You'd be hard pressed to find a gentleman with a more mundane occupation than Vernon Potter.'

'But he must have encountered all sorts in his line of work,' Miss Busby countered. 'Knocking on doors. Taking payments from people. There'd be some element of potential intrigue there, surely. Danger, even.'

Evelyn Simpson recoiled slightly.

Miss Busby feared she may have gone too far. 'Not from your sister-in-law, of course,' she added hastily. 'I just wondered if his occupation may have been a little risky in some respects.'

Mrs Simpson relented. 'Well, yes, and you've only to look at the new houses going up along the street, heaven knows what sort will be moving into the town...' She paired a meaningful pause with a knowing look. Miss Busby thought she could only be referring to the modest group of houses that were being constructed on the site of the old Woollen Mill. She refrained from comment, choosing instead to clear her throat politely.

'But, no, not for Vernon Potter,' Evelyn went on. 'He always knew exactly who he was dealing with. He was that sort.'

'That sort?' Miss Busby sat a little straighter in her chair. It had taken more time, and tea, than she'd anticipated, but they were getting to the heart of the matter at last.

'Yes.' Impatience flared in Evelyn's tone. 'The man was self-absorbed. Handsome, of course, and used to being fawned on, and quite charming, or so they said. But I thought he was shallow.'

'Really?' Miss Busby encouraged.

'Harold knew him better than I. He wanted to sound the fellow out when he first approached Frances. He had to make sure it was all above board. Frances has been enough of a burden to us, and the last thing we needed was for her to put herself into an even worse state. But

Potter seemed perfectly legitimate, and he had similar dealings with other ladies of suitable standing.'

Miss Busby nodded encouragingly, not wishing to interrupt the flow.

'Oh, you know the type, genteel women, widows…' Evelyn continued. 'And spinsters who'd fallen on hard times.' She narrowed her eyes suddenly at Miss Busby. 'Women such as yourself.'

Miss Busby was rather taken aback. 'I did not have a policy with Mr Potter. I never even met the man.'

'I wasn't referring to that, I meant that you are alone, without a man, and you must fend for yourself.' Evelyn Simpson's beady eyes were gleaming with something difficult to discern. 'After all, you were once engaged to be married to the heir of—'

'That was a very long time ago,' Miss Busby cut in, her tone quite firm. 'And I have fended for myself perfectly well ever since.'

'Hum.' Evelyn pursed her lips. 'Well, as I was saying, ladies left alone were Vernon Potter's bread and butter. It was no secret. He supposedly had a whole flock of them.'

Miss Busby composed her voice into neutral tone. 'But what possible need would these women have of life insurance? As you say, they are alone, who would they leave their insurance money to?'

'Ah, but Miss Busby, you're looking at it quite the wrong way. Vernon didn't sell insurance on their lives, he sold policies *on his own life.*'

Whatever Miss Busby had been expecting, she was quite sure it wasn't this.

'Good Heavens,' she managed, before sitting back in her chair. 'How on earth would he have done that?'

'Oh, it's quite simple. Harold went through it all with Potter at the very onset. The man had suffered ill-health after being gassed in the war – he was forever coughing – and proposed that Frances took out a policy on *his* life. He assured us it was all perfectly legal, and it would allow her to benefit when he died. Harold encouraged her to go ahead because it didn't seem as if Potter was long for this world – not incorrectly, as it turns out…' Evelyn Simpson turned her gaze towards the fire, and fell silent for a moment.

Miss Busby waited politely, then broke into the reverie. 'His death must have been a terrible shock, despite the…' she cleared her throat delicately '…silver lining?'

'Indeed. Frances will receive a nice lump sum now,' Evelyn rallied, 'which means she may finally be inclined to move out of the vicarage. In fact, we're rather hoping she'll move to the coast…' She looked dreamily into the distance, before coming back to herself. 'You must excuse me, Miss Busby,' she said, flushing slightly. 'It has been a most trying morning.'

Miss Busby acknowledged the apology with a wave of her hand, before letting her own gaze drift to the brightly burning fire, her mind beginning to tear freshly through the gears.

CHAPTER 3

Much as she would have liked to step into the church and ask Miss Simpson a few questions, Miss Busby had to concede that now was not the time. She had, after all, learned a great deal already, courtesy of the forthright Mrs Simpson, and her initial thoughts on the man's death had been turned on their head.

Why on earth would he have been selling policies on his own life? And how many had he sold? The list of people who might benefit from the man's death could be endless.

She thought back to when she was drawn into the mystery up at Bloxford Hall, and remembered discussing motive with Major Heathcliff Lennox. *The road*, she'd assured him, *was laid by reason*, and the road in this case could be an extremely busy one. Surely Potter must have been rather careless to encourage significant numbers of women to want him dead? Perhaps Evelyn had been onto something in suggesting he hadn't been as clever as one might assume.

As she walked along the high street, Miss Busby continued past Lily's Tea Rooms to arrive at Little Minton Police Station. Built of cotswold stone under a slate roof, the station was discretely set back from the main street behind a black painted railing backed by a tall privet hedge. Its dark blue front door was gleaming in the winter sunshine; she pressed the brass doorbell and entered the sparse reception area.

'Good morning, Miss Busby.' Bobby Miller looked over from behind the long wooden counter. 'Nice to see you.' The lad gave a lopsided grin; smartly turned out, thick black hair neatly combed, buttons polished, and with a look of newfound confidence about him. He'd been one of her slower pupils, but she'd spent many hours after school teaching him the three 'r's until he had grasped the principles.

'Thank you Bobby.' She smiled in return. 'How are you settling in?'

'It's smashing, Miss. I passed my basic training, I'm a proper constable now.' He straightened up, the better to show off his smart new uniform.

'Well done, I'm so pleased for you.' Her eyes shone, as her former young charge's grin widened.

'Thanks Miss. There's lots more happening here than in Bloxford.'

'I can imagine. I hear there was a death at the lake,' Miss Busby began in innocent fashion. 'It must be keeping you busy.'

Bobby Miller glanced over at a young lady Miss Busby

hadn't initially spotted. Dressed in a tailored camel coat, the collar turned up against her dark hair, she was apparently absorbed in reading the 'lost and found' board.

'Yes, and no, Miss,' he admitted.

Miss Busby looked at him in schoolmarm fashion.

'I mean, it *was* busy…' He glanced again at the young lady, then lowered his voice and said with hushed pride, 'I fingerprinted the dead man's car yesterday. It was found up the lane by the lake and they brought it back and parked it in the yard. Worked on it all afternoon I did, and used a whole pot of powder.'

Miss Busby made sure to look suitably impressed. He really had done well for himself. 'Did you find anything significant?'

'No, it was just his prints everywhere, but it's put the cat among the pigeons. There's a detective inspector been sent over from Oxford, he's had the two new chaps, Sergeant Brierly and Constable Lewis, out searching for clues, and knocking on people's doors. And them not even knowing who lives where. Plus *he's* new, and *foreign…*'

'Bobby, just because someone is foreign…' She was about to dress him down, when Bobby held up his hands. 'It wasn't me said that, it was Sergeant Brierly. His nose is out of joint because Inspector McKay has been sending him running all over the place. It's the inspector's first detecting job, and he's from *Scotland*, with red hair and an accent and everything. He's a real stickler. We haven't stopped since he turned up.'

'Well, at least there is a detective here, now.' She nodded, pleased to hear that something was being done. 'But, you implied you were less busy now?'

Bobby's excitement faded. 'They can't find anything suspicious, Sarge says, so it's just an accidental drowning, and that'll be that.'

'Surely it's too soon to come to such a conclusion?' Fear suddenly grew that this new inspector would prove no better than her useless nephew.

Bobby leaned on the counter; he still had a smattering of freckles across his nose. 'You're not worried it's like them murders up at the Hall, are you, Miss? Because it weren't, the bloke just slipped on some ice and fell in.'

'How can you be certain?' Miss Busby didn't like to be taken for an hysteric, particularly by a young ex-pupil, but questions surely needed to be asked. 'What did the doctor say?'

'He said the gentleman died from drowning. There was a bit of a bump and a graze on his head, but that was probably nothing significant. They're doing the post mortem today and that should settle it.' Bobby adopted a mollifying tone, which failed to mollify Miss Busby one iota.

'The inspector does know about the life insurance policies, doesn't he?' she asked, her tone a little sharper than she'd intended.

'I don't know, Miss.' Bobby glanced at her, then reached for a pencil and the large ledger lying open on the desk. 'But if it'll rest your mind, I'll make a note about it.'

Miss Busby took a slow breath, and composed herself. 'That isn't necessary, Bobby, I shall discuss the matter with the inspector myself.'

'He's not the chatty sort, Miss, and if you've got any information, you have to tell us,' he lectured, clearly feeling more confident now Miss Busby had tamed her temper.

'Oh, I'm sure he must be aware of the situation,' she replied. 'Are you expecting him later?'

'Sorry, Miss, I don't know.' He finished writing and put the pencil down, then gave her a solemn look. 'Now, you're not to repeat anything I've said. It isn't a secret or nothing, but I don't want anyone thinking I can't hold me tongue.'

'Of course, Bobby, I shan't breathe a word,' she promised, and after asking about his parents' health, congratulated him once more on his promotion and bid him good day.

Ten minutes later, Miss Busby entered Lily's Tea Rooms, where a cheery fire crackled in the cast iron grate and the chattering of a small crowd of customers greeted her. The room offered a cozy setting, plush green velvet furnishings, a large bow window overlooking the high street and a dozen tables and chairs gathered in convivial groupings.

A Christmas tree in the corner added to the cheer and it occurred to Miss Busby, as she hung her coat and hat on the rack by the door, that she should think about taking her own festive ornaments from the box under the stairs.

'I've a nice table just come free by the window, if you'd like to be seated?' The waitress led her between the crowded tables. 'Shall I bring tea and a menu?'

'Please,' Miss Busby agreed, already feeling much more her usual self.

The door opened just after she sat down and a dark-haired young woman paused to shrug off her long camel coat. She looked about, spotted Miss Busby, and weaved through the customers towards her.

'Would you mind if I join you?' She smiled. 'I know it seems a little presumptuous, but I rather hope we may be able to help each other.'

'Not at all.' Miss Busby nodded, and waited as the woman took the chair opposite. 'Did you find what you were looking for?'

'Sorry?' She appeared confused.

'The lost and found board,' Miss Busby explained. 'You seemed quite engrossed.'

'Oh, yes…I mean, no, actually. I was hoping to talk to the inspector, but he was elsewhere…' Her accent was educated, her clothes in tailored style; a wool jacket nicely trimmed at the waist, a mid-length skirt in the same chocolate brown as the jacket, and a dark red sweater over a pretty white blouse. 'I'm a reporter for the *Oxford News*. My name is Lucy Wesley.'

'Miss Busby.' They shook hands, then smiled as it seemed overly formal in the setting.

'Vernon Potter…' Lucy began.

'You suspect a story?'

'I suspect you do too,' Lucy replied. Her face was too long to be beautiful, but an expression of candour, with a ready smile, lent her an attractive air.

'I've only very recently found myself apprised of the situation,' Miss Busby replied carefully, before relenting, 'but yes, I believe there may be more to it than meets the eye.'

The waitress arrived with tea for two. 'I saw you arrive Miss and thought I'd best bring an extra.' She placed a polka dot tea-set on the table and then handed them each a printed card. 'Here's the lunchtime menu to take a look at, if you're interested. I'll be back shortly.'

'I heard you mention insurance.' Lucy poured tea for them both.

Miss Busby picked up her cup to wrap cold hands around its warmth, carefully considering the young woman. Bobby had clearly not wanted her to overhear anything, but Potter's occupation was hardly a secret.

'Yes,' she replied after a pause. 'Mr Potter was an agent for the Prudential.'

'Not just for the Prudential, he acted for a number of other companies too,' Lucy elaborated.

'Ah.' Miss Busby felt a little foolish regarding her concern. The young lady was apparently well informed, but then if she worked for the newspaper, that should not have been a surprise. She deliberated for a moment, taking a sip of tea. 'Yes, that makes sense.'

'Does it? Why?' Lucy asked.

Miss Busby placed her cup back onto its saucer. 'I really would prefer not to be quoted in the newspaper.'

Lucy quelled a smile. 'No quotes, I promise. I'm merely trying to determine facts.'

Her words, *We may be able to help each other*, resonated, but nevertheless, she hesitated. It took a few more sips of tea to decide that it was time to act, because secrets would not help the matter. 'Vernon Potter sold insurance on his own life,' she said, watching the young woman for her reaction.

Lucy paused with her cup in her hands, her lips forming an 'o' of surprise.

'Rather disingenuous of him, don't you think?' Miss Busby continued.

'I'd have said suicidal.' Lucy recovered quickly. 'Who was he selling these policies to?'

'Elderly ladies, as I understand it,' Miss Busby replied. 'I suppose he thought them unlikely to pose a danger.' She picked up her menu and glanced through it, aware of Lucy's gaze on her.

'Are you one of his…?'

Miss Busby looked a little affronted, before laughing at the implication. 'No, I'm merely taking an interest.'

'Why?' Lucy took a sip of tea.

Miss Busby decided she admired the woman's openness, but settled for a white lie in response.

'On behalf of a friend.'

Lucy nodded. 'Do you know how many ladies are involved?'

'I'm afraid not. Although, I believe there are at least five, locally, and I do hope they will be properly considered. They may now be in dire straights, and I do feel something must be done for them.'

'Absolutely.' Lucy nodded agreement.

The waitress returned. 'Now, what are we having?'

'The soup, please, followed by a slice of Dundee cake,' Miss Busby replied.

'I'll have the same, please,' Lucy said.

'Right you are.' The waitress picked up the menus, wavered for a moment as though in indecision, then went off again.

'Has your newspaper reported Mr Potter's death yet?' Miss Busby asked, comfortably convinced now that she had found an ally.

'Only a statement that a body has been found in the lake at Little Minton.' Lucy leaned forward and lowered her voice. 'He doesn't seem to have any surviving family, but we have to be careful, we don't want to upset grieving relatives,' she said, then added, 'or close friends.'

'Has there been any mention of...foul play?' Miss Busby kept her voice even lower, although the other occupants of the cafe were more interested in their lunches than anything else.

'No, and I don't think they'd have sent me if there were,' Lucy replied. 'I'm only a junior, you see, but I did think there may be more to this than meets the eye. That's why I was at the police station.'

Miss Busby sat back in her chair, she had found an ally indeed! With her faith restored in her abilities after something of a shaky start, she began to run through all the questions tumbling in her mind. She picked a simple one to begin with. 'Do you know how old Vernon Potter was?'

'Fifty-two, according to the lady I spoke to at the Prudential.'

Miss Busby took another sip of tea. 'Apparently he'd told his clients he was in ill health,' she said. 'Because he'd been gassed in the war.'

'He's hardly likely to have been fighting at the Front at his age,' Lucy replied. 'And there was no mention of a war record.'

The reappearance of the waitress with steaming bowls of pea and ham soup, and soft buttered rolls, brought them to a halt.

'Fresh pot of tea?' she asked.

'Yes, please,' Lucy answered before Miss Busby could draw breath.

They ate in silence for several moments.

'You mentioned a friend who was one of Potter's clients.' Lucy glanced at Miss Busby with pretty brown eyes.

A light flush rose in her cheeks; the white lie had caught her out. She dabbed delicately at her mouth with a napkin before replying. 'She's really more of an acquaintance.'

'Do you think I could speak to her?' Lucy was quick to ask.

'Oh, I'm afraid she was dreadfully upset,' she prevaricated.

They continued to spoon their soup, a sliver of tension rising between them.

'I'm not terribly good at being pushy…' Lucy smiled. 'It's rather a drawback for a journalist.'

Miss Busby couldn't help but smile herself. 'Well, there are ways to ask for things without appearing pushy,' she replied. 'A direct question will often elicit a direct answer.'

'Yes, but if the answer is "no", what am I supposed to do?' Lucy finished her soup. 'I'd really like to talk to one of Potter's clients, but I don't know who they are.'

'But you spoke to the Prudential, surely they, and the others you mentioned, could furnish a list?'

'They've cited client confidentiality.' Lucy looked rather crestfallen.

Miss Busby sympathised, but attempted a diversion. 'Where did Potter live?'

'Cheltenham, in a flat near the racecourse. I spoke on the telephone to the concierge, he said Potter was a widower. Charming, and attentive to the ladies, but never entertained any at home.'

Miss Busby nodded, it fitted the picture Evelyn Simpson had given. 'Perhaps your search should begin there?'

'I'm going this afternoon, but I believe the mystery lies here in Little Minton.'

Miss Busby agreed. She gave the matter some thought. 'Is it actually possible to simply slip on ice, fall into a lake, and drown, do you think?' The pair ate their slices of Dundee cake companionably, while discussing the odds.

'There was mention of a bump on the head,' Lucy said.

Miss Busby glanced up at that. 'You overheard that in the police station?'

Lucy was unabashed. 'I did,' she admitted. 'And that he had a graze, too. It sounded quite suspicious to me.'

'Quite, and why was he there?' Miss Busby puzzled. 'I really don't see how such a thing can happen by accident. After all, he wasn't particularly old, and despite the supposed cough, there didn't seem to be any disability as far as I'm aware.'

'I suppose the water must have been freezing.' Lucy played devil's advocate. 'And he would have been wearing a winter coat.'

They continued to debate the theory of how one could accidentally fall into icy water until Lucy glanced at her watch. 'I'm afraid I must be off.' She smiled at Miss Busby. 'You've been terribly kind, thank you.'

Miss Busby returned the smile. 'You know, we may be able to help each other, and indeed, I think we should.'

'I'll do whatever I can,' Lucy assured her.

'I'm sure you will.' Miss Busby gazed up at her. 'And

perhaps if you were to ask at the local vicarage, you may find someone who could enlighten you further.'

Lucy beamed. 'Thank you, Miss Busby!'

CHAPTER 4

For some time after Lucy had left, Miss Busby sat in quiet contemplation. The eliciting of information from those who held it was a delicate matter, and an interesting one. Should she have mentioned the vicarage to Lucy? Surely there was no harm in the disclosure – the intelligent young woman would have discovered the name Frances Simpson on her own, given time. And Miss Busby now had gained the knowledge that Potter had worked for other insurance companies. If knowledge was to flow both ways, then it seemed she'd have to accept the notion of sharing, albeit with appropriate caution, she thought to herself.

The tea room was slowly emptying, people were returning to their shopping or homes, and she began to wish she'd brought her book. Dennis was almost certain to be late, he'd never outgrown tardiness at school and was unlikely to have changed now. Nursing her fourth cup of tea, she wasn't sure she could take any more on board when the waitress reappeared.

'I think I'm at capacity,' she admitted apologetically.

'Oh, don't you worry, dear.' The woman smiled. A plump lady in black frock and white apron with a cap carefully pinned onto thick brown hair.

Miss Busby nodded gratefully in response, but still the waitress hovered. Despite her best efforts, she found she was beginning to fidget under the woman's gaze.

'It's Miss Busby, isn't it? I don't mean to intrude, but...' The waitress came a little closer. 'I'm Maggie Trounce, you taught my Milly. Do you remember her? She's married with little 'uns of her own now.'

'Ah...yes.' Miss Busby had to wrack her brains. 'Of course. A lovely girl...' She had taught so many children over the years, and a fair few Millies to boot, but this was always a well-received response.

'She was, and still is.' The waitress, Maggie, nodded approvingly. 'Now, did I hear you mention the gentleman who drowned in the lake?'

'Oh, yes, a friend of mine knew him.' Miss Busby made a careful reply.

'Well, they're saying he slipped on ice while he went to feed the ducks, but I don't believe it for one minute.'

'Feeding ducks? Really?' Miss Busby replied, wondering who 'they' were.

'He wasn't the type to feed ducks. No-one's wanting to say anything, but there was something going on, I'm sure of it.' The waitress looked over her shoulder as though she feared being overheard, although the only other occupants were a middle-aged couple eating toasted teacakes while not speaking a word to each other.

'What sort of something?' Miss Busby lowered her voice to encourage the woman.

'Well…I couldn't tell you exactly, but my husband, Derek, bought his insurance from Mr Potter. Now, he only came to collect the premiums twice a year, but I heard Potter visited his old ladies once a month, at least.'

'Oh, that seems…unusual…' Miss Busby felt she was treading a fine line, and resolved to proceed one careful foot at a time. 'Which "old ladies" in particular, if you don't mind me asking?'

'Her Ladyship up by the railway, for one.' The waitress sniffed in blatant disapproval.

Miss Busby frowned. 'Do you mean Dorothy Cranford?'

She nodded. 'Yes, *Her Ladyship*, although I doubt she's allowed to use the title anymore. If she ever was in the first place.'

Miss Busby sighed. People had such long memories in the countryside. Dorothy Cranford had never really been "Her Ladyship", but certain people had taken unkindly to her marrying above her station, and refused to let her forget it. The death of her husband and the awful business with his family at Cranford Manor had been quite a scandal at the time.

'Poor Dorothy, it was so unfortunate,' Miss Busby replied, half to herself, then asked, 'Why would Mr Potter visit her quite so often?'

'I don't know the answer to that, but I thought perhaps, as you're taking an interest, you may want to ask her yourself.'

'I'm sure the police inspector will have spoken to her…'

'Well, that's as may be, but nobody knows this new one, do they? Your nephew may not have been much good, but at least we all knew where we stood with him. I'm not one for pointing fingers, Miss Busby, and if it weren't you, I wouldn't say a word. But there's something not right and someone needs to do something about it.' She looked around again. 'Now, I'd best be getting back to my work.'

'Before you go, Maggie, I wonder if you could set aside a slice of ginger cake for Bobby Miller, and have your delivery boy drop it at the station?'

'I can do that, Miss.' She nodded.

'And could I trouble you to also bring me a vanilla slice, to take away?'

'O' course, Miss.'

Miss Busby, left alone once again, returned to thoughts of the divulging of information and the question of sharing. It was quite clear that one generally didn't like to share with those one didn't know. Which meant Lucy, and the new inspector, might have a rather difficult time convincing the close-knit locals to open up.

* * *

'Did you know Bobby Miller is now a proper constable?' Miss Busby asked a harassed-looking Dennis when he finally appeared.

'No, I didn't know, but it dun't surprise me,' Dennis said. 'Getting ideas above his station, I heard.'

'Quite literally, it would seem.'

'Eh?'

'Never mind.'

Dennis was in the driving seat, his nose almost pressed to the windscreen as he battled to keep the wheels from skidding on the icy lanes.

They slid slowly round the final corner, clipping the frosted grass verge.

'Well, here we are then,' Dennis said as they pulled up outside Lavender Cottage. Dusk was drawing in and her home appeared somewhat lonely, with no lights in the windows or smoke pouring from the chimney. She hadn't taken the time to bank the fire properly before leaving, and suddenly found herself missing the warmth and brightness of the tea room she'd left behind – as well as the company.

When did I stop inviting people in? she wondered. It didn't seem too long ago that Lavender Cottage was always bustling with friends and neighbours calling – she'd barely had to actually invite anyone – but lately the path to her door had remained largely untrod, other than by her own boots.

Perhaps, she thought, *the older we get, the more effort we must make.* The problem being, the older one got, the less inclined one somehow felt to make an effort. She'd lived alone a long time, and had mostly been content. She still missed Randolf, naturally, even after all these years – she always would – but she'd managed perfectly well on her own. Sometimes, though, it was the sort of thing that got to you.

'Miss Busby?' Dennis was eyeing her with concern.

'Oh, of course. Thank you, Dennis. Before I forget…' She delved into her handbag and pulled out the brown paper bag. 'A small treat.'

'For me? Gosh, thanks, Miss!' His eyes lit up.

'You're most welcome,' she said.

'Vanilla slice! My favourite!' Dennis's nose was already in the bag.

'So I recall. Do enjoy it. Oh, and Dennis?' Miss Busby turned back to face him.

'Yes, Miss?'

'Would you give me a knock tomorrow, with the first post? I'd appreciate a lift to the lake at Little Minton.'

'Yes, Miss.' Dennis devoured the pastry in a few bites, then licked his fingers as Miss Busby stepped from the post van with as much dignity as possible.

As Dennis puttered off into the distance, Miss Busby stood for a moment, then turned away from her own gate and headed instead for Holly Cottage, two doors down. Bracing herself for the inevitable, she pushed open the gate, the squeak setting off the ever alert Barnaby inside.

The terrier spotted her from his seat on the front window sill and yapped boisterously with tail wagging madly as she approached. He was the standard white type with black and tan patches on head and tail. Bright eyes, button nose, far too tubby, and with tufted hair that sprang out at all angles.

Mary Fellows appeared at the window alongside him, her eyes large in her lined face. She smiled weakly, and raised a thin hand in greeting when she saw her visitor. Miss Busby wished she'd had the foresight to purchase an extra vanilla slice. Mary's poor health meant she rarely left her cottage these days; she would no doubt have appreciated a pastry. As the front door opened, Barnaby barrelled out, his barks becoming almost hysterical.

'Barnaby, quiet,' Miss Busby ordered in her best schoolteacher voice, and to her satisfaction, the dog instantly obeyed. She patted his head, he was no doubt as much in need of company as his owner.

A good hour later, having enjoyed a pleasant tête-à-tête mostly about local comings and goings, and without any mention of unexpected death, Miss Busby made the short walk home feeling much happier.

Pudding awaited her on the kitchen table, his large amber eyes narrowing in disapproval at her lateness.

'Things are afoot in Little Minton,' she informed him, going straight to the cupboard in search of something to appease him. 'You may need to apply some patience, Pud.' Pudding's tail twitched, he held no truck with patience.

Opening a can of salmon, Miss Busby dished out a generous helping to make amends, lifted him off the tablecloth and put him on the tiled floor. Then she pulled the curtains against the growing chill, chivvied the smouldering fire, warmed a pot of stew that she'd made the day before, and finally sat down feeling altogether more cosy. There were things to do, she decided over her supper. Major Lennox came to mind once more: he'd employed a number of tools to detect the terrible murders at Bloxford Hall and they'd proved really very useful.

The remainder of the evening was spent collecting a notebook, a few coloured pencils, a pen, some blotting paper, and a magnifying glass she sometimes used when footnotes in novels were typed in an absurdly small font. She returned to the kitchen and sought out three empty jars, gave them a good wash and left them to dry on the draining board. Then she went to sit as her desk, carefully extracted a page from her blue notebook, and began a list…

CHAPTER 5

Following a simple breakfast of a boiled egg accompanied by toast and a pot of tea, Miss Busby busied herself before making another sortie to her frail neighbour. Mary Fellows, at Holly Cottage. This time she carried a tin of shortbread biscuits to share with the occupants. An hour later she returned home to pick up her book and wait for Dennis's frantic yells to break the rural quiet. They weren't long in coming.

'That's my cue, Pud,' Miss Busby told the cat as he watched proceedings from the window sill.

Quickly donning her coat, hat, gloves, and thick boots, Miss Busby left with a determined tread.

'First post, I said, Dennis, not second,' she admonished as she strode along the path, her breath white in the clear cold air.

'This…gah, gerroff me…this *is* the first post, Miss Busby. Roads are dead icy again, slows me down dunnit? I can't help the weather. Argh! Help! He's gone right through me trousers!'

'You could set off a little sooner.' Miss Busby turned her attention to the dog. 'Barnaby. No.'

Barnaby promptly detached his teeth from Dennis's trouser leg and trotted to Miss Busby's side, then sat and stared up her, adoration in his brown eyes.

'Good boy.' She bent to ruffle his ears. His focus never left her pocket.

'What...but...' Dennis trailed off, clutching his trouser leg.

'We had some time together this morning, didn't we, Barnaby? And we discovered that someone is extremely fond of biscuits. Watch.' Miss Busby pulled a biscuit from her pocket, and said, 'Down, Barnaby.' The Jack Russell flew to the ground. She broke off a small piece of shortbread and handed it to the dog, who devoured it in a flurry of white beard.

'Good, isn't he?' Miss Busby smiled. 'We've reached an understanding.' She held a gloved finger aloft. 'Barnaby, wait.' The dog waited. 'Now, Dennis, if you could just pop him in the van.' Miss Busby turned to pick up a large handbag.

'Pop him in the...? That's not coming with us, is it?'

'Really Dennis, there's no call to be rude. Barnaby is a he, not an it. I'm sure he'd thank you to remember.'

'But, Miss! He's bitten clean through my trousers!'

'Nonsense. You were unprepared, that's all. Here.' She broke off another piece of biscuit and handed it to him, before heading for the post van, the contents of her bag clinking.

'But…?' Dennis floundered.

'Just try, Dennis,' she called over her shoulder.

'H-here, boy,' Dennis stuttered, offering the titbit gingerly. A low growl became audible. Miss Busby *tsked*, and turned to call the dog herself. Barnaby responded by launching himself aboard with gusto. Dennis muttered under his breath then ate the biscuit himself.

Once all three were settled and en route to Little Minton, the young man broke his injured silence.

'So, why d'you bring it—him, anyway?' Dennis asked.

'I promised Mrs Fellows I would take him for a walk today. I've decided it will be around the lake at Little Minton. I thought he'd like that.'

Dennis thawed. 'Aw, that's nice. I s'pose he dun't get out much as it is.'

'No, I suppose he doesn't,' she agreed. 'Now, I'd like to go to the police station first, and then the lake.'

'But, Miss! I'm already late. I ain't got time to go back and forward like that,' Dennis protested.

'Nonsense, of course you have. It's hardly far; I'm not asking you for a lift into Oxford.' She squeezed the tiniest hint of threat into the remark – she hadn't done her Christmas shopping yet, after all.

'But people are waiting for their post and I'll get in trouble if I keep driving around where I'm not supposed to,' Dennis panicked. 'Please, Miss…'

'Oh, very well,' she relented. 'Just drop me at the police station.'

* * *

'Good morning, Miss Busby. I didn't expect to see you back so soon.' Bobby was once again behind the long wooden counter, and leaned over it as he spotted Barnaby. 'Oh, you've got a dog – he's nice…he's not lost is he?'

Barnaby growled by way of greeting.

'No, he belongs to Mrs Fellows at Holly Cottage,' Miss Busby explained. 'Quiet, Barnaby. Now, Bobby, I have a little favour to ask.'

'Oh, Miss…' Bobby looked wary. 'If it's about that dead bloke, I'm not allowed to say anything.'

'Of course you're not. No, it's just a few items I'd like you to obtain for me.' She opened the bag and extracted the list she'd written the previous evening.

'Oh, alright, Miss.' Bobby took the proffered page with his customary grin. The boy was resourceful when it came to the real world. It was simply school he'd struggled with. 'Miss…' The wary look resurfaced as he read the list. 'You can't—'

Two uniformed policemen, presumably Sergeant Brierly and Constable Lewis, emerged from a door leading to the rear of the station. Barnaby instantly raised his hackles, a rumbling noise building in his chest.

'Time we were off for our walk,' Miss Busby said, scooping up the dog and heading towards the front door before an incident ensued. 'And thank you, Bobby. I shall pop back later for those items.'

She set off with a determined tread, Barnaby pulling

ahead, and they soon left the high street behind. A few cottages lined the lane to the lake, but they were replaced by a high wall guarding the extensive grounds of Lambert House. She noticed a small wooden gate, half hidden between shrubs and trees growing against the frost glazed wall.

Miss Busby continued along the cinder path and paused to catch her breath as she arrived at a slight rise overlooking the broad expanse of water. Having reached her goal, she suddenly realised that she had no idea where the body had been discovered. For all her careful note-taking and preparation, she had made the most elementary error.

'It seems I'm not quite ready for my deerstalker and pipe just yet, Barnaby,' she admitted. Barnaby looked up at her, ears pricked, unperturbed and eager to continue. She sighed and headed for a bench set before a line of shrubs bordering dense woodland.

The bench proved chilly and Miss Busby gazed about for several moments, hoping that something would indicate the whereabouts of Potter's death. It didn't. The lake's still surface mirrored the clear blue sky; ice crusted its rim, and reeds gathered in spiky flotillas where nests would no doubt be hidden. The path followed the meandering shore. There were no boats, nor bandstand, nor ice cream booths; it had once been a quarry dug deep over the centuries, and was now a secluded country lake where townsfolk strolled when time and occasion allowed.

Barnaby gave a sharp bark and wagged his tail meaningfully.

'Absolutely not,' Miss Busby told him. 'I need a moment's respite, but you may have a wander by yourself.' She pulled a biscuit from her pocket. 'Provided you come back the moment you're asked.' She broke off a small piece and gave it to him, then let him off the lead.

She watched as he pattered off, his white-tipped tail held high, ears pricked, and nose to the ground.

Lacking inspiration, she turned to her bag and dug inside to pull out her blue notebook and pencil, then proceeded to write a number of questions regarding how and where the body was discovered. She would aim these at Bobby, she decided. Then she constructed another list concerning Potter's general movements, and wondered if the overbearing Evelyn Simpson would answer those, or perhaps her sister-in-law, Miss Frances Simpson, if she were sufficiently recovered. She pondered a little more and then added, "Dorothy Dent, The Station Master's House" under the heading of "Persons of Interest".

She was just eyeing her jam jars and wondering where she might start hunting for clues, when a rustling from somewhere, followed by a harsh cough, made her sit up. She reached into her capacious bag and pulled out the small loaf she'd thought to bring as cover for her activities.

The bank was muddy as she made her way to the

edge of the lake to look about for ducks. There was one sleepy-looking mallard in a cluster of reeds off to the left. It was hardly the flock she'd expected. Still, determined to make a good show of it, she waved the loaf and called, 'Breakfast!'

The duck quacked in alarm, causing Barnaby to reappear at speed and hare toward the bird, barking loudly in the still air. Miss Busby tried calling, cajoling, and offering a biscuit, none of which worked.

Having failed to lure the terrier out of the reeds, she turned, and was shocked to see an unkempt man looking inside her bag.

'You there! Stop!' she shouted. 'I have a dog with me. Barnaby! *There's a man*! There, look!'

Barnaby remained absent.

'Typical,' she muttered, and pulled her shoulders back, hefted the uncut loaf and advanced with as much menace as she could muster.

The man looked up and raised both hands. 'I weren't takin' nothin',' he said. 'I heard clinkin', that's all, an' wondered if you had a drink with you.'

'I most certainly do not,' Miss Busby replied indignantly, still wielding the loaf.

'Why've you got empty jam jars for?' he asked, rheumy eyes looking up into hers.

'I…tadpoles,' she stammered, caught off guard.

'In December?'

'Yes. That is, no. I… now, wait just a minute.' Miss Busby recovered herself and lowered the loaf. 'It's no business of yours what I carry in my bag, and you have no right to look in it.'

He sniffed, and hung his head. 'Lookin' was all I was doin'. Saw you down by the water. Just wanted a drink, that's all.'

Miss Busby paused to observe the man now the immediate threat had passed. Bent and painfully thin, his clothes were ragged and far from clean. Hair and beard long and shaggy, ungloved hands misshapen by arthritis. He was no threat, she realised, and decided in that moment she'd have given him a drink if she'd had one.

'I'm sorry,' she said. 'You startled me.' She sat down on the bench beside him. There was…an aroma… which she did her best to ignore.

'S'alright.' He sniffed again. 'Don't normally see anyone up here this time o' year. S'why I like it. No-one bothers me. Last couple o' days though it's been like Piccadilly Circus.'

Miss Busby's senses fired.

'The body, you mean? Were you here when they found it?' she asked.

The tramp nodded, and she looked at him intently. He wasn't looking at her, she noted, he was focused on the loaf of bread in her hands.

'Are you hungry?' she asked. 'It's only yesterday's; it's still fresh. I baked it myself.'

'You brought fresh bread for the ducks?'

She flushed. 'I did, yes.'

'And you don't want it?'

'No, not at all. Please.' She handed him the bread, and watched as he tore off a chunk and chewed on it.

'Much 'preciated,' he mumbled through a mouthful.

Miss Busby found herself at a loss. She knew Oxford had plenty of tramps, but places like Bloxford and Little Minton were too far off the beaten track. Questions swarmed in her head – was he from the town and fallen upon hard times? Perhaps he didn't want to leave his former home. She peered at his face as surreptitiously as she could. She didn't recognise him, but with the beard and the grime it was hard to tell what he actually looked like.

'He'll catch his death,' the tramp mumbled.

Pulled from her thoughts, her mind immediately shot back to Mr Potter. 'He did, I gather.'

'Eh?'

'The man they found. The body.'

'No, not 'im. Your dog.'

Miss Busby looked up. A despondent, shivering Barnaby was approaching with a wet weed plastered on his head like a limp beret.

'Oh, dear Lord.' Miss Busby stood up in panic.

'Wait 'ere a minute, Miss.' The man disappeared into the woods behind the bench. His home, Miss Busby thought with a pang. In this weather. How awful.

Barnaby trailed over to her feet and hung his head. The weed slithered to the ground.

The tramp reappeared, clutching some sort of grey cloth.

''Ere,' he said, holding it out to her. Miss Busby involuntarily recoiled. The man shrugged and crouched down beside the dog instead.

Wrapping the filthy cloth firmly around him, he rubbed vigorously. Barnaby emitted little huffs of what sounded like delight.

Removing the cloth, he turned it around and swaddled the dog like a baby. Then he lifted him to set him on his lap on the bench, wrapping his arms around him for extra warmth. The ungrateful dog started growling. 'I think he'd best be with you,' he said and carefully handed Barnaby to her. 'He'll be alright in a bit,' he assured her.

'Yes, thanks to you,' she said, pulling Barnaby onto her knees. 'You must let me wash your cloth and return it.' She could smell its damp aroma, along with the scent of wet dog. 'Do you... that is to say... are you staying for a while?'

'Might be, but you can keep the cloth,' he said. 'Ain't mine anyway.'

'Oh. Well, if you're sure. Thank you. That's very kind.'

'It musta been hers.'

'Whose?'

'The old lady what killed 'im.'

Miss Busby's eyes widened as she stared at him.

'Didn't catch 'is death,' he said. 'And he weren't there, either.' He nodded to where Miss Busby had been standing by the lake's edge. 'He were up over there.'

A crooked finger pointed to a clump of laurels further along the shore. 'And she followed 'im in.'

He took another mouthful of bread.

'Who followed him?' Miss Busby's breath was coming quickly, her brain racing to keep up.

'The old lady,' he said between chunks of bread. 'My eyesight 'int what it was, but she was definitely old. Stooped, sort of. She followed the bloke in wearing the cloth over her head, like a shawl. Sun was behind them, just goin' dusk it was. Wind was gettin' up.' He shivered at the thought.

Miss Busby looked down at Barnaby in horror. Mary's dog was wearing vital evidence in what was now almost certainly a murder case.

'What happened?' she managed to say.

'Dunno.' He shrugged. 'Couldn't see from 'ere. She came out though, after a bit. 'E didn't.'

A frenzy of questions tumbled in Miss Busby's head.

'Did you mention this to the police?'

The old man frowned and looked down at his worn boots. 'I don't talk to police. Don't trust 'em. Never have.'

'But…you must! You may have been the only witness to a murder!'

'Ain't none of my business, is it, what other folks do. Just didn't want to see your dog freeze, that's all.'

'You are sure it was a woman?'

'Looked like one to me alright. And it was him for sure, I saw him pulled out next mornin'. Wearin' the same clothes, he was, but all wet and mudded.' He shrugged then stood up. 'Thanks for the bread, Miss. Be seein' ye.'

He stood up and shambled off quickly towards the wood before Miss Busby had a chance to organise her thoughts.

'Wait!' She rose to her feet, Barnaby still bundled in her arms. 'How did you get hold of the shawl?'

'She musta' dropped it,' he shouted over his shoulder.

'But did you see—'

It was no good. The man had already disappeared deep into the maze of overgrown shrubs and the woodland beyond.

'I don't even know his name,' she told Barnaby, bemused, horrified, and excited all at once.

CHAPTER 6

Miss Busby tried to follow the tramp into the dense bushes, but gave up when she slid in a patch of mud, almost dropping the shivering dog in her arms. Footsteps in the distance caused her to turn about.

'Hello?' she called out, and went back to stand on the path.

'Aye, hello there,' a deep, rich voice replied. A tall, handsome young man with a stern face and red hair, fiery in the sunlight, strode towards her with a determined air. Well dressed in a smart grey suit and long charcoal overcoat; blue eyes glinting with intelligence, he was clearly not the type to be trifled with. 'Can I help you?'

The accent, he was a Scot. 'Inspector McKay?'

'Yes.' He stopped a few yards away, frowning in puzzlement.

'Inspector, I can't tell you how pleased I am to see you. Now, the man I was just speaking to, did you see him? If you're quick, you'll catch him. He went—'

'I'm sorry, madam, but I didn't see any man.'

'But you must have done, it was only moments ago, you must go and find him. He is witness to the murder—'

'And what murder would that be?' He sounded terse.

'It's…well, the death of Mr Potter,' she stammered, and then got a grip. 'Inspector McKay, I am Miss Busby.'

'Is that so?' He raised a red brow. 'I heard you have been asking questions at the station, and now here you are.'

She bristled at the implication. 'I am simply walking my neighbour's dog.'

The inspector shot a look at the animal in her arms.

'Well, I was, until…Look, Inspector, I appreciate you're new to the area, but my nephew was the previous police inspector, and–'

'Ah, that explains a thing or two. I need to talk to you, Miss Busby.' His tone was as stern as his expression, and his habit of cutting her off mid-sentence was beginning to rankle.

'Whatever for? I mean, it's fortuitous, as it happens, because I have some vital information regarding the death of Mr Potter. My dog, that is, my neighbour's dog, is wearing crucial evidence.'

Confusion flickered across Inspector McKay's face, before he resumed his sharp gaze. 'I beg your pardon?'

'I know it sounds a little unhinged, but you really must find the tramp. He's in the woods, over there.'

She pointed as best she could, given the wet dog in her arms.

'Miss Busby.' McKay sought to regain his authority. 'I understand you hold information relating to the death of Mr Vernon Potter.'

'Yes, I know, I've just said…' It was Miss Busby's turn to be confused.

The inspector pulled a piece of paper from his pocket. 'You came into the station and spoke to Constable Miller?'

Miss Busby nodded. Understanding dawned. 'Yes, but that was different, that was about the life insurance. He sold it against himself, you see, but the shawl is more important, and the tramp. You simply must find him.'

To her dismay, he made no attempt to find the tramp, and instead turned over the piece of paper in his hand. 'And you requested a list of items from Constable Miller this morning.'

'Really, Inspector, I fail to see—'

'Lockpicks?'

'Ah.'

'Possession of lockpicks is a criminal offence.'

'Is it? But a very good friend of mine uses them…' She stopped, realising this wasn't helping. 'I will remove them from my list,' she promised. 'But the important thing is that the tramp saw the murder, he is an eye witness.'

'I cannot–'

'Oh, then I will,' Miss Busby snapped, utterly out of patience with the young man and deciding it was her turn to cut him off. 'Just hold onto the dog, please.' She thrust Barnaby towards the inspector, who stepped back smartly as the dog bared his teeth.

'No, I'll go, but please remain here.' He stalked off in the direction Miss Busby had indicated. Ten minutes later he returned, looking even sterner than before. 'There's just a few muddy footprints and some empty whisky bottles.'

'Oh dear, he must have heard you arrive.' She sighed, then thought of something. 'Why are you here? Not to find me, surely?'

'No, I wanted a quiet look at the …' He stopped.

'The scene of the murder?' Miss Busby finished his sentence.

'It hasn't been designated a murder.' The inspector was sharp in reply.

'But it will be, won't it?'

'I'll be wishing you a good day, Miss Busby,' he said, making to leave, before adding, 'And should I find you in possession of the aforementioned lockpicks, I shall be forced to take action,' he lectured, then strode off, his long coat flapping in the breeze.

She put Barnaby down; his shivers had lessened and he growled at the departing inspector, a sure sign he was recovering, and that he was indeed an excellent judge of character. She'd been tempted to growl at the man herself. *Take action*, indeed!

'Come along.' Miss Busby slipped the dog's leash back on, and followed the inspector at a distance. He'd turned off the path and gone behind the tall stand of laurels, their evergreen leaves glossy in the winter sunlight.

Miss Busby stopped to quietly observe the inspector kneeling on a grassy bank churned with mud; he was examining an exposed root through a magnifying glass. As she watched, he bent and stared more closely at the twisted wood.

She decided to give the young man a second chance. 'I have jam jars if you need to collect evidence,' she offered.

He didn't flinch – he must have known she was there. 'I have envelopes, thank you.' He scraped a few slices from the root with a penknife and carefully placed the shavings in the palm of his hand, then turned them over with his thumb before slipping them into a brown envelope.

'The tramp said this is where the woman followed Mr Potter in.'

McKay stood up. 'Did he now.'

Miss Busby decided to switch tack. 'You must have brought a car, Inspector. I would very much appreciate a lift back to my cottage. My age, you see,' – she wasn't above playing on it, on occasion – 'and it really is terribly cold.'

The inspector opened his mouth to object, but Miss Busby was building up a head of steam and wouldn't be stopped now.

'I would like to explain everything and I'd much rather do so in my cottage in front of a fire, where the poor dog can warm up and I can sit down,' she said, and headed determinedly up the path towards the lane, calling over her shoulder, 'And we can dry the wet shawl, because it's evidence in the murder of Mr Potter.'

Inspector McKay stalked back to the road with bad grace. He was still in gruff mood as he steered his grey Alvis motor car along Bloxford's icy lanes, with Miss Busby and Barnaby in the front passenger seat.

'So kind of you,' Miss Busby said cheerily into the silence. *A force to be reckoned with,* Randolf had always said of her, usually with a gleam of pride in his eyes. Oh, how she missed those eyes. How she missed everything about him, she thought as a sudden longing swept over her. 'I'll make some tea,' she said briskly, fighting off the sting of tears. She could be a pleasant force, after all, she reminded herself. 'Turn left, just up here. And I'll explain everything. And another left.'

The inspector drove without a word.

'That's Lavender Cottage, there.' Miss Busby pointed to the classic Cotswolds house amid the row of sturdy cottages.

'Miss Busby, I really—'

'Do come in, and I shall tell you all about it.'

Some minutes later Barnaby was lying in front of the fire and Miss Busby had set the kettle to boil while the inspector stood glowering in the living room with his hands in his pockets.

'Here we are.' She arrived carrying a tray with tea things and a plate of butter biscuits to place on the low table.

'Miss Busby, I need to return to the station.'

'Of course. Do sit down. Sugar?'

Inspector McKay agreed to two lumps and sipped his tea in her favourite armchair in determined silence as she began to recount the morning's events.

She wished she'd had time to take notes so she could appear more authoritative, although she didn't think she did too bad a job, considering. When she came to the end of the tale, she plucked the cloth from the fireguard where she'd draped it to dry, and handed it over triumphantly.

She expected the inspector to look impressed, or grateful, or, well… anything other than more annoyed than previously.

'I've heard you out, Miss Busby,' he began, holding the grey material in his hands and glancing at it cursorily. 'And it's time to put an end to this. This is clearly some sort of child's blanket, not a shawl. And I can assure you my constables have already searched the area thoroughly. They wouldn't have missed anything as obvious as this.' He dropped the cloth back over the fireguard.

'No, because the tramp had already picked it up, of course,' Miss Busby rejoined, 'although apparently your constables missed the tramp entirely…' she trailed off, the implication clear.

'This tramp of yours is hardly a credible witness,' the inspector went on, his tone hardening. 'You admit he was in search of a drink.'

'Well,' Miss Busby managed, the wind dropping from her sails. 'Yes, but—'

'I appreciate that I'm new to the job, but I'm fully qualified and I'm no idiot, madam. Protocol was followed to the letter, and no suspicious circumstances were determined.'

'Of course, but the matter of the insurance policies is surely—'

'It's unusual, aye, but there isn'ae anything illegal in it as far as I can understand.' His Scottish accent seemed to accentuate with his irritation.

She sighed, suddenly downcast; she wasn't used to feeling the fool, but perhaps her experience with Major Lennox had given her a false sense of her abilities. Had the tramp simply spun her a drink-addled story and she'd wanted to believe him? It wasn't like her at all, her judgement was usually sound, but the excitement, the sudden sense of *purpose*...had perhaps carried her away...

'But why would Mr Potter even have been at the lake in the first place?' She realised she was questioning herself as much as the inspector.

'He'd probably gone to feed the ducks.'

Miss Busby remembered the waitress mentioning as much, and dismissing it.

'Did you find any bread on his person?'

'No. He would have thrown it to the ducks.'

'A paper bag? Crumbs about the area? Duck prints in the vicinity of his fall?'

'Duck prints? Really, Miss Busby.' He gave her a withering look.

She refused to be withered.

'What about the bump on the back of his head?' she asked, remembering Bobby's words and triumphantly blurting it out before considering whether or not she'd get him into trouble.

The inspector narrowed his eyes.

'People talk, Inspector, in small towns and villages such as these.'

'Aye, and never more so than when they shouldn't.'

Miss Busby's eyes darkened. 'It's only natural for people to be concerned. And if you can honestly tell me there's nothing suspicious about an elderly lady being at the scene of the death of an insurance salesman known to sell policies benefiting elderly ladies, well, I shall be very surprised, and not a little concerned, Inspector.'

She paused for breath, not certain she'd phrased that to the best of her ability, but surely under the circumstances it must be obvious.

'This "elderly lady" is only mentioned by a tramp known to like a drink. No-one else has reported seeing such a person.' The inspector shook his head. 'The most likely cause usually *is* the cause, Miss Busby. It was icy, the bank is steep, Potter could easily have slipped and fallen.'

'But the bump was to the back of his head, surely he would have fallen forwards if he were to plunge into the lake.'

'Not necessarily. The lake is very deep where he went in, plus he was wearing a thick winter coat, which would had weighed him down.'

Miss Busby refused to concede. 'Why did you visit the lake today and take samples of the root, if you're convinced Potter merely fell in?'

The inspector ignored the question and leant over towards the little table beside her chair, picking up the novel lying there. 'Fond of mysteries, are you?' he asked. 'I am, too,' he went on before she could answer. 'Conan Doyle, Buchan, Chesterton, I've read them all. But I'm afraid real crimes, in my experience, bear little resemblance to their fictional counterparts.' He put the book down and forced a reassuring smile.

That, Miss Busby thought, was quite enough of that. Possibly making a mistake was one thing, but being patronised was quite another.

'And what experience is that, exactly, Inspector?' she asked, tilting her head slightly as her eyes bored into the inspector's own. 'This is your first case, I understand?'

The man's lips tightened into an angry line. 'As everyone in the vicinity likes to remind me, aye,' he managed through clenched teeth. 'But I spent enough time at my studies to be able to assure you I—'

'—didn't miss a key witness at the scene? Didn't condemn a man as a drunk, despite having never met him?' Miss Busby interjected, getting into her stride. She'd given the man her finest homemade biscuits, after all. 'I may enjoy fiction, Inspector, but I helped the police solve the murders up at The Hall, which I'm sure you've heard about.'

The inspector admitted he hadn't.

'There, you see? Something else I need to tell you about. This will necessitate another pot of tea.'

She stalked through to the kitchen, deaf to the inspector's objections. And as she recounted the awful events, detailing how she and Major Lennox, alongside Inspector Swift, had solved the mystery, she sensed something change in his demeanour. And with it, something in her own attitude began to shift. The man really was at a disadvantage, being new to the area, and his first encounter with her had seen her accompanied by a sodden animal, a filthy piece of cloth, and full of enthusiastic tales of a tramp nowhere to be seen. Perhaps, she realised, they'd both been at fault.

'So you see, Inspector, I do have a little experience of my own, and I wasn't sure if anyone would investigate after my nephew left, but—' She held up a hand before he could interrupt '—I also appreciate I may have got a little carried away. Perhaps we could start afresh?'

The inspector sat back in the armchair, and released a long breath, seeming to relax for the first time since she'd encountered him. 'Aye, I think that would be for the best, but you must understand that it's not safe for you to get mixed up in this sort of thing.'

'What sort of thing?' Miss Busby pressed.

'Murder and the like,' Inspector McKay replied.

'Ah, so you *do* have a suspicion.' Miss Busby sat back, triumphant.

The inspector flushed. 'I just mean, in general terms, it's not safe for civilians to involve themselves in police business.'

'I may be a "civilian", Inspector, but I taught half of the surrounding villages for decades, and you'll find that most people will be much more likely to talk to me than your new men from Oxford. And the tramp is a case in point.'

'That's as may be, but there's no legal weight behind such conversations.'

'But I am a witness to what he said,' she persisted.

'And many people tell us much the same sort of thing.'

'Ah.' The penny dropped. 'The type referred to in the newspapers as "cranks"?'

'Exactly, and they waste a great deal of police time.'

'Hum,' she mused. 'But if I pass the information to you, and you discover it's valid, that will carry the required weight, will it not?'

The inspector sighed. 'Are you always this... determined?'

'Unfailingly so.' Miss Busby smiled, wondering if he'd been about to select a less flattering term, but he was at last getting the measure of her.

There was a moment's silence as the inspector gazed

into the fire. 'My mother used to teach,' he said. 'Forty years. Another determined woman. Formidable, even.'

Miss Busby nodded appreciatively. 'A necessary quality in matters of education. She must be very proud of you.'

He shook his head. 'She has no idea. She's not well. Alzheimer's Disease, they call it. She's in a home in Edinburgh.'

'Oh, I'm so sorry.' Miss Busby had read about the disease only recently, and remembered thinking how awful such an affliction must be. 'That must be dreadful for you.'

'Aye, and it happened while I was away at the war, when I came back...' He sighed, keeping his gaze fixed on the flames. 'I'd have stayed up there after I'd finished my studies, if it'd been something they could cure, but as it is she's no idea if I'm there, here, or anywhere else. She doesn't even recognise me.'

Miss Busby gave a pained sigh, and looked determinedly into the flames herself, to spare the inspector any inkling that she might have seen the glint of tears in his eyes.

He cleared his throat, before continuing, 'So when the post became available here I applied straight away. I write to her every weekend, and the nurses read her the letters. Who knows, one day she might realise.' He shrugged. Miss Busby's heart ached for him. A teacher of forty years, his mother must have been in possession of a fiercely keen mind. The loss would be unimaginable.

'And your father?' she asked gently.

'Visits her every day,' the inspector replied. 'It's hard on him, but he's stalwart. A better man than I, at any rate.'

'Nonsense,' Miss Busby said, attempting to bustle her way through the upset her questions had caused. 'You're pursuing your chosen career; it's a credit to you, and I'm sure you'll be returning for Christmas?'

'Aye.' That brought the ghost of a smile to his face. 'For Christmas and New Year. There's nothing like a New Year's celebration in Edinburgh.'

'How wonderful.'

'Will you be away for Christmas yourself?' he asked, getting to his feet.

'I shall probably visit my sister and her family,' she said without enthusiasm. The inspector clearly needed to return to work, and now that she felt she'd explained herself sufficiently she was happy to let him do so.

'Thank you for the tea, Miss Busby,' he said. 'I'll allow Bobby to find the items on your list for you, minus the lockpicks,' he added. 'But I strongly suggest you leave police work to the professionals.'

Miss Busby smiled. 'What are our next steps?' she asked, walking the inspector to the door.

He raised an eyebrow. '*Our* next steps? Have I been talking to myself?'

She had made her decision. This Inspector was a considerable cut above her useless nephew, but he was new and unknown to the neighbourhood. 'Two heads are better than one, Inspector, and I'm sure I can be of help to you.' She'd picked up the grubby cloth and held it out for him.

He took it, shaking his head. 'There's to be a memorial service for Mr Potter tomorrow morning at Little Minton church.'

'Tomorrow…? I've heard no mention of it.'

'That's because I only recently suggested it. I'm primarily concerned with seeing his former clients.'

'Oh…' She stopped, realising the implication. 'You're going to bring the suspects together. How very clever!'

'I'm not quite as green as some may think, Miss Busby,' he replied dryly, and then left with a smile playing on his lips.

Miss Busby leaned back against the door and took a moment to catch her breath. What a morning it had been! A scratching sound interrupted her thoughts. She was just about to let Pudding into the sitting room when she remembered the sleeping Barnaby by the fire. In fact, she realised, he hadn't moved for quite some time. *Oh, Dear Lord, I've killed Mary's dog*, she thought.

'Barnaby!' she called.

Nothing.

'Barnaby?' She hurried over and bent down to place a hand on his back, whereupon he twitched, snorted, and rolled over, beginning to snore loudly.

Miss Busby decided that both dogs and suspicious deaths could be hard on the nerves. With that in mind, she donned her coat, picked up the sleepy animal and returned him to Holly Cottage, taking a bag of biscuits for good measure.

Upon her return home, she released Pudding and gave him the rest of the salmon, then heated some leftover stew before settling by the fire.

Her mind drifted back to the unfortunate murders at the Hall, and Major Lennox:

'Investigating requires the gathering of information and evidence. There is very little evidence, but someone with an enquiring mind may be able to offer information.'

'Well, Pud,' she said, scratching the ginger tom's ear. 'If there's one area in which I could never be said to be lacking, it's in the enquiring mind department.

CHAPTER 7

'She fell in with the wrong sort,' Dorothy Cranford called from the cramped kitchen later that afternoon. 'A dreadful shame, I'm sure you'll agree. The girl could have been anything she wanted. She could have even gone to university.'

'Mm,' Miss Busby murmured diplomatically. To the best of her recollection Dorothy's niece, Jennifer, had been the epitome of 'the wrong sort'. And Barnaby had more chance of going to university than that silly girl. But people rarely saw things as they were when it came to their relatives. Which wasn't such a terrible trait, when you came to think of it. Inconvenient, perhaps, but understandable.

'Married an awful man called Arthur Lucas. Heaven only knows what she sees in him, and thanks to him, she's estranged from her father. The rat doesn't want her around people who tell her the truth about him.'

'Goodness, he certainly sounds unpleasant.' Miss Busby was gazing out of the window across the railway track and over toward the roofs of Little Minton. Snow had begun to fall at noon, by one o'clock it had blanketed everywhere in a fine layer of white and then mercifully stopped. The reappearance of the sun had encouraged Miss Busby to flag down Dennis and once more request a lift to Little Minton. 'Does she have children of her own?' she called.

'Two.'

'How lovely.'

'Not really.' Dorothy appeared with a laden tray supporting a mismatched tea set. 'Unpleasant little devils, the pair of them. They take after their father,' she said tartly, and set the tray down on the coffee table with a bang.

The Station Master's House was actually Dorothy's brother's home, and stood next to a row of smaller railway cottages. It was all quite charming in the usual Cotswold style, but far removed from Dorothy's previous home at Cranford Manor. She'd moved there many years previously, having been unceremoniously expelled from the Cranford family home upon her husband, Patrick's, death.

Patrick and Dorothy had met at the local opera society (during a performance of *Aida*, Miss Busby recalled, it being her favourite). He had fallen for her almost instantly, but Dorothy was several social rungs below him; so far below, in fact, that he'd been roundly condemned by his entire family. It didn't help that Patrick was the ineffectual sort, and hopelessly incapable of standing up for himself, or his vivacious young wife.

Lord and LadyCranfordhad made no attempt to hide their feelings on the matter. They'd eventually permitted the couple to marry and grudgingly allowed them to occupy the Dower house in the grounds. But according to Adeline Fanshawe, who knew about such things, their solicitor had inserted some trickery into the marital contract, ensuring Dorothy would never inherit a penny of the Cranford fortune.

Patrick had adored Dorothy and she'd adored him, his status, and casual affluence in equal measure; she'd taken to the aristocratic life like a duck to water. Miss Busby had always suspected Dorothy believed she would eventually charm her way around Lord and Lady Cranford, but it never came to pass. Patrick succumbed to influenza, and Dorothy lost everything in one awful sweep of fate.

Her brother, George Parker, the station master, had been widowed and generously made room for his sister. He'd forgiven her airs and attitude, although there were many in Little Minton who had not.

More recently, George had fallen gravely ill with consumption and was being nursed in the local sanatorium. Miss Busby supposed the railway authorities would want the house back when George died, and she wondered what Dorothy would do then.

'We'll let it steep a little.' Miss Busby indicated the tea.

'Yes, I think we should.' Dorothy slipped into the armchair beside her. She'd grown a little heavier since her youth, although there was still a hint of glory about her. Miss Busby knew the silver curls falling gracefully to her shoulders were a wig, although it was very discretely done. With her high cheekbones, large eyes of violet blue and pert nose, there was still a feminine allure in Dorothy's ready smile. She'd been in a drab frock when Miss Busby had arrived but insisted on changing into a dress of pale blue with a glittering necklace in honour of the visit.

'I'm afraid I suffer with my hips these days,' she said, trying to find a comfortable position.

'Oh, I'm so sorry to hear that,' Miss Busby commiserated, recalling how Dorothy used to sway with a catlike walk.

'I'll consult a specialist as soon as the insurance money comes through.' She sighed. 'I feel old, Isabelle, and of no interest to anyone anymore.'

'Don't you have anybody to help you?' Miss Busby asked. She'd noticed dust in a few places, and frayed threads on the overstuffed armchairs.

'If only! No, I lost my maid and everything else all those years ago, and poor George is so desperately ill, and now Vernon is dead. Although Vernon is still helping me, in his way…'

'Vernon Potter?' Miss Busby's brows shot up. She certainly hadn't imagined him 'helping' anyone. Despite Inspector McKay's assurances regarding the insurance policies, she found it hard to think of Potter as anything other than a predator circling elderly women.

'Yes, Vernon was a dear, and such a gentleman.' Dorothy's face lit up with a smile. 'He used to bring me little gifts, flowers, you know. We laughed together… Such a shame he's gone.' She sighed again. 'It's so rare that I have anyone to talk to. Well, there are the neighbours, of course, but you know what I mean.' She fell silent for a moment, then rallied. 'Isabelle, do you remember when we used to go to concerts about town, and take trips to the theatre? And your Randolf would come, when he wasn't away soldiering. My goodness he was a handsome man. And such a catch! Just think what your life would have been, you'd have thrown us all into the shade.'

'Oh, nonsense.' Miss Busby was dismissive. It had been such a long time ago and she'd long since reconciled herself to her life, but they were pleasant memories nonetheless.

'You always were the stoic, and a good thing too, in the circumstances. A shame though, for us both; our lives could have been so much easier…and now I spend my days just looking at four walls. I barely go anywhere… Life can become so terribly drab. Vernon made me feel alive again.' Dorothy's hand suddenly flew to her mouth, and she stifled a sob. Miss Busby had rarely felt more off balance. It was so unlike the Dorothy she knew of old. Could her predator have actually been a protector, after all? This was the second lady the man's death had left in tears, although Dorothy's reaction wasn't quite as extreme as Miss Frances Simpson's.

'I'm so sorry, Dorothy. I heard what happened at the lake, but I hadn't realised you and Mr Potter were close.'

Dorothy drew out a handkerchief and blew her nose delicately, then a little more forcefully, as if growing in confidence. 'We weren't, to begin with, but when George became ill Vernon came to see him, and together they cooked up a plan to help me, given my straitened circumstances.'

Miss Busby felt her cheeks flush, and she fidgeted in her seat.

'Oh, Isabelle, it's no secret, and I feel no shame. That horse bolted years ago.' Dorothy waved a tired hand. 'I made my choice, and now here I am. I've had a good run, after all. Anyway, Vernon approached the problem with unflinching honesty and I've learned to do the same.'

'Well, he certainly seems to have been a popular chap,' Miss Busby said, choosing her words carefully. 'I hear there's to be a memorial service for him tomorrow.'

'Yes, I had a visit from the police yesterday afternoon and they mentioned it. I shall be there, of course.' Her eyes took on a faraway look. 'Vernon had quite the mind for difficult situations.' She gave a tremulous smile. 'He was determined to turn my fortunes around, and make sure Jennifer didn't get her hands on any more of George's money.'

Miss Busby's head tilted in interest.

'He and George were old acquaintances. I don't know what either of us would have done without him.'

Miss Busby leaned across to pour the tea, which was now in danger of being stewed. 'Milk?' she asked.

'Yes, please, and I think a little tot to keep the cold at bay.' Dorothy slipped a flask from her pocket and poured a noggin into her cup. 'Would you…?'

'No, no, thank you.' Miss Busby shook her head, glanced at the clock on the mantel, and held her tongue. It wasn't even three o'clock in the afternoon, but time did strange things to you when you lived alone, especially in such difficult circumstances.

She sipped her tea, giving herself a moment to consider her words. There seemed a lot to unpick here, and she didn't want to pull the wrong thread and have the whole thing unravel to nothing. 'So Vernon had sold George insurance, previously?'

'Yes, years ago. But then Jennifer landed herself in trouble and George had to help out. He never thought she'd marry such a weasel. Well, one wouldn't, would one?'

Miss Busby suspected most people would, actually.

'Anyway, it was *him,* Arthur I mean, who was in trouble, but it was Jennifer who paid the price. Quite literally, I'm afraid. She had the bailiffs banging on the door for loan repayments and all sorts, and he was never anywhere to be seen. Well, George didn't have much in the way of savings, and I…well…you know my situation.' Dorothy took a sip of tea. 'Poor George cashed in the policy. Naturally he lost a lot in the process, but Jennifer promised she'd pay it back in instalments…'

Miss Busby feared she knew where this was going.

'And, of course, he never saw a penny of it.' Dorothy sniffed, then blew her nose again.

'Oh dear,' was all Miss Busby could think to say.

'It's not Jennifer's fault,' Dorothy stated firmly. 'Not really. It's that bounder she took up with. She was a good girl before she met him.'

This was what worried Miss Busby. Her own recollections of Jennifer were quite the opposite – and with that in mind, could she really trust that Dorothy's opinion of Mr Potter wouldn't be equally clouded?

'Dear me,' she muttered again.

'I'm sorry, Isabelle, here I am rambling on. It's just that I'm on my own so often these days that I go overboard whenever anyone comes to call. Can I find you a biscuit?' she asked, making to rise from her chair.

'No, thank you, Dorothy, the tea is sufficient; please don't get up. I'm often alone, too, these days, so I quite understand. Do go on.'

Dorothy's smile returned. 'Well, if you don't object to my rattling. Vernon came round shortly after George was admitted to the sanatorium. He said a few papers needed signing – loose ends over the old policy. We began talking, and Vernon said he and George had discussed an idea to secure me a little nest egg.'

Miss Busby sat up straighter. This was the meat of the matter, at last. Mr Potter was surely about to reveal his true colours.

'Did he really?' she murmured over the rim of her cup.

Dorothy nodded. 'He sold me a policy – on his own life, as it happens. Vernon explained his lungs were badly damaged from being gassed in the war, and George had offered to pay the premiums, as I couldn't.' She shrugged. 'And with a bit of careful wording added to the policy, it meant Jennifer couldn't get her hands on any of it. It was Vernon and George's way of looking after me. They thought of everything. Poor, dear Vernon, he knew he wasn't long for this world; he had really quite an awful cough. I thought it was terribly heroic of him...'

'Yes, it sounds it.' Had she misjudged the situation so badly? *A fine detective I make*, Miss Busby thought, *leaping to conclusions so quickly.*

'So, there you have it,' Dorothy declared. 'But I'm sure you didn't come all the way here to listen to me chatter on, Isabelle. Was there anything in particular...?'

'Not at all, I was simply concerned for you, Dorothy,' Miss Busby replied. It was true, actually. Concerned, and curious, and perhaps out to prove a point to her newfound Scottish acquaintance. A point it now appeared she may have to concede. 'As I said, I heard what happened to the fellow at the lake, and Maggie mentioned you'd known him. Then I realised how long it is since I've seen you...'

'Maggie from the tearooms? Oh, I expect she had a thing or two to say!' Dorothy gave a throaty laugh. 'Nice enough, but she's led such a dull life. I may not have achieved much, but at least there was adventure in it.'

'Yes, indeed there was.' Miss Busby smiled, then finished her tea and put the cup down on the mismatched saucer. 'One last thing, Dorothy, if you don't mind me asking, but were the payments George made to Vernon each month awfully expensive?'

'I don't mind *you* asking, no. I drew the line at that officious new sergeant– Brierly, he said his name was – asking me the very same thing. I told him it was none of his business. I don't know him from Adam.'

'Yes, I know what you mean,' Miss Busby sympathised. 'My nephew explained it's a new idea in the police force, they've begun to move their people around to gain experience, but it seems to me they rarely think how it affects the locals.'

Dorothy huffed her agreement. 'I would've had a decent chat with the old sergeant.'

'Exactly so,' Miss Busby agreed.

'But anyway,' Dorothy continued, 'the insurance premiums were a guinea a month.'

'Ah.' Miss Busby was taken aback. That did seem a great deal. 'And what would be the value of the...?' She wasn't quite sure how to phrase the question.

'Payout? Five hundred pounds,' Dorothy said, with a hint of satisfaction.

'Well, that is a silver lining, indeed,' Miss Busby replied quietly. She smiled and thanked Dorothy for the tea and company, wondering as she left if she mightn't perhaps have been right about Mr Potter all along. And what a grave mistake he had made in putting such an enormous price upon his own head.

CHAPTER 8

Miss Busby trod carefully through the snow along the lane toward Little Minton. A glint of sunshine reflecting off the surface of still water caught her eye, and she stopped for a moment to gaze across the white expanse of fields to a gap through the trees. The lake was only a few minutes' walk from here, ten perhaps at the most. Almost the same distance as it was from the vicarage, although that lay in the opposite direction entirely.

A train came whooshing past, engine thrumming in rhythmic roar, shattering the peaceful quiet of the countryside; dense smoke greying the air for a moment until it dispersed in specks of soot and ash. It broke into her musing and she turned to continue down the hill.

If there had been a train to the village of Bloxford, Miss Busby would have returned on it, but there wasn't and so she made her way back to the high street with her mind full of Dorothy's tale.

A bustle of shoppers, browsers, and happy meanderers gave animated colour to the cobbled street. Today was market day in Little Minton, and stallholders offered all manner of goods, including wooden toys, colourful figurines, nativity sets, delicate glass baubles, gold painted stars and bright tresses of tinsel. They'd been joined by purveyors of seasonal fare, and the scent of roasted chestnuts, mulled wine, and hot chocolate filled the crisp cold air with delicious temptation.

She wandered between the busy stalls, pausing to chat to various old friends and acquaintances as she searched among the glittering Christmas cards for a box to her liking. Then she added two packets of crepe paper and, after much deliberation, finally chose a pine Christmas tree to place on order.

A pleasurable hour later, having completed her festive endeavours, she found Dennis waiting for her in the post van. He complained of this and that en route, but Miss Busby found herself distracted by the days events and almost forgot to give him the bag of roasted chestnuts she'd bought for him as a treat. He set her down and motored slowly off while she made her way indoors. Dinner was a dish of chicken shared with Pud, before she settled at her Davenport desk to make notes.

A tiring day, she thought some time later, having written as much detail as she could think of under Dorothy's name, listed under the heading, "Persons of Interest" in her notebook. She put her pen down, blotted the ink dry and then sat back against the cushioned chair. She was now thoroughly enjoying her foray into sleuthing, feeling firmly on the front foot once more.

Pudding reminded her with a complaining 'mew' that he was overdue a visit outdoors; opening the kitchen door onto the garden and orchard beyond, she waved a hand in the direction of the layered snow. He stared at the pristine whiteness, then up at her as if she were quite mad, and turned on his tail to go back into the warmth.

She remained for a moment gazing out over the hills behind the cottage, the stars shining like the most delicate of Christmas lights spread across a clear night sky. All was peaceful and calm; the virgin snow appearing to simply wait for the first footprints of the new day to fall upon it. Where they would lead, Miss Busby didn't know, but as she closed the door she was certain they would be crisp and satisfying and really quite exciting.

* * *

'Oh, drat, should we be wearing black?' Adeline Fanshawe asked as she and Miss Busby trod the snowy path toward Adeline's white Rolls-Royce parked outside Lavender Cottage.

'I don't see why,' Miss Busby replied. 'It's not a funeral, and besides, neither of us actually knew the man. Anyway, it's too late now.'

They climbed in. Miss Busby gritted her teeth as her friend started the car. Adeline had no need for such a large and expensive vehicle, nor would she have chosen to drive one if it weren't for her late husband. He had purchased it on the principle that a Rolls-Royce was utterly reliable and didn't require a crank start. It was such a shame he'd died shortly afterwards, and never had the chance to enjoy either his car or his meticulously planned retirement.

Adeline generally drove too fast, but with Miss Busby in the passenger seat, she now proceeded at a more stately pace.

'Was there anything else mentioned in the *Oxford News*?' Miss Busby asked, one gloved hand gripping the interior door handle.

'No, just the notice stating that there was a memorial service today at ten o'clock. I knew you'd want to go.'

'The new inspector arranged it.'

'Really?' Adeline turned to stare. 'What on earth for?'

'Eyes forward, Adeline,' Miss Busby reminded her and took a sharp breath as they veered around a bend. 'It's to draw in the suspects.'

'Suspects?' Adeline's eyes slid across to her friend's again, and then darted back to the snow-covered road. 'You mean, Vernon Potter truly was murdered?'

'There's not a doubt in my mind.'

'Well, why has nobody said anything?'

'It's all very cloak and dagger at the police station now, not like when my idiot nephew was in charge. Even young Bobby Miller is frightened to let anything slip, and I've yet to hear a good word about the new sergeant. I suppose the inspector has to be certain of his facts, and he didn't even know about the tramp, or the elderly woman until yesterday.'

'The… What?'

'Watch the road, Adeline,' Miss Busby instructed, then informed her of the details as they motored along the quiet country lanes. As they entered Church Way, they encountered a plethora of parked cars.

'Good heavens, Isabelle, just look at it!'

There weren't actually above a dozen, but it was quite a crowd for the narrow road.

'Potter *must* have been popular,' Miss Busby remarked with surprise as they drew to a halt.

'Rubberneckers, as Tom would have said.' Adeline was eternally forthright.

'Oh look, there's Lucy.' Miss Busby spotted the young reporter filing into the church among the crowd. She was wearing her customary camel coat over a tartan dress and matching scarf. 'Come on, Adeline.'

They were among the last stragglers and took an oak pew toward the rear of the ancient church. There were only a few flowers placed on the stone altar, and no coffin, of course, because Potter was still in the mortuary.

They waited quietly, the air above them stippled with motes of dust drifting in rays of filtered sunlight. Remnants of mediaeval paint clung to huge oak trusses supporting the roof. The walls, too, had once been coloured with lively frescos, although these had faded over centuries to become ghostly shades in red, blue, and yellow on flaking whitewash.

A hush fell; the brief moment when the spirit of sanctity slips into the soul, and reminds one that this is the house of God. Miss Busby whispered a prayer under her breath; *To those who are gone before, to those who are yet to come, may God bless thee and keep thee. Amen.*

'Isn't that Belinda Tasker?' Adeline asked, dispelling the spirit of sanctity as quickly as it had arrived. 'The florist from the high street?'

'Hmmm?' Miss Busby opened her eyes. 'Yes. And Dorothy, too. I was worried she wouldn't be able to walk all this way.'

'Couldn't she have caught a bus?' Adeline was whispering because the vicar had arrived, dressed in formal black and white, wearing an air of solemn piety.

'There aren't any local buses, Adeline,' Miss Busby replied, having told her many times before. She shook her head at her friend's cosseted ignorance.

Lucy, presumably on hearing a familiar voice, twisted around in her seat and raised a hand in a brief wave. Miss Busby smiled and waved back.

'Look, there's Letitia Lambert! I haven't seen her in years,' Adeline hissed as the vicar turned toward the altar.

Miss Busby straightened up to peer over at a rotund figure dressed in a mink coat and dark silk scarf. 'Good Heavens, so it is.' Shifting slightly in her seat she could also see Evelyn Simpson and Miss Frances Simpson, the latter of whom appeared still completely anguished, gazing about with puffy eyes, shoulders heaving every now and then with fresh, silent sobs.

The door behind them opened, letting a cold draught blow through, then closed again with a bang. Inspector McKay slid into a pew at the very back of the church just as the vicar turned to face the congregation and made the sign to begin.

Some thirty minutes later, after a dull service with little insight into Potter's life – with no reference to loving family, or service to country, Miss Busby noted – they filtered out to form small gaggles between snow-laden yews. The inspector was among the first to exit and found a strategic position not far from the lych gate. He wore the same smart grey suit and long dark overcoat of yesterday, close-fitting across his broad shoulders, his red hair subdued under the shade of a trilby pulled low over his eyes.

The vicar waited by the door, muttering glum words and forcing a smile to those who appeared in expectation of it. His wife and sister stood to one side; Frances Simpson gazed at the crowd, whereas Evelyn Simpson was po-faced and stiffly aloof.

Lucy came out with a group of elderly ladies. Miss Busby didn't recognise them; they all seemed rather decrepit, leaning on walking sticks, or each other.

'The Martin sisters from Long Compton,' Adeline proclaimed. 'Three of them are anyway, I've no idea about the other one.'

'Look, there's Enid Montgomery.' Miss Busby turned

her head to indicate a lady of formidable demeanour marching determinedly towards the gate, ignoring all around her.

'I can't have ever imagined she'd be a client of someone like Potter,' Adeline said. 'She used to be worth a small fortune.'

'So was Letitia Lambert.' Miss Busby watched the plump lady in the mink coat pause to speak to the vicar and his wife. Evelyn bustled forward to dominate the conversation, Frances stared down at her snow-covered boots, the vicar nodded mutely, barely given the chance to open his mouth.

The inspector had been silently observing the ebb and flow of movement: those who paused to talk, others who shuffled away with heads down and collars pulled up. Miss Busby noticed his eyes stray toward Lucy now and then, although Lucy didn't appear to notice. She was looking particularly attractive in the freshness of the day, the cold air having brought a blush to her cheeks, her dark hair gleaming in the sunshine. Miss Busby did wonder about her choice of tartan though…

McKay remained until the crowd thinned out, and he nodded to Miss Busby as she and Adeline passed him on their way to the Rolls-Royce.

'Well, that was all rather exciting.' Adeline smiled. 'Now what shall we do?'

'Lily's Tea Rooms,' Miss Busby declared. 'Where we can decide what to make of it all.'

The place was busy once more, although not from any of the church crowd, from what Miss Busby could see. They were fortunate to find a recently vacated table next to the fire.

'Hot chocolate and buttered muffins, please,' Adeline ordered for them both.

'Right you are.' Maggie, the waitress, smiled and nodded.

Lucy arrived a moment later; the waitress took her order as she removed her coat and scarf, before making her way over to them.

'That was quite illuminating!' She beamed.

'And clever of Inspector McKay to organise it,' Miss Busby added.

Lucy gave a curt nod. 'Yes, although we were informed by the vicar's wife. She made it sound as though it was all her idea.'

'That doesn't surprise me,' Adeline said dryly.

Miss Busby made the introductions.

'I adore your car,' Lucy said as the waitress arrived with a tray of steaming mugs and warm muffins.

'I've been very fortunate,' Adeline replied with a contented smile.

Miss Busby was more interested in the events of the morning. 'How many of the people at the service were Potter's clients, do you think?'

Lucy blew on her drink. 'I'd guess most of the ladies were. I'm compiling a list with the help of the insurance companies.'

'I thought you said they weren't very helpful,' Miss Busby recalled.

Lucy glanced sideways, a gleam of mischief in her eyes. 'They weren't, but they're having a change of heart.'

'Oh?' Miss Busby raised her brows.

'None of them realised Potter had taken out life insurances with other companies,' Lucy said with some small satisfaction. 'They only uncovered the full extent when I told them, so now they're a little more inclined to cooperate with me.'

'And how did you find out?' asked Adeline, with her customary forthrightness.

'A good reporter never reveals her sources,' Lucy replied lightly.

Adeline paused, buttered muffin in hand, as she gave the young woman a careful stare before nodding in approval.

'So, Potter's policies were against the rules?' Miss Busby asked.

'No, they were within the rules, that's what had upset them. He'd found a loophole,' Lucy confided.

'Really?' Miss Busby's eyes grew wide. 'However did he manage that?'

Lucy's smile slipped a little. 'I haven't gleaned all the details yet, but he was an agent for five different companies, and the policies were spread among clients in different locations. He had about eighteen in total, I think.'

'Surely each company would have noticed multiple insurances against the man's life?' Adeline quibbled. 'They keep records. It must have been obvious.'

'Yes, I raised the same point,' Lucy agreed, 'but they wouldn't discuss it. I think they're running internal investigations.'

'There could be a simple explanation.' Miss Busby's mind had been busy with its customary whirring. 'We are right on the border of three counties: Cheltenham is in Gloucestershire, Long Compton is in Warwickshire, and Little Minton is in Oxfordshire. If Potter took the insurances out with different companies in three different counties, it's quite possible that nobody at the various branches would have put two and two together.'

'Oh, how clever of you!' Lucy gave a throaty laugh. 'Of course, that's how he did it. He had five ladies here in Little Minton, six in Long Compton, and seven in Cheltenham.'

'And which of them attended the service?' Adeline asked as she finished her muffin.

Lucy pulled out a slim notepad. 'All five Little Minton ladies were present, four from Long Compton, and only two from Cheltenham.' She ran her finger down a neatly written list as she spoke.

'The Long Compton ladies were the Martin sisters,' Adeline affirmed. 'I saw them.'

'Yes, they were with their neighbour, Mrs Benedict. They all came together in a taxi cab. They're quite frail, poor souls,' Lucy replied.

'I wonder how they all knew about the service, with it being at such short notice,' Adeline mused.

'The local papers, of course.' Lucy looked a little affronted. 'We all co-operate to publish notices and announcements.'

'We recognised everyone from Little Minton,' Adeline rattled on, entirely oblivious to Lucy's affront. 'Frances Simpson, Belinda Tasker, Enid Montgomery, Dorothy Cranford, and... *Letitia Lambert*!'

'I must say, I was surprised to see Letitia there,' Miss Busby admitted.

'Which one was she?' Lucy asked.

'She looks like Queen Victoria in a 'we are not amused' mood,' Adeline answered and pulled a smugly superior face.

Lucy laughed. 'Why were you surprised she was there?'

'The Lambert family used to own most of the town, in fact, they still own quite a lot of it,' Adeline told her.

'Including the lake,' Miss Busby added. 'And Lambert House is almost right next to it.'

'Really?' Lucy made a note.

Something had been bothering Miss Busby. 'I'm surprised the insurance companies were suddenly so helpful. Particularly now that they realise they will have to pay out on Potter's policies.'

'Ah, but they don't think they will,' Lucy replied.

'Why?' Miss Busby and Adeline asked together.

'Because they believe it is about to become a murder

enquiry, and if it does, they will only have to pay out if the murderer is caught,' Lucy explained.

'Oh, Isabelle, is this all because of your tramp?' Adeline instantly accused her. 'Just think how those ladies will struggle without their insurance money.'

'Adeline,' Miss Busby hissed in horror. 'He is not *my* tramp, I'm simply trying to get to the bottom of things.' She felt a stab of guilt thinking of Dorothy in her dying brother's house, and her heart sank. 'Murder cannot simply be covered up just because someone may lose by it,' she reasoned, 'however unfortunate that loss may be. Truth will out.'

'It will if you keep digging for it,' Adeline shot back. 'And you should have been more careful…'

Lucy cut in to the developing tiff. 'Actually, it was as a result of the post mortem.'

'Why? What did they find?' Miss Busby asked with a feeling of relief.

Lucy lowered her voice. 'One of my colleagues knows an assistant at the mortuary, and apparently there were splinters of wood driven into the bump on Potter's head.'

'The inspector was taking samples from a root by the lake, yesterday,' Miss Busby said.

'What does that mean?' Adeline sounded puzzled.

'It means they're trying to discover if the bump and splinters were caused by Potter being dropped onto the root when he was dragged from the water, or if he was hit over the head with a branch or some such,' Miss Busby surmised.

'How do you know this?' Adeline turned to her friend.

'Actually, it's an educated guess,' she admitted.

'And it's probably a good one,' Lucy said in support.

Adeline nodded. 'You really can be quite clever, Isabelle.'

'Thank you, Adeline,' Miss Busby replied dryly.

'But now you simply *must* find the murderer, or nobody will be paid,' Adeline continued.

'Well, it isn't entirely down to me,' Miss Busby replied tartly.

Lucy had been making notes, but stopped to look up. 'I haven't heard the story about the tramp. Perhaps you could tell me?'

Miss Busby did so, including the details of the blanket.

'There was a notice on the board at the police station,' Lucy recalled, 'somebody had lost a child's blanket.'

'Really? How interesting,' Miss Busby replied, then immediately thought of something else she'd been meaning to ask. 'Have you managed to interview Inspector McKay yet, Lucy?'

Colour flushed on her cheeks. 'He refused to talk to me. He was quite rude actually.' She pushed a long strand of dark hair behind her ear.

'Yes, he can be quite acerbic,' Miss Busby murmured, remembering her own encounter with the man.

'Oh, just look at the time.' Adeline shot a look at the grandfather clock ticking in the corner of the cafe. 'I must hurry, I'm catching the two o'clock to London.' She stood up.

'You're going to see Jemima?' Miss Busby asked.

'And the boys, yes.' Adeline brushed crumbs from her navy skirt. 'I promised to take them to Hamley's, they're at an age where they like to choose their own toys for Christmas.'

'No Father Christmas for them, then?' Lucy smiled.

'They're a little too old for that now, I'm afraid.' Adeline looked about for the waitress, who came over immediately.

They settled the bill between them, left a tip and weaved through the crowded cafe to collect their coats and scarves.

Lucy headed for a red Sunbeam sports car parked just outside, having to disperse the small crowd of young boys admiring it before she could get in. 'Keep an eye out for tomorrow's newspaper,' she told Miss Busby, before tearing off down the high street, heading back toward Oxford.

'Isabelle, would you like a lift home?' Adeline enquired.

'I think not. I didn't quite complete my Christmas shopping yesterday.'

'As you wish. I will see you on my return. And I think you had better spend some time on this dead Potter, because you're involved now, Isabelle. And it's a serious business for all concerned. There's people's financial futures at stake.' And with that stern lecture delivered, she went off.

CHAPTER 9

The town had grown even busier, it seemed Christmas shopping had begun in earnest and there was still a week to go.

The police station was actually Miss Busby's first port of call; Bobby was once again behind the long wooden counter, writing carefully in the open ledger, his mouth moving as he wrote.

'Oh, Miss Busby, you've caused a real stir,' he said when he spotted her.

'Have I?' She raised her brows.

'When the inspector got back yesterday, he was in a right mood.' Bobby leaned forward across the counter to talk to her. 'Sergeant Brierly hadn't bothered to find the tramp, even though one of the people living nearby had mentioned him. The inspector was hoppin' mad and tore a strip off him good an' proper. So now they're all down at the lake searching for him.'

Miss Busby smiled. 'Well, perhaps old ladies do

know a thing or two after all. Is there any information about the blanket I gave the inspector yesterday?'

'It's locked in the Evidence Room, Miss.'

That raised her brows even further.

'Actually it's only a store cupboard, but the inspector says it's to be treated as evidence.'

A warm, satisfied feeling settled in Miss Busby's chest. 'Has the inspector looked at the notice board recently, do you know?'

'I shouldn't think so.' Bobby shook his head slowly. 'The notices are for people to come in and look at.'

She walked over to the board and scanned it quickly. There were only four notices pinned onto it. She pointed to one of them. 'This is a note from Josie Lloyd, who lost her child's comfort blanket near the lake on Sunday. That was the same day Mr Potter drowned. Perhaps someone would like to visit Josie and ask her one or two questions?'

Bobby's mouth dropped open, before he hurriedly raised the counter top and came to join her. 'Ooooh, so it is.' He nodded, and his eyes widened. 'Now that's really clever of you, Miss, he's not going to like missing that, neither.'

'I can't take the credit, I'm afraid; it was the reporter, Lucy Wesley, who told me it was here. I understand she has tried to speak to the inspector, but found him less than amenable. I suggest you inform him he'd do well to take time to listen to people who are willing to offer him information.'

'I can't say that to him, Miss Busby, or he'll tear a strip off me, too.' He reached up and carefully unpinned the notice from the board. 'I'll be sure he sees it though. Is there anything else I can help you with?'

'Yes, the post mortem results...'

'Oh, no.' He scurried behind the counter and banged the top back down. 'I'm sayin' nothing about that. You'll have to ask him yourself, Miss. More than my job's worth, that is.'

She smiled. 'Then I will do just that. Thank you, Bobby. Goodbye.'

'Bye, Miss.' He offered a cheery wave, and she left feeling really quite pleased with herself.

There was one item she'd failed to purchase yesterday, having feared she'd overload herself with shopping.

She entered the florist's to the cheery tinkle of the bell, which seemed somewhat misleading given the dimly lit and decidedly uncheery situation within. A meagre fire burned in the grate, a few flowers and evergreens drooped in buckets on shelves set along the walls to her left and right. A scarred trestle table was set up near the back wall, furnished with pad and pencil, a few sheets of brown paper, scissors, secateurs, and reels of ribbon and twine.

It was plain to see that Belinda was struggling, and Miss Busby's heart sank. It was all very well thinking herself clever, but if the insurance companies had their way, this poor lady – and quite a few others – wouldn't receive a penny from them. And she was now responsible for adding grist to their mill. The warm feeling from just moments ago froze to ice in her chest and dropped to her stomach.

She sighed as she waited for Belinda to appear, and tried to tell herself not to be silly – a crime couldn't be left unpunished. And besides, once the culprit was discovered, there was no reason to think the money wouldn't flow exactly where it ought. Truth would out, with or without her, and justice would follow, she told herself firmly.

'Hello?' she called, the bell still not having brought anyone forth. 'Mrs Tasker? Belinda?'

Belinda finally emerged through the door behind the trestle table, her grey hair tied back, highlighting her worn, plain face, now pale and drawn. She'd changed from her best coat and hat of this morning into a dark, shapeless frock with a green apron fastened over it. Her eyes were red and puffy, but met Miss Busby's own with steely determination nonetheless.

'Yes?' she asked briskly. 'Christmas wreath, is it?'

'Please, if you have the time,' Miss Busby replied in a friendly tone.

Belinda leaned closer. 'Miss Busby, isn't it?'

'Yes, good afternoon, Mrs Tasker,' she replied with a bright smile.

'I haven't see you for a while,' Belinda observed, and picked up the pencil to make a note. 'With or without dried berries?'

'With, please, and tied with a red ribbon.'

Belinda wrote down the order. 'I don't usually see people anymore until either something good happens, or something bad. Bad, more often than not.'

Miss Busby glanced around at the sparse offerings on display and felt a stab of regret that she didn't call in more often. 'I hadn't thought of it like that,' she replied, realising she hadn't spoken to Belinda since she'd ordered a bouquet for Lady Caroline's wedding at the Hall last year. Like a lot of people in rural areas, she had her own garden which furnished her with all the blooms she required day-to-day. 'How have you been keeping, Mrs Tasker?' she asked, concern in her voice.

'Oh, so-so. Still missing my Daisy, of course.' Her eyes glazed over momentarily. 'But life goes on, doesn't it?'

'It does.' Miss Busby nodded sadly. So many women in the area, Belinda, Dorothy, Adeline, even herself, had lost so much. How much easier might things be, she wondered, if they could somehow find a way to ease their grief, and loneliness, together. But perhaps she was simply projecting her own feelings onto others. And it wasn't like her, she thought, to be feeling this way. She'd always tried to keep her days, and her mind, full. It just seemed to become harder, somehow, with age. As if the isolation crept slowly upon you with each year that passed.

Belinda ran her eye over the buckets of evergreens. 'I'm afraid we only have a limited supply of holly.

Everyone wants it, but it grows so slowly. I could add some pine to plump it out?'

'That would be perfect, Mrs Tasker. Thank you.'

'Do call me Belinda, it's so much easier.' She tried a wan smile.

'Of course, thank you, Belinda. I wonder if I might wait? Or are you terribly busy?'

Belinda seemed to soften. 'I'm busy enough coming up to Christmas.' She indicated the Windsor chair in front of the fire. 'But do sit down. You can tell me how you'd like it made up. Bill from the market does the deliveries for me, it'll be easier than you struggling home with it.'

Miss Busby nodded her thanks and sat with her handbag on her lap. 'You don't have anyone to help you?'

'Not any more. I had to let my assistant go only last month.' Belinda gathered sprigs of holly, pine, and cedar from the buckets and placed them on the table. 'There just hasn't been enough work for two of us. She was such a lovely girl, I hated doing it, but since Daisy... well. Things haven't been the same.' Her gaze turned back to Miss Busby. 'But they could be worse, I suppose.'

'Indeed. Take poor Mr Potter, for instance.'

'Oh, I doubt he was poor.' Her words were as sharp as the holly she was threading into the wreath with deft movements.

'Possibly not,' Miss Busby agreed. 'I saw you at the service this morning.'

'Oh, you were there? I didn't spot you, but there were more people than I'd expected.' Her reply was noncommittal.

'There was a notice in the *Oxford News*,' Miss Busby continued in conversational tone.

'Was there?' Belinda snipped the end from a long stem. 'I don't take it. I heard about it from Evelyn Simpson.'

'Evelyn told you?'

'Yes, she dropped by. She knew Potter too, of course.'

'Oh?' Miss Busby feigned surprise. 'How interesting. What was he like? Everyone I've spoken to seemed quite fond of the man.'

'Didn't you know him?' She looked up from the wreath in surprise, as Miss Busby gave a small shake of her head. 'Why did you go to the service then?'

It was a misstep, she realised, but quickly rallied. 'I went with Adeline.'

'Oh.' Belinda frowned at the secateurs in her hand. 'Well, I suppose he seemed nice enough.'

'He was very knowledgeable about insurance, I gather,' Miss Busby continued. 'And I'm told he's ensured his clients will be well cared for now that he's...'

'Dead?' Belinda glared at her, before dropping her eyes back to the wreath. 'I'm not sure he was terribly competent at all. He advised me to...' Her voice suddenly cracked. 'I...I can't discuss it with you. I should never have agreed to it. I might be...might... oh, I just don't know what I've got myself into.'

'You mean with the insurance?' Miss Busby probed gently, leaning forward in the chair.

Belinda sniffed, holding back tears. 'The police came here, asking where I was on Sunday. I told them I was visiting my daughter's grave at the Methodist Chapel, and then one of them asked about my policy with Potter, and I said I didn't have one, but...but...' Tears ran down her thin cheeks; she dashed them away with the back of her hand.

'Oh, Belinda, I'm so sorry.' Miss Busby rose to put a hand on Belinda's arm, and noticed the woman was trembling. 'You're frightened, aren't you, but I'm sure there's really no need.'

'There is.' She took a handkerchief from her apron pocket and blew her nose. 'I've done something terrible.'

Miss Busby's heart began to race as she wondered if a confession was imminent.

'You did have a policy with Potter, didn't you,' she asked softly.

Belinda tried to stifle her sobs. 'But it was a cheat, I knew it was. I'm too old, over sixty. Potter said it was perfectly fine, that it wasn't hurting anyone and as long as I made my payments then why shouldn't I have my money? He said I needn't worry about a thing, and he made it sound alright, but now he's dead and I can't do anything but think about it. What if they prosecute me for fraud? I will lose everything.' She buried her face in the handkerchief and sobbed loudly.

'There now, Belinda, they won't.' Miss Busby forced

confidence into her voice. 'I have heard that the loop-hole in the insurance company's system Mr Potter discovered was genuine.'

There was a pause in the sobs. 'Truly?' She removed the handkerchief.

Miss Busby nodded authoritatively.

'Oh, I've been so worried. I haven't been able to sleep, or think of anything else… You are sure? You're not just saying that?'

'I am sure,' Miss Busby pronounced, hoping to good-ness that Lucy was right.

'But even if it is legitimate, they are still refusing to pay out.' She tucked the handkerchief away with a final resounding sniff. 'I had a letter from the Prudential, it was here when I got back from the service.'

'What did it say?' Miss Busby asked, although she had a horrible feeling she already knew.

'That Mr Potter's death was "unexplained" and that given the circumstances my claim may not be upheld.'

'Well, that will depend on the outcome of the inves-tigation.'

'That's what Mrs Montgomery said.'

'You've spoken to Enid?' Miss Busby tried to keep her tone calm, even as the scent of fresh information hung in the air.

'Yes, as soon as I opened the letter I went straight round to see her.' Belinda cleared her throat and pulled herself together. 'She knows I'm worried about being involved in a fraud, but she said Potter was clever enough to know what he was doing. She was concerned about his death though.'

'Why?'

'Because she thought it could be foul play, and then we really would be in trouble. And she never believed he was ill, of course. Even with that coughing performance he put on. And she'd know, wouldn't she? Oh, I've been *such* a fool.'

Miss Busby sighed. Things were indeed becoming rather serious.

'I'm sure the matter will be cleared up soon enough. And if it truly was something sinister, the culprit will be found and the money released.'

'Well, you're surer than I am,' Belinda retorted sharply. 'But then I suppose you can afford to be.'

Miss Busby drew back a little in shock.

Belinda immediately relented. 'Oh, I'm so sorry. I spoke out of turn. You've been so kind, but it's been dreadful, you simply can't imagine, and on top of everything else... I met Potter soon after losing my Daisy, you see, and now I wonder if I was in my right mind when I signed the policy. I think he chose people like me, people who'd suffered a loss, or tragedy. I know I haven't been myself since it happened. Please, do forgive me Miss Busby. I truly did not mean what I said.'

'No need to apologise.' Miss Busby genuinely felt for the woman. 'Daisy was such a lovely girl.' She recalled Belinda's daughter, and her terrible death from polio. She'd only just turned thirty.

Belinda looked down at the wreath on the table, then reached for the roll of red ribbon. 'I wish I'd never met the man. I think he was a scoundrel, always trying to bend the rules. There was something off about him. If I'd been more myself I'd have seen it right away. But you'd think that a church-going woman would know better than to associate with his sort.'

'Frances? I'd imagine she was just as vulnerable to his sales techniques as anyone else.' Miss Busby watched as Belinda finished the wreath in a few quick movements.

'No, not Frances.' Belinda's eyes flashed furiously as she looked up. 'Evelyn – the vicar's wife. She was the one who sent Mr Potter my way. I scraped together every spare penny to pay the premiums and now I'm likely to lose it all. I wish I'd never met the infernal man, and if it hadn't been for her meddling, I never would have done.'

CHAPTER 10

The following morning arrived without any news, but as Miss Busby didn't take the *Oxford News*, this was hardly a surprise. She'd quite expected Adeline to arrive with it, but perhaps she'd stayed longer in London than expected.

More snow had fallen in the night and after toast and marmalade for breakfast, she carried Pudding into the garden and put him down near the compost heap where warm ashes kept the ground clear. She waited in the cold for him to perform the delicate task of his toilette before carrying him indoors again. He flicked his tail, but then jumped up to settle on her lap and rumble loud purrs. He may have seemed a curmudgeonly cat, but in reality he was just a big softy.

She gazed through the window deep in thought as she rubbed his ears. What was happening? Had Potter's death been declared a murder? She glanced at the clock on the mantelpiece, it was after eight, which in the countryside was a perfectly reasonable time to call on one's neighbours. She gently lowered the cat to his favourite spot by the fire and went to don her coat and boots to tramp through the snow to Holly Cottage. Mary Fellows always had the newspaper delivered, and that would answer the question.

'Mary? Barnaby?' she called out as she approached the cottage. No frantic barking met her knocks on the front door, no curtain moved in the front window. Indeed, the curtains were still drawn. She noticed the newspaper was still in the terracotta pipe set in the garden wall. She tugged it free, brushed away the snow and carried it into the house, still calling out as she stepped inside.

The house seemed strangely quiet, and far too cold. She placed the paper on the hall table, glancing briefly at the large lettering declaring more snow was on the way.

'Mary?' she called out again. No answer came, and a sudden fear caused her to dash upstairs.

'Oh, no,' Miss Busby murmured as she crossed the bedroom to kneel by the old lady lying on the floor. Barnaby was curled up the other side of her, misery written in his dark eyes. She paused to give his head a consolatory rub, then lifted Mary's wrist, and was surprised and relieved to feel the faintest of pulses.

'Oh, Barnaby, thank heavens,' she whispered, her mind racing into action. 'There's hope.' Pulling the pink candlewick cover from the bed, she tucked it around Mary, then carefully manoeuvred a pillow under her head. 'I'm going to fetch help,' she said into the old lady's ear. 'Just hold on. Barnaby, stay,' she added, although the dog was already settling himself back into place, alongside his mistress. 'Good boy,' she whispered. The extra warmth would help.

Rushing back down the stairs, she flew from the cottage and across the road to follow the bridleway to Oak End Cottage.

Nurse Delaney was outside, vigorously sweeping snow from her steps. She looked up the moment she heard her name called, her eyes widening in surprise at the figure rushing towards her.

'Miss Busby?' she called. 'Slow down, for goodness' sake! You'll fall and break something in this weather!'

Bloxford's sturdy community nurse for many years, Nurse Delaney was nearing retirement but never baulked at a plea for help from her neighbours. From skinned knees, to the harrowing outbreak of Spanish Influenza, the woman was a dependable and knowledgeable pillar of the community. Miss Busby had never been so glad to see her, and breathlessly informed her of poor Mary's situation.

With a shouted instruction into the cottage that Mr Delaney should telephone the doctor without delay, the nurse fastened her thick cardigan over her navy uniform and hurried with Miss Busby back to Holly Cottage.

'It's freezing in here, we need to light all the fires in the house,' she instructed, before pounding up the stairs.

This task kept Miss Busby occupied until Dr.

Stephens arrived in his motor car, followed by assorted curious and concerned neighbours. Miss Busby shooed the well-wishers out, promising to inform them how Mary fared, just as soon as there was news.

'Was it a fall?' the doctor asked as he headed straight up the narrow staircase, his substantial weight causing the treads to squeak.

'Possibly. Nurse Delaney doesn't think there's anything broken.' Miss Busby followed him.

'This cold doesn't help.' He went to the bed, where Mary now lay. She'd been picked up bodily by the no-nonsense nurse and propped by pillows to help her breathe more easily. Despite these ministrations, Mary remained unconscious and deathly white, her frail frame seeming to have shrunken even further.

'Hospital,' Dr. Stephens pronounced and gazed over his pince-nez at Nurse Delaney.

'I'll go home and telephone for an ambulance,' the nurse agreed. 'Unless there's a phone here, or...' She looked to Miss Busby.

'I'm afraid not,' she replied with a brief shake of the head.

'Well, Miss Busby,' Dr. Stephens lectured in a rather pompous tone, 'you should consider installing one, because the consequences of living alone without any means of communication can be very serious.' He indicated the poor patient.

'I will consider it most carefully, Doctor,' Miss Busby replied, feeling rather like one of her former pupils after a telling-off. 'Is there anything more I can do here?'

'You may sit and talk to the Mrs Fellows until the ambulance arrives,' he said, as the nurse bustled out. 'She's beginning to come round, but is weak and will be confused. She must have lain there for hours. It will have taken a toll.'

'Yes, of course. Was it her heart, do you think?'

'Most likely. Her angina has been worsening this past year. It was only a matter of time.' He gathered his leather bag from the marble washstand. 'I would wait with her myself, but I'm on duty and should stay near my telephone. You know where to find me if you need me.'

Miss Busby felt a weight of sorrow descend. Mary had always been such a stalwart. And then a thought occurred to her.

'Doctor?'

'Yes?' He turned, bushy brows raised.

'You didn't happen to attend the death at the lake, did you?'

He frowned. 'No, it was one of my colleagues. I've heard tales, though, that the victim was involved with some sort of insurance shenanigans.'

'As have I, I'm afraid, and I believe there is quite a lot resting on the outcome of the investigation.'

He nodded. 'Were you or Mrs Fellows one of those affected?'

'No, but I'm afraid a friend of mine...' Another white lie, her conscience reminded her. Although, did it count as another, given that she'd used it previously?

'It's best left to the coroner to decide, Miss Busby. None of the locals would want to cloud the issue.'

She wondered what that meant. 'Mr Potter's injuries weren't consistent with slipping and falling, were they?' She threw caution to the wind.

He shook his head, before catching himself. 'As I said, it's best left to the coroner to decide.' He placed his felt hat on his white hair, bid her good day, and left.

Miss Busby remained with Mary, talking quietly to her. The poor lady didn't seem to hear, and began to softly snore, which was at least reassuring. Barnaby remained steadfast at her side.

Nurse Delaney returned a short while later and bent over the patient. 'Hello?' she said as Mary's eyes flickered open. 'You'll soon be feeling better, my dear. Miss Busby found you.'

Mary tried to whisper a reply.

'Sweet tea may help,' Nurse Delaney declared, looking pointedly at Miss Busby.

'Yes, of course.' She instantly jumped up and went downstairs. The newspaper was lying where she'd left it on the hall table. She picked it up as she headed for the kitchen.

Waiting for the water to boil, she searched the front page – there was no mention of Potter, or murder. That was strange, Lucy had seemed so certain yesterday...

Despite copious amounts of milk and sugar, Mary was unable to do more than sip a mouthful. The nurse may have been a matter-of-fact type but she was a comforting presence, and monitored Mary's pulse and ensured she was warm enough.

Miss Busby searched for a spare nightgown and some toiletries to pack for Mary. 'She'll want her own things,' she told the nurse, who nodded. The two of them chatted encouragingly to Mary while she drifted in and out of consciousness. Barnaby refused all offers of food and attention, and Miss Busby's heart broke a little when the nurse asked what would happen to him.

'He must come and stay with me, of course,' she said. 'Until Mary is better.'

There was no consoling the animal when his owner was carried to the ambulance. Miss Busby held him close while Nurse Delaney went with her, declaring she'd see her settled and comfortable at the local cottage hospital.

The neighbours were reassured as much as possible, Miss Busby insisting Mary had a much better colour now than when she'd found her, and that she'd even managed to squeeze her hand before she left.

An hour later, after a quiet cup of tea, along with some ginger snaps, she sat in her favourite chair with the dog at her feet and the cat perched on top of the dresser.

A sharp rap suddenly sounded on her front door, making her jump and causing Barnaby to bark frantically.

'Oh no, Miss, what's 'e doin' here?' Dennis complained loudly as he popped his head through the door and Barnaby launched himself forward.

'Barnaby, no,' Miss Busby shouted, which stopped the dog in his tracks. He turned with his tail between his legs, and padded back to the hearth.

'What is it, Dennis?' Miss Busby asked.

'Have ye' heard, Miss? I thought you'd want to know. Summat terrible's happened.'

'It's not Mrs Fellows is it?' She instantly thought of Mary.

'No, why would it be?' He looked puzzled.

'Because she's just been taken to hospital.'

'Ooooh! It's all happening today, in't it?' His eyes rounded.

'Yes, I suppose, but what have you come to tell me?'

'They've found a body!' There was a distinct note of relish in his voice. 'Down by the lake. That's the second in less than a week. This is gettin' like them picture shows, in't it? There must be someone ever so sinister about the place.'

'Who is it?'

'Dunno, that's what they got to find out, afore anyone else snuffs it. Maybe if Bobby Miller did a bit more proper work...'

'I meant who died, Dennis.' She tried not to sound exasperated.

'Ooooh. Dunno. Just a body, they said.'

She was about to reach for her coat when a car drew up at the kerb, it was an elegant grey Alvis, and Inspector McKay stepped from it as Dennis watched in open-mouthed astonishment.

'Miss Busby.' McKay strode down the now well-trodden path.

'I'd best be goin',' Dennis squeaked. 'I'll see ye' later, Miss Busby.' He dashed off toward the red post van parked further down the lane.

'Inspector, I hear there's been another tragedy,' she said as he stopped in front of her.

'Aye, there has, and I'm afraid I need to ask for your immediate assistance.' He looked down, his eyes shaded beneath his hat. 'Could you come with me, please?'

Dennis was right, she thought to herself, it really *was* all happening today. 'Let me fetch my coat...' She suddenly thought of Barnaby. 'And the dog,' she added.

'No, not the—' Inspector McKay called, too late.

A moment later she was following him back to the car with Barnaby under her arm. The dog didn't seem particularly keen to go, but she felt he oughtn't be alone given the circumstances.

'May I ask in what way this concerns me?' Miss Busby settled into the passenger seat with Barnaby on her lap.

McKay's lips were drawn in a tight line. 'A body has been found at the lake.' He started the motor. 'We think it's the tramp.'

Her hand flew to her mouth as her heart sank to her boots. 'Oh, heavens.'

'I'd like you to identify him, if you can bear it. You are the only one who heard his statement.'

'So, this *is* a murder enquiry now?' She felt shaken, but was determined to maintain her composure.

'I think it most probable, although we still don't have definitive evidence.' He drove skilfully around a sharp bend, avoiding the snow drift built up against a thick hedge.

'What about the samples you took from the root?'

He glanced sideways at her. 'It was the same type of wood as the splinters found in Potter's head wound, but that doesn't prove he was hit with a branch. It's equally possible his head was actually dropped onto the exposed root when he was pulled from the water.'

'Implying the branch he *may* have been hit with, would have been laurel.' She recalled the bushes growing in the vicinity.

'Exactly, and please, do not repeat that information to anyone.'

She was pleasantly surprised he had confided in her, but then again, he'd probably come to realise she'd find out one way or another. 'And the tramp?' she asked. 'How did he die?'

'We don't know yet. He was found early this morning on the bench, apparently asleep, but he had actually frozen to death.' The inspector turned into the lane leading to Lambert House and the lake beyond.

Miss Busby felt a chill run down her spine. That poor man. Imagine being so alone, so forgotten, that you could simply lie down and die from exposure to the elements. She remembered, with a fresh pang, the kindness he'd shown Barnaby when the poor dog had been shivering. If only someone could have done the same for him.

The unexpected and upsetting events of the morning were taking their toll, she realised as she pulled her coat tighter together. She wasn't the sentimental or melancholy type, but her usual equilibrium had been thrown out of kilter. Feeling hopelessly sorry for the man would do him no favours now. Her mind raced to catch up with events, and worked instead to help him in the only way she could – by getting to the bottom of things.

'He must have been used to managing in this type of weather,' she said, thinking aloud. 'And surely he'd have known he could have taken shelter in the church if need be. Why would he have been sleeping out on the bench in such terrible conditions?'

'Drink,' the inspector concluded glumly. 'There was a half bottle of whisky in his hand.'

'It would have taken more than a half bottle, surely.' Miss Busby knew that hardened drinkers built up a tolerance. The inspector would know this too, she realised, and would surely have taken it into account. She shot a sideways look at him. His expression was grim.

'You suspect a substance of some sort,' she surmised softly.

'The bottle will be sent for testing.' He stopped the car next to the high stone wall and pulled on the handbrake.

An ambulance was parked just a little way along the lane. Two men sat in the front. A policeman in sergeant's uniform spotted the Alvis and walked toward them.

'Lewis is still scouring the area, sir. Haven't found anything yet.'

'Then go back until you do,' McKay snapped.

The sergeant nodded. 'Yes, sir.' Then stalked back along the trampled tracks in the snow.

McKay muttered something under his breath as he turned to Miss Busby. 'Perhaps you could leave the dog in the car?'

'I fully intend doing so, Inspector.' She told Barnaby she wouldn't be long, and that he'd be warmer where he was, before closing the door on him. He instantly jumped up to stare through the window, his breath misting the glass.

One of the ambulance men climbed down from the front cab. 'This the lady, sir?'

'It is.' McKay led Miss Busby to the rear of the ambulance, a fairly modern vehicle, unlike the ex-army van that had transported Mary Fellows away earlier.

Two ambulances in one day, she thought to herself, *how very extraordinary.*

The medic was dressed in a drab brown coat, the ambulance painted white with a red cross on its doors and the word 'ambulance' writ along its sides, just to avoid any doubt.

'This is a formal identification, Miss Busby,' McKay said, and entered the rear of the vehicle.

'Careful now.' The medic offered his hand to help her climb the two metal steps.

The body lay under a white sheet on a bed fixed to

the side panels. A frosted window allowed light to enter the confined space. McKay lifted a corner of the sheet. Miss Busby stared in sadness at the grey face of the tramp, his hair still damp and plastered to his head, grey bristles on his chin, mouth and eyes closed, he looked strangely at peace. She nodded mutely.

No more was said until they were both back in the Alvis, Barnaby once more on her lap.

'It can't be a coincidence,' she began.

'No,' McKay agreed. 'I'd like you to come to the station, if you would, and write out a statement.'

'You should have asked me to do that two days ago.' She was angry, not with him – or not entirely – but with whomever had carried out such a cruel act on the poor homeless soul.

'I know, and I apologise for it.'

They were both subdued and remained in silence for the few minutes it took to reach the station. Miss Busby insisted on bringing Barnaby in with her, and the dog sat patiently at her feet in the inspector's meticulously neat office while she wrote a concise statement of her encounter with the tramp. It didn't take long and she sat in silence for a while, waiting for McKay to return.

The inspector had actually been quite solicitous, he'd insisted on switching on three bars of the electric fire to keep her warm, and ordered Bobby Miller to provide her with a mug of sweet tea. She knew the inspector was based in Oxford and assumed his official office was there, but there was no sign of dust, even the black candlestick telephone was wiped clean, and the blotter and inkstand were placed precisely in the centre of the plain oak desktop. She had heard of 'incident rooms' and wondered if this were one, although if it were, there wasn't much to distinguish it.

She placed the empty mug on the desk and handed the precisely written statement to him when he strode in. 'I've written everything I could think of, including the blanket,' she said. 'Did you interview Josie Lloyd?'

'Sergeant Brierly spoke to her. She told him the child had been carrying the blanket and must have dropped it on the path around the lake sometime about two o'clock the same day Potter died. The killer must have found the blanket sometime after then and before Potter's arrival.'

She noted he used the word 'killer' but didn't remark on it. 'The tramp said he saw Potter and the woman as dusk was falling.' She gathered up Barnaby's lead as she rose to leave.

'That would've been around four o'clock.' McKay opened the door for her, a cold draught wafted in from the corridor. 'Would you like me to drive you home, Miss Busby?'

'No, thank you. I'm sure you will have plenty to occupy you.' Their conversation was stilted, shock and anger taking effect.

'I will,' he agreed. 'But I'll try to keep you abreast of the situation. You are an important witness now, Miss Busby.'

She looked up at him.

'And the tramp was probably murdered,' he continued, his face set very serious. 'I must remind you, for your own safety, to take care.'

'Did he have a name?' she asked quietly.

'One of the medics believes he was known as Joe Tucker, but there's no way of confirming it just yet.' He sighed. 'We made a thorough search for him yesterday, and he chose to avoid us, but I'm still sorry for what happened.'

'I know.' Her anger suddenly dissipated to be replaced by simple sadness. 'He was frightened of the police, I think.'

'Possibly, or authority, anyway,' McKay said quietly. 'He had a shack deep in the woods. We spoke to the gardeners at Lambert House. Apparently he came around this time every year, although they'd only catch sight of him now and then.'

'Did you speak to Letitia Lambert?' Miss Busby's eyes sharpened.

'We did, but she's quite reclusive and didn't seem to know what was happening around her.'

'Hmmm,' Miss Busby murmured. 'But she was one of Mr Potter's clients, wasn't she?'

McKay frowned. 'Miss Busby…'

'Don't worry, Inspector, I'm quite capable of looking after myself,' she said, and left the station with Barnaby at her heels.

CHAPTER 11

Miss Busby decided lunch was required. She wasn't at all hungry, but it was midday and she couldn't call on anyone at such a time, so she might as well while away the hour at Lily's Tea Rooms.

'Now, soup, sandwiches, or we've got welsh rarebit today if you fancy a treat,' Maggie, the waitress, told her once she'd settled at the table by the fire.

'Welsh rarebit would be very welcome,' Miss Busby agreed. Barnaby stared out from under the tablecloth in pitiful fashion.

'I have some hard biscuits, if he'd like one.' Maggie indicated the dog.

'That's very kind, thank you.'

Maggie hovered in indecision, looked about and then lowered her voice. 'There's been another body found at the lake.'

Word had spread quickly, Miss Busby thought. 'So it seems.'

'There's something funny going on,' Maggie continued. 'Derek said there's talk at the railway.'

Miss Busby recalled Derek was Maggie's husband. 'Why at the railway?'

'Derek works there, he's head porter.' The waitress's eyes darted about again and she lowered her voice even further. 'A while back, one of the stable lads let drop that Mr Potter was fond of a flutter on the horses.'

'Really?' Miss Busby's brows rose.

'But you'd best not tell anyone,' Maggie added.

'No, of course not,' Miss Busby assured her, lowering her brows to 'soul of discretion' level.

'It's just that things are turning serious, and no-one wants to talk to the police.'

'Why ever not?' Miss Busby felt quite exasperated. She could understand people being reluctant to talk to new officers they didn't know, but really, with it now being a two-body concern there ought to be a line. Why couldn't people just tell the truth? *Secrets*, she reminded herself, *and secrets beget lies.*

'Because some of the porters earn themselves a bit extra as runners for the bookies.' Maggie finally spilled the beans. 'There's no harm in it, but it could get them into trouble. All sorts of rules on the railway, and half of them make no sense.'

'Ah, I quite understand,' Miss Busby said in confidential tone as comprehension dawned.

'I knew you would. And I thought *someone* ought

to know, someone sensible, so they can do something about it.'

Miss Busby was about to point out that there really wasn't anything she could do if she wasn't to tell anyone, but Maggie had further details to impart.

'Anyway,' she went on, 'word at the railway was that Mr Potter used some of the insurance money he collected to put bets on; big ones, more often than not. It's been going on for months apparently, and his horses had a tendency to win,' Maggie confided. 'The lads had started to follow his bets, and it was getting a bit out of hand. My Derek is head porter, as you know, and he was thinking of telling the station master, but he's not well…'

'You mean George Parker, Dorothy Cranford's brother?' Things were beginning to drop into place.

'Yes, but with him not there, Derek was at a loss, and now Mr Potter's dead, and there's another one today – well, it's set them all by the ears.'

'I can imagine,' Miss Busby said, then cast a quick glance towards the couple at a neighbouring table, who remained safely engrossed in their soup. 'How could Derek be certain Mr Potter was using some of the insurance money?'

'Well, he couldn't be absolutely *sure*, but he truly believes that was what was happening.'

'But why?'

'Mr Potter came here to Little Minton at least once a month to collect his money from the old ladies, and he always came on the train, even though he had a car. The railway people all know each other up and down the line, and the head porter in Cheltenham is a friend of Derek's. He said Mr Potter would park at Cheltenham, take the train over to here, go and see his ladies, and then return to the station. That's when he gave his bets to the lads, well it was actually two of them, Den and Kevin. He'd take a bundle of cash from his wallet, tell them which horse, and which race to put the money on, then say he'd see them next time for his winnings. And win he did! Me and Derek don't think anyone could win all the time, not without someone giving him a tip. No-one's *that* lucky.'

Miss Busby didn't know a thing about horse racing but assumed one would not wager a large amount without good reason. 'But he lived not far from Cheltenham race course.'

'Exactly, so why did he make bets through the lads at Little Minton Station?'

The bell above the tea room door jangled, making them both jump. Maggie looked over her shoulder to see a portly gent removing his coat and hat, and closing her mouth into a tight line, she darted off.

Miss Busby pondered the unexpected news. What was Potter up to? Making money was the obvious answer, but why did he need to involve the porters? Perhaps if he were seen to be consistently winning, questions would be asked at the racecourse about where the tips were coming from. Using the young men at the station would presumably allow him greater winnings with a lesser risk. And Potter seemed the type who was familiar with calculated risk.

So, where *were* the tips coming from? Despite the unhappy events of the morning, she suddenly felt a frisson of excitement. New leads would bring her closer to the truth, which could only allow for the relief of the unfortunate ladies such as Dorothy and Belinda.

Once the welsh rarebit arrived, along with Barnaby's biscuits, Miss Busby found she did indeed have an appetite after all. She'd rather expected Lucy to appear, given the discovery of the tramp that morning, but the reporter must have been busy elsewhere. Perhaps it was the reason there'd been nothing pertaining to the case in the newspaper this morning? When the grandfather clock in the corner struck the hour, she delicately wiped her lips with a napkin, gave Barnaby the last biscuit, and decided it was time to make a move.

* * *

The Grange lay within five minutes' walk of the high street; tall trees with bare branches crusted in snow followed the line of the curving drive. Yew hedges enclosed the formal front gardens. A tennis court set among mature trees bordered the rear, along with an extensive lawn, shrubs, and herbaceous borders, all enveloped under an expanse of white.

She should have taken her new snippets of

information straight to Inspector McKay, who may, or may not, have welcomed them. But there was someone she was keen to talk to first, because she knew the lady in question also had a certain penchant for calculated risk.

'Good afternoon?' A maid in grey and white opened the door, then smiled at the dog. 'And a warm welcome to you.' She bent to give him a pat on the head. Barnaby wagged his tail in delight.

'Could you inform Mrs Montgomery that Miss Busby is here, please?'

'Of course. Would you like to step in, and bring your little doggy with you?' The maid opened the door wide. 'Nasty weather this, don't like it at all. Can never keep the house warm enough. Shall I take your coat?'

'Thank you.' Miss Busby allowed her coat to be carefully slipped from her shoulders and folded over the maid's arm.

'Now you come with me, and I'll tell Cook to put the kettle on for a nice cup of tea, and a treat for the little one.' The maid led her out of the lofty hallway, through a tall arch and along a thickly carpeted passage to a polished mahogany door. The maid gave a light knock and walked straight in. 'Mrs Montgomery, it's Miss Busby for you, and her little dog.'

Enid Montgomery's sharp eyes fixed on Miss Busby and Barnaby as they entered the finely furnished drawing room. Despite the weather, and the maid's fears, the room was like an oven.

'Isabelle,' Enid said. 'How interesting to see you, we haven't spoken in an age.' She rose in a quick movement from a cream damask sofa, where she'd been shuffling a set of cards. 'And who is this fine fellow?' She smiled down at Barnaby but didn't bend to pat him.

'Barnaby. He's my neighbour's dog. I'm caring for him.' Miss Busby advanced to where Enid was poised. 'He's quite sweet under the gruff exterior.'

'I'm sure he is. Do sit down, Isabelle.' Enid Montgomery had been a handsome woman in her day, with auburn strands still visible amid the white of her thick, swept-back hair. She held herself as stiffly upright as age and health allowed and was dressed in richly colourful style; a green and yellow silk jacket and skirt with an ivory blouse and a jade brooch fastened at the high neck. She resumed her seat on the sofa.

Miss Busby sat down too. Barnaby flopped at her feet and closed his eyes. A hush fell as the women faced each other.

'I know why you're here, Isabelle. It's Vernon, isn't it? And now some other man. Two dead in a few days, whatever's the place coming to?'

'It is rather a commotion for Little Minton,' Miss Busby agreed.

'Sherry?' Enid offered.

'Your maid mentioned tea.'

'Oh, she would, she's such a conventional soul.' Enid was dismissive. She went to the decanter on the gleaming walnut sideboard. 'Dry or sweet?'

'Dry, please.' Miss Busby gazed about the elegantly decorated room as Enid picked out two sherry glasses and put them on a silver tray. She had only visited The Grange a few times in the past, mostly fundraising parties for local good causes. They'd been great fun actually, with much animated talk, plentiful food and fine wines. Enid's husband had been a banker in London before they'd retired to their Cotswolds home. He had died three years ago after a short illness.

'Here you are.' Enid placed the glass almost brimming with amber liquor on the table in front of her.

'Thank you.'

Enid took a sip and regarded Miss Busby with shrewd green eyes.

'Do we know who the other dead man is?'

'Yes, it seems he was a tramp known to visit the area at this time of year,' Miss Busby replied.

'And is it a coincidence that he died at the lake?'

'I rather doubt it.' Miss Busby tried the sherry. It was really rather fortifying. She tried a little more.

'That doesn't surprise me. There are new people coming from the city,' Enid replied. 'They bring their nasty habits with them.'

'Really?' Miss Busby thought that a bit rich considering Enid had moved here from London.

Enid *tsked*. 'Of course. That's why I always liked Little Minton. Much smaller. A proper place. You know who's who, what's what, and where you are. Or rather, you used to.'

'Oh, I doubt it was a stranger.' Miss Busby was dismissive.

'Yes, and if you thought so, you wouldn't be here to ask me questions.' Enid drained her glass, then rose to fetch the decanter and fill it back up. 'A top-up?' she offered.

'No, thank you.' Miss Busby shook her head, having the feeling she may need to keep her wits about her where Enid was concerned. 'Were you at the memorial service for Vernon Potter yesterday?'

'You know perfectly well I was.' Enid appeared to be enjoying crossing swords.

'And has the insurance company been in touch with you?'

'No, why would they?' She shrugged, then sipped more sherry.

'Because you were one of Vernon Potter's clients.' Miss Busby decided it was time to come to the point, before Enid got any further through the bottle.

'Nonsense,' Enid retorted sharply. 'I'd expected better of you, Isabelle.'

Miss Busby knew Enid's name had been on Lucy's list of Potter's clients, and wondered why she would deny it. She decided to try another tack. 'Belinda Tasker mentioned she'd come to see you with the letter from the insurance company.'

Irritation flashed across Enid's face. 'The poor woman merely wanted me to read it. Needed a shoulder. She was upset. The blighters are trying to avoid paying out.'

'And they'll have all the more reason to do so now,' Miss Busby sighed sympathetically, trying a less confrontational approach.

'The dead tramp, of course. Hmm.' Enid nodded, then reached to pick up the pack of cards she'd placed on the table. 'Do you do Tarot, Isabelle?'

The question surprised her; she'd never have thought Enid the type. 'I don't think I have the talent.' She tried a diplomatic response. It had the desired effect.

'Well, you are in luck, because I do,' Enid replied and began to lay the cards on the table. 'These cards will represent the present. I am only using Major Arcana…' She became absorbed in spreading all the cards in a neat, straight line, each overlapping the next.

Miss Busby leaned forward to watch, bemused and intrigued in equal measure at the unexpected turn.

'Now, you must choose six.' Enid glanced up. 'Do not rush, allow the cards to direct you.'

Miss Busy wondered quite how they'd manage that, but decided against asking. 'Should I turn them over, or remove them from the row?'

'Draw them one at a time, and leave them face down in front of you,' Enid instructed.

Miss Busby hesitated, doing her best to imagine each card 'calling' to her. It felt rather surreal. She chose six cards and slid them toward her until they were lined up.

'Tea and macaroons, ma'am.' The maid entered and broke the tension.

'Oh, Jilly, we have just started a reading,' Enid told her.

'Well, I'm sure the fates'll not mind me,' the maid replied in friendly fashion. 'And tea's a better alternative to liquor!' She shot a disapproving look at the glasses at their elbows. Miss Busby felt herself duly scolded.

'It's sherry. It doesn't count as liquor,' Enid replied tartly. Despite her acerbic manner, it was clear she had an amicable relationship with her maid.

Jilly busied herself with the teapot, pouring each of the ladies a cup and placing it at their respective elbows, then added a small plate of macaroons each. 'And don't forget what the doctor said,' she admonished Enid as she left.

Enid knocked back the remains of her sherry and put the empty glass down with a bang on the table. 'Interfering busybodies,' she muttered.

'Your maid, or the doctor?' Miss Busby asked as she picked up her teacup.

'Both,' Enid replied and extended a hand to point at the first card Miss Busby had picked from the pack. 'This card represents how you feel about yourself at present. Turn it over.'

Despite her scepticism, Miss Busby found herself intrigued.

'The Fool.' She read the name of the card. 'Well, I suppose that about sums it up.' She forced a smile as her heart sank.

'It's not to be taken literally.' Enid's focus remained on the card. 'It's actually auspicious.'

'Is it?'

'It means you are uneasy. There is a certain discontentment in your life and you are searching for something new. A new purpose perhaps, or an adventure of sorts. The direction is not clear to you, but the unexpected could offer a path, which you may choose to follow.'

'Oh.' Miss Busby sat up. 'How interesting,' she said, and found herself surprised that she meant it.

'Do you believe you are searching for a new beginning?' Enid looked her directly in the eye. 'As a detective of sorts, perhaps?'

A flush rose in Miss Busby's cheeks. 'I did help Major Lennox with those dreadful murders at the Hall,' she said in her own defence.

Enid was direct, as ever. 'And it's why you are here, Isabelle.'

'As you are well aware, Enid. And you weren't telling the truth when you denied you were one of Vernon Potter's clients.'

It was Enid's turn to blush. 'That may well be.' She waved a hand at her. 'Turn the next card.'

'The Wheel of Fortune…' Miss Busby read, then frowned. 'Does that mean I should have a flutter on the horses?'

Enid shot a look at her, which caused Miss Busby to stifle a smile. She'd hit a nerve.

'No, I've told you,' Enid recovered herself quickly, 'do not give them literal meaning. The second card depicts what you want in life. The Wheel of Fortune represents a turning point, when events combine to guide you in a new direction. Circumstances that seem to be coincidental are actually synchronicity; it is destiny setting you on your path.'

'Does that mean I am destined to become an amateur sleuth of sorts?' Miss Busby smiled.

Enid had the grace to smile back. 'Possibly.'

'Did Vernon Potter seem ill to you?' Miss Busby asked, hoping to catch her sparring partner off guard.

Enid let out a bark of laughter, which ended in a harsh cough. 'Oh dear, that man will be the end of me…' She wiped her mouth with a handkerchief, red lipstick and a thin smear of blood stained the white linen. 'I'm more ill than he ever was, although he tried to pretend otherwise. Offering up that awful attempt at a cough whenever he remembered. I was quick to tell him not to take me for a fool. I'm too long in the tooth for sweet-talking charmers.'

'Oh Enid, I'm so sorry to hear that you're unwell.' Miss Busby's concern was genuine. The thin stripe of blood had dismayed rather than alarmed her. She'd heard Enid's health was failing, but the woman did such a good job of not showing it that the reminder was stark, and timely.

'One's steps are measured, Isabelle, and the path is only so long.' She looked suddenly downcast. 'Do you remember Daniel, my husband? He was a fine man, everything one could want really.' She sighed. 'He made a mess of things, of course, common knowledge, but it was a genuine mistake. He wasn't a crook, although it ruined him all the same, and left us without any surplus. I'm living off savings, and there are debts which I can't repay.' Miss Busby moved to interject, not wanting Enid to put herself through a painful rendition of the details, but she waved a hand to dismiss it. 'People speculate all the time, and it doesn't take a genius to work it out. When I'm gone, and it won't be long, Jilly and Cook and the boot boy will have to find new jobs and a roof over their heads. Heaven knows what will become of them.'

Miss Busby bit her lip, she imagined very few employers worried about their servants after their death. 'Don't they have their own homes?'

'No, they've always been with me. I have no-one else left now, they've become my family. I know they will care for me to my last breath. That means a lot, Isabelle, and I wanted to secure their futures for them, provide them with a pension for their old age. That's why I took out the insurance with Vernon. And why I don't consider it *my* policy, even though it is in my name.'

Miss Busby finished her tea and put the cup down. 'But you knew you were ill, why didn't you take a policy out on your own life?'

'My age, of course! Really, Isabelle. And the insurance company would have written to my doctor, who would have been duty-bound to tell them about my condition. They would never have insured me.'

'Ah.' Miss Busby nodded. Enid was clearly quite aware she was cheating the system, even if it was actually Vernon doing the deed. Miss Busby was certain they were all aware of that, each of the individuals concerned being perfectly intelligent women. With the possible exception of Frances Simpson, although the vicar must have known. She determinedly put these thoughts aside for later. 'But if you had gone before Vernon,' she reasoned, 'surely the policy would be ended and your money have been wasted?'

'That's the entire nature of insurance, is it not?' Enid's eyes sparkled with mischief, despite the disapproval evident in her tone. 'There's always a risk to be weighed. Not unlike life as a whole, of course. One must take a risk every now and then, if there's anything at all to be gained.'

Enid looked her in the eye for a moment, before continuing. 'And now you have wheedled the truth from me. I'm not sure which of us has triumphed. I suspect neither,' she finished.

Miss Busby was momentarily stuck for words, not a situation she often found herself in.

'Turn the next card over,' Enid ordered, and picked up a macaroon.

'The Moon,' she read from the card, which showed a full moon over a monochrome landscape.

'These are your fears,' Enid said as she took a bite of the biscuit. 'The moon will light your way, you have no need to fear the path ahead of you. You fear being lied to, and you mistrust what you are being told, but if you step back with an open mind, all will become clear.' She pointed at the next card. 'Carry on.'

But Miss Busby didn't carry on. She sat for a moment, a forgotten macaroon halfway to her lips, as her mind whirred. How on earth could a mere trifle like selecting a card possibly reveal so much of what went on in her mind? She gave her head the tiniest shake. It couldn't, of course, she told herself. It was mere coincidence. She took a nibble of macaroon before reaching for the next card.

'Justice,' she read. 'Which I do hope will be the outcome.'

Enid raised her eyes. 'Isabelle, must I keep repeating that you are not to take the cards literally.' She tapped a finger on the card showing a picture of blind Justice with her balanced scales. 'This is the force currently working in your favour. It is a positive force, a reward for past behaviour. It will guide you as you approach your current difficulties. It will instil in you calm and logic, so that you may retain a balanced view of the situation.'

'Ah,' Miss Busby said, thinking it just the sort of thing she needed, although it was quite extraordinary how the cards had fallen. She reached for the next card and turned it over. 'And what does this indicate?'

'The Empress,' Enid muttered, a frown deepening the crease between her brows. 'She is the force working against you – that is the meaning of the fifth card. She is not to be feared, but it does suggest that conflict will swirl around you for a while. You must not overreact to that conflict, even if it causes you distress and you are tempted to act rashly.'

'Hum.' Miss Busby liked to think rashness wasn't in her nature, but one never knew. Especially after a day like this one. She reached for the last card and carefully exposed it. 'The Sun.'

Enid's delight was instant. 'Now that is probably the best card you could hope for. The sixth card is the outcome of your endeavours. The Sun indicates success!' she exclaimed, and then became serious. 'And I truly want you to be a success, Isabelle, because nobody will be paid out unless you are.'

'I will do my best, Enid, and it would be a great deal easier if people were a little more forthcoming,' she chided.

'Well, you have extracted all I can offer,' Enid replied, shuffling the cards back into the deck.

Barnaby snuffled loudly on the rug and suddenly sat up looking confused, a cue for Miss Busby to make ready to leave.

'Thank you Enid, it was most illuminating, but there was one more question – do you ever put bets on the horses?'

Enid laughed throatily. 'Whoever told you that?'

'An intuitive guess. And you did mention a risk ought sometimes be taken, if anything is to be gained.'

Enid regarded her with a fresh spark of respect, and

nodded curtly. 'Well, you do have good intuition, I will grant you that. The answer is yes, it's my little vice,' she admitted. 'But it's only ever small amounts, Lord knows that's all I have to spare, and it's merely to keep life entertaining, you understand.'

Miss Busby was struck by a sudden thought. 'Enid, the cards... do they...? That is to say, they surely don't...?'

'Lord above, Isabelle. How many times? The cards cannot be taken literally. And even if they could, they are hardly likely to provide me with horses' names, are they?'

Miss Busby flushed. 'No. Of course. Do forgive me, Enid. I got carried away.'

Enid *tsked*, but nodded, a glimmer of amusement in her eyes.

'These bets, did they involve Vernon Potter?' Miss Busby pressed, wondering if she might be really pushing her luck.

There was a small pause, before Enid nodded.

'He placed them for me, and returned with my winnings – when there were any. Sometimes he would advise me. He was very knowledgeable, and we'd often have a lively debate over form.' Enid accompanied her, and Barnaby, toward the mahogany door.

'Really?' Miss Busby didn't know what 'form' was. 'But his tips were winners, weren't they?'

'Yes, for the most part. Almost unfailingly, in fact. As I said, he knew what he was about.' She sighed. 'I was quite fond of him actually, he had panache, you know. You don't get much of that around here.'

They arrived in the spacious hall. 'No, I suppose you don't.' Her mind drifted back to Randolf; he'd had panache, and style, and he'd made her laugh. Despite him being the heir to Bloxford Hall, and destined to be the next Earl of Bloxford, he'd always had his feet on the ground.

'He owed me twenty pounds.'

'Who?' Miss Busby's mind had wandered.

'Vernon, of course. Do pay attention, Isabelle.'

'Yes, sorry... Twenty pounds is an awful lot of money.' Particularly in Enid's situation, she thought, but refrained from saying so. 'Why did he owe it to you?'

'It was my winnings. A horse had come in the day before he died. He was supposed to bring it to me, we were going to have dinner together, but he didn't come. He was dead, as I realised later, but no-one has mentioned my money.'

'Have you asked the police?'

'No, I feared it might open a can of worms, what with the chicanery around the insurance, although it looks like that's gone with the wind now. Perhaps you could mention it to them, Isabelle?'

'I will,' she promised and left with one certainty in her mind. The answer to the question as to whether Vernon Potter was protector or predator was quite clear, the man was a scoundrel of the first order.

CHAPTER 12

Miss Busby picked her way carefully along the snowy pavement. It was after three o'clock, and she knew that if Dennis weren't at the post office already, he soon would be. Barnaby hopped alongside, his short legs battling through powdery drifts – perhaps he needed a little knitted coat, and possibly stilts, although that was outside her abilities, she thought with a smile.

She knew she ought to call into the police station and inform the inspector of all she'd learned, but the wind was picking up and her mind was fixed on returning to her fireside.

The rumble of an engine sounded behind her. She pulled Barnaby in close and turned to see Lucy's red Sunbeam sports car approaching, headlights gleaming in the gathering dusk.

'Miss Busby,' she called from the window as she pulled to a stop alongside. 'I was just on my way to pay you a visit.'

'How fortuitous, I was hoping to talk to you, and a lift would be most welcome.' Miss Busby bundled

Barnaby in first then gratefully climbed in after him. Ten minutes later they arrived at Lavender Cottage and entered its comfortable confines.

'Please sit down, I'll put the kettle on,' Miss Busby called as she entered the kitchen. She returned to the sitting room to find Lucy had poked the fire into blazing life.

'I wanted to ask you more about the poor tramp, Joe Tucker,' Lucy said as she extracted her notebook and pencil from her shoulder bag.

Miss Busby sat opposite. 'I only spoke with him for a short while.'

Lucy readied the pencil above an open page. Miss Busby noticed that the young woman's notes were immaculately organised and incredibly detailed. Although they weren't quite as she would have expected.

'I'd heard journalists used shorthand,' she said.

Lucy glanced up. 'You're right, they do.' She looked sheepish. 'I'm ashamed to admit that I simply cannot master it. I've tried and tried...I can write awfully quickly, and I'm neat. I just hope that it's enough...'

'For you to keep your job?' Miss Busby finished the sentence for her.

She blushed. 'I'm not going to lose my job, Miss Busby, but I must prove myself competent. It's important to me, I want to convince my father I'm able to do something – something useful.'

The whistle of the kettle broke in. It took only a few minutes for Miss Busby to return with tea and a plate of toast and jam, having decided she'd had quite enough biscuits for one day.

'Why would your father need convincing?' Miss Busby asked, her head tilted very slightly to one side.

Lucy let out a long sigh. 'He owns the newspaper. My older brother will take it over one day, but he's injured – well, he's recovering, I mean.'

Miss Busby sipped tea and digested the news. 'Your father is Sir Richard Lannister?'

Lucy nodded. 'I use my mother's surname. I didn't want the other reporters to know.'

'They wouldn't be terribly good reporters if they haven't found out,' Miss Busby remarked dryly.

Lucy smiled. 'You're quite right, it didn't take them long to uncover my secret, but it's all the more reason to do well, you see. I don't want them to think I'm playing at it.'

'No, indeed,' Miss Busby agreed and reached for a slice of toast. Barnaby watched her every move. 'I thought you had prepared an article or some such for this mornings' newspaper, but I didn't notice anything...?'

'I'd written about the possibility of Potter's death being murder, but the editor decided we needed something more concrete, and then we heard the news about the poor tramp,' she explained. 'Is there anything you can add to that, do you think?'

Her mind returned to earlier; the shock of identifying the body, and then writing her statement in McKay's office.

'I fear it really can't be anything but foul play.' *And wonder if I'm somewhat to blame*, she thought, not wanting to voice the fear aloud.

'What makes you suspect foul play?' Lucy asked in a professional manner.

'I'm not a great believer in coincidence.'

Lucy nodded. 'Nor am I, and I understand the whisky is being tested.'

Miss Busby arched a brow. 'You've spoken to the inspector?'

Lucy's cheeks flushed pink. 'No, despite my best efforts, he's been difficult to pin down – actually he has made it quite clear he doesn't want to talk to me. Fortunately I have my own sources.'

Miss Busby gave a crust to Barnaby. Lucy was the sort of bright young woman who exuded life's possibil-ities – she reminded Miss Busby of herself at the same age. She'd rather hoped she and the young reporter would become friends, but now she wondered if she was simply just another 'source'.

Stirring her tea, she said softly, 'Then I'm quite sure you don't need me.'

Lucy's colour heightened. 'Oh, truly I do! I really enjoy talking to you, Miss Busby. I think you've been quite heroic actually, trying to help Potter's victims – they are so often overlooked in these cases.'

Miss Busby felt a surge of relief, her usual strength and vigour returning.

'The tramp had a shack in the woods by the lake,

and he would stay there at this time each year, according to the inspector. He had that information from the gardeners at Lambert House,' she explained, noting Lucy's keen gaze at what was clearly fresh information.

'And Letitia Lambert was one of Mr Potter's ladies,' she mused. 'How interesting. Lambert House is right next to the lake, isn't it?'

Miss Busby nodded. 'I understand Letitia has been questioned, but I wonder if she'll warrant a repeat visit, given the circumstances.'

'Would she be likely to talk to me, do you think?' Lucy asked, then bit into a slice of toast.

'I shouldn't imagine so. Letitia has become rather reclusive in recent years. I might attempt a visit tomorrow.'

'May I come with you?' Lucy asked.

'I think it's better if you don't, as she doesn't know you...' she tried to say it kindly, but Lucy looked crestfallen nevertheless. She quickly added, 'I have spoken to Belinda Tasker and Enid Montgomery since I last saw you, though. And Dorothy Cranford was my first visit.'

Lucy perked up. 'Shall we compare notes?'

The pair moved to Miss Busby's desk by the window, where she proceeded to apprise Lucy with much of what she'd learned from the ladies. She made no mention of the Tarot cards because somehow that had unnerved her a little. She'd never taken any interest in such things, and yet Enid's reading had almost precisely distilled her hopes and fears. She shook the thought away and fixed her attention back to Lucy.

They cross-referenced and swapped information with increasing confidence. Miss Busby knew she ought to have waited until she'd spoken to the inspector, but Lucy filled in several gaps in her theories, and the inspector would ultimately benefit when she passed them on to him. He'd get a much clearer picture in the long run.

'Only the Lower Minton Ladies could be suspects,' Lucy explained when Miss Busby queried the point. 'There aren't any trains on Sunday afternoons, so the Cheltenham ladies couldn't have managed the journey. And the Long Compton ladies really are far too frail to be in the frame.'

'What about taxis?' Miss Busby asked, remembering the arrival of the Martin sisters at the memorial service.

'I already checked with the local firms,' Lucy said. 'None travelled to Little Minton that day.'

Turning to her "Persons of Interest" list, Miss Busby was pleased to see three of the five suspects, Dorothy Cranford, Belinda Tasker, and Enid Montgomery, all had detailed notes of their circumstances and respective dealings with Potter.

'Only two left,' Lucy said, glancing down at the paper. 'You have been busy.'

'Yes...' Miss Busby tapped her pencil on the page. 'Each of them had motive, all of them are in great need of money. Dorothy perhaps the most. I don't believe she quite accepted she was doing anything wrong. And she definitely *was* doing something wrong.'

Lucy nodded. 'Morally wrong, perhaps, but not illegal. I had to ask the legal bod at the paper to look into the details and then explain them to me. Potter's clever loophole was entirely legitimate, although his name would have been mud among the insurance industry…'

'Possibly, but at that point he would have been too dead to care,' Miss Busby observed wryly.

Lucy laughed. 'True. But even so, I'm certain the policy holders were aware they were bending the rules, including Dorothy Cranford. The ladies were too old for a life insurance policy, and Enid was too ill.'

Miss Busby nodded. 'And yet they went ahead all the same.'

'I doubt it was entirely their fault,' Lucy said. 'Potter was an absolute charmer by all accounts. Pleasant to look at too, which always makes it harder to resist.'

'Like Inspector McKay?' Miss Busby said.

'He's hardly a charmer,' Lucy was quick to retort.

Miss Busby quelled a smile. 'I can see Dorothy falling for Potter's charms, she always was susceptible to flattery, but Belinda and Enid really should have known better. Did know better, in fact, and Belinda was frightened she could be prosecuted.'

'No, she couldn't, although her fears weren't irrational, because without legal advice, one couldn't be sure.'

'Well, that's a relief.' Miss Busby gave a small sigh. She'd been almost certain when she'd reassured Belinda, but felt more confident now that things had been clarified. 'What about the vicar?'

Lucy glanced up at her. 'Difficult to say, he wouldn't talk to me. None of them would.'

'Ah,' Miss Busby had wondered how Lucy's visit to the vicarage had gone. 'Not even Evelyn Simpson? She usually has plenty to say.'

'Virtually mute, almost hostile, actually.'

'I think they are rather banking on Frances receiving her insurance payment,' Miss Busby suggested.

'Yes, and have now realised it may be in jeopardy,' Lucy replied. 'And now the insurance company will have every reason to assume it's murder.'

'With the poor tramp's death,' Miss Busby agreed. 'And if one of his ladies is responsible…'

'Fears over fraud will be the least of their concerns,' Lucy finished her sentence for her.

Miss Busby felt a shiver up her spine. It didn't bear thinking about.

'Whoever it was, must have felt themselves in dreadful need,' Lucy continued.

'I'm afraid so.' Miss Busby suddenly realised what had been niggling at her. 'But how would Potter have known about their desperate circumstances?'

'I had the impression it was fairly common knowledge in the town?'

'Yes, but Potter wasn't from the town. He lived in Cheltenham,' Miss Busby said.

'Well, then someone local must have been passing on information.'

'Evelyn!' Miss Busby blurted the name out with

unthinking relief. Of course! With all the revelations and the tramp's death she'd quite forgotten what Belinda had said – Evelyn was the one who'd sent Potter her way. What if she'd done the same for all the others?

Lucy gripped her pencil and waited for more, but Miss Busby held back. She'd told Lucy what she felt necessary, but this was something that needed further investigation.

'You must forgive me, Lucy. It's all getting terribly jumbled in my mind.' She feigned a yawn. 'And it's been such a long day.'

Lucy didn't appear convinced.

'It's only that Evelyn mentioned her brother looking through Frances' papers,' Miss Busby battled on. 'And Dorothy's brother knew Potter too. So there could be a connection there. Potter getting to know the men. It just popped into my head.'

'Do any of the other Lower Minton ladies have brothers he may have consulted?'

'Not that I'm aware of.' It felt painfully weak to Miss Busby's mind, even as she was saying it, but Lucy took fresh notes all the same, seemingly appeased for the moment.

A loud, discordant mewl from the direction of the stairs caused Lucy to look around in surprise.

Miss Busby, immune, simply checked the clock.

'It's Pud's tea time,' she confirmed, getting to her feet as her large and clearly agitated ginger tom stalked into the room, his amber eyes full of recrimination.

'Oh Heavens!' Lucy jumped up. 'I should be back at the office or my piece will never make tomorrow's edition. Thank you for the tea, Miss Busby! You've been so helpful.'

'Not at all.' Miss Busby cast a wary eye at Barnaby, who was in turn casting a wary eye at Pud.

'I do look forward to seeing you again soon,' Lucy said, closing her notebook and making for her coat and gloves in the hallway.

'Yes, very soon,' Miss Busby said distractedly, as an audible rumble built in Pud's substantial chest.

'I've an appointment to see a chap from the Prudential in the morning. Perhaps we could meet afterwards?'

Turning to the reporter's fresh face, Miss Busby found herself struck with a sudden idea.

'Do you enjoy game pie, Lucy?'

'I… yes,' she replied, a little taken aback.

'And are you free tomorrow evening?'

'I believe so.' Lucy was searching for her car keys in her shoulder bag

'Perhaps you would meet me at The Crown at around six?'

'I'd love to,' Lucy agreed with a beaming smile, and left, closing the door firmly behind her.

Some time later, with Pud fed and having stomped back upstairs, thoroughly disgusted at the continued presence of Barnaby, Miss Busby wondered what she and the little terrier would have for tea.

Finding her appetite diminished after the toast

and other snacks she'd eaten during the day, she cast an eye around the room and decided it was woefully in need of some Christmas cheer. Perhaps it would be the perfect antidote to the horror of two deaths virtually on one's doorstep. Not to mention the awful fright of finding Mary this morning – and she suddenly realised she hadn't enquired after her neighbour's recovery yet.

She chided herself. The doctor had been quite right: she really must do something about installing a telephone line. It would make things so much easier – although, she decided, it was hardly a task for this evening. Delving into the under-stairs cupboard, she searched for her box of Christmas decorations, but before she could make a start a sharp rap on the door set Barnaby off.

'Barnaby, no,' she scolded, his piercing yaps going right through her. 'You really must stop this. Go and lie down.' She pointed toward the living room, and the dog mooched off to flop in front of the fire.

'It's only me Miss,' Bobby Miller called from the doorstep. 'Got summat for you from the inspector. Brought it back from Oxford, earlier. He's been racing about, here, there and everywhere since that body was found dead.'

Miss Busby had opened the door to find the young constable dusted with snow, including his helmet. He had a large parcel clasped in his arms. 'What is it, Bobby?'

'He said you'd know what it was.' He handed a parcel over, wrapped in brown paper and tied with string. 'I can't stop, I'm on my way to see Mum, and—'

Miss Busby had a thought. 'Come in. Just for a moment.'

'No, Miss, like I said I—'

'You can use the boot scraper.'

Bobby walked as far as the hall, brushing snow from his shoulders.

Barnaby gave a grumpy growl, before dropping back to sleep on the hearthrug.

'There's something I wanted to…aha, yes,' Miss Busby said, flicking through the pages of her notebook. 'Who found Potter, at the lake?'

'What? Don't you know, Miss?'

Miss Busby *tsked*. 'I would not be asking, if I did.'

'Sorry Miss. I just thought everyone knew. It was Ron and Stan what found him.'

Miss Busby gave a disapproving frown, they were a notorious pair. A father and son team, their only contribution to the locality lay in the poached pheasants they were forever attempting to sell. She feared she could guess the answer to her next question.

'And did they report finding any money on Mr Potter's person?'

'No, Miss, and I've already said, if you've got evidence you're supposed to—'

'Yes, thank you Bobby. Please be assured I will do so. Do give your mother my regards.'

With the cottage to herself once more, and the chain securely latched against further visitors, Miss Busby settled herself into her favourite chair and carefully opened the parcel. Inside she found the most beautiful brown leather bag containing a jar of fingerprint powder, the soft shaving brush that accompanied it, a torch and penknife, along with a leather-bound notepad and a set of pencils. Attached to the notepad was a short missive in a neat, precise hand.

Miss Busby.

Please accept this with my apologies. We set off on the wrong foot. Grateful for your assistance.

Regards,

Alastair McKay.

Her breath caught in her throat – it was a thoughtful gift, and really too much. She'd forgotten even asking for the items with all that had happened, and now found herself quite emotional.

'Oh, bother,' she muttered, wondering if he might want the present back as soon as he read tomorrow's newspaper.

CHAPTER 13

Freshly fallen snow overnight had coated Miss Busby's garden and the orchard beyond, and she felt a frisson of renewed festive spirit when she opened the curtains next morning. The little terrier was clearly more settled, and must have come to some sort of arrangement with Pud, as there hadn't been a single growl or hiss between them in the night.

Having fed the pair leftover scraps, she chivvied the cat outside just long enough to complete his requirements. Barnaby took a more leisurely approach and followed her to the log store to nose through the stock of wood. He found a stick and insisted on carrying it with him, tail happily aloft, as she filled her wicker basket with stout logs to resurrect the fire.

'Drop it, there's a good boy.' Miss Busby held a hand out for the stick, whereupon the dog gave a muffled yip, then darted off up the stairs.

Deciding not to humour the animal by engaging with the game, she placed three logs on the fire and trusted the embers to do their work. Then enjoyed a leisurely breakfast of tea and honey on toast.

Thus fortified, she opened her box of Christmas decorations, and soon had the sitting room festooned with reams of bright-coloured crepe paper, china snowmen, wooden figures of Father Christmas and his little elves, angels with swan-feather wings and homemade felted reindeer. The nativity took a little longer as the donkey's leg had fallen off and she had to hunt for glue to stick it back on again.

As more snow began to fall softly against the window, she found herself humming *Good King Wenceslas*, and once she'd finished most of the decorating, she decided to move over to her desk to make a start on the Christmas cards.

The sound of tyres crunching to a halt a few moments later, followed by footsteps stomping up the path, broke the peaceful mood.

'Oh, lord,' she muttered, having almost forgotten.

Several loud raps sounded on the door. Barnaby flew downstairs, grumbling and whining but clearly making a heroic effort not to yap.

'Clever boy, you remembered,' she told him, while contemplating not answering the door at all.

She did so, with a heartfelt sigh.

'I suppose you're behind this?' Inspector McKay thrust a copy of the *Oxford News* towards her.

"Second body found at Little Minton" the headline proclaimed, with a sub-heading reading, "*Two dead. Police clueless.*"

It was quite clever really, she thought. Clues were indeed thin on the ground, after all.

'Do come in, Inspector. I believe the author of the piece is listed at the end of the article,' she said and held the door open wider. 'Tea?'

'Miss Busby, this is a serious matter. And I know very well who wrote it.' He stalked inside. 'I also know she was seen leaving your cottage late yesterday afternoon. Constable Miller said she almost ran him off the road.'

Miss Busby arched an eyebrow. 'I hadn't thought you so thin-skinned, Inspector.'

The inspector's lips tightened in barely concealed anger. Barnaby let forth a low growl.

'Miss Wesley has undermined an ongoing police investigation,' he said through gritted teeth, with a wary glance at the dog. 'She has made fools of the force, and I'm in no doubt as to who aided and abetted her.'

'Really?' Miss Busby kept her tone level, thinking it best to let him run out of steam before attempting reason. She turned and went through to the kitchen, calling, 'Milk and sugar?' over her shoulder.

'I put my trust in you, Miss Busby,' he called after her. 'I shared information with you in good faith, and did not expect to find that information plastered all over the local rag this morning.'

'I don't appreciate your tone, Inspector,' she replied as she returned to the living room while the kettle boiled.

'And I do not appreciate news of Joe Tucker's whisky being doctored plastered all over the newspaper before we released our official statement. We still have further enquiries to make, and are going to say as much later today when we officially declare both his, and Potter's death suspected murder.'

'So you *are* going to declare it murder?' Miss Busby felt suddenly lightheaded, and put an arm to the door frame to steady herself.

'Yes, but I don't appreciate the postulating being set out for all and sundry in such an irresponsible manner.' He cast the newspaper down onto the little table beside her armchair with far more force than necessary.

Miss Busby opened her mouth to protest, but found her breath increasingly hard to catch. Thoughts darted around her head faster than she could keep up with them.

If I hadn't gone to the lake and talked to the tramp, if I hadn't started digging into all this, Joe Tucker would still be alive, the ladies would have their money, and Potter would still be dead either way. Oh, lord, what have I done?

'I was simply trying to help,' she managed weakly. 'I didn't know this would happen…'

The inspector hesitated, concern suddenly replacing his anger. 'Perhaps you ought to sit down? You're looking rather pale, are you alright?'

'Yes, I…the tea…'

'I'll see to it.' Guiding her to her chair, he divested himself of overcoat and scarf before going to the kitchen and rattling about with teapot and cups.

Miss Busby sat, hands in her lap, trying to compose herself. He returned with a cup full to the brim – no saucer, she noted.

'I put sugar in. It's good for shock.'

'Yes,' she said, taking a sip and wincing at the sweetness. 'Thank you.'

He cleared his throat, then added, 'Perhaps I may have…' He trailed off, clearly struggling. 'Could I fetch you a biscuit?'

Barnaby instantly sat up on hearing the word, which brought a tremulous smile to her lips.

'Two, perhaps,' she answered. 'Three, if you'd like one. And pour some tea for yourself. There are things we ought to discuss. May I see the article?'

He retrieved the newspaper and handed it to her, then went to clatter about, looking for biscuits. Barnaby followed him into the kitchen to keep an eye on proceedings.

Several moments later, she sighed as she put the paper down. 'Lucy knew an awful lot more than I did. Although I am rather flattered you think me clever enough to have wheedled information directly from the insurance companies. And to have a "source" at the lab.'

He shuffled uncomfortably in his chair. 'I just assumed…possibly incorrectly…'

Miss Busby let him suffer for a moment, before relenting. 'I may have become carried away, and discussed too much with her. But I would have shared the information with you, had you given me the opportunity. And I believe Lucy tried to talk to you on several occasions.'

Irritation flashed again in his eyes, the blue turning steely grey.

'I don't talk to reporters. You can't trust them.'

It took Miss Busby a moment to place who the words reminded her of.

'That is precisely what Joe Tucker said of the police,' she said softly. 'And yet, had either of you overcome your distrust, he may well have still been alive today.'

Several uncomfortable moments passed. She wasn't sure if the Scot's temper would flare again, but would hold no truck with it if it did. Instead, he raked a hand through his hair as if trying to shake loose the right words.

As the silence drew on, she took charge. 'All three of us – you, Lucy, and I – have made mistakes along the way, Inspector, yet we are all working towards the same goal: a murderer is among us, and must not be permitted to get away with their crimes.'

'Aye, and they've killed twice now.'

'Yes, indeed. Would you pass me my notebook? It's on the desk. Let me tell you what I learned yesterday.'

Miss Busby made a precise and detailed report, although she realised almost everything had been cleverly referenced in Lucy's article. No names had been printed in the paper – something Miss Busby had insisted upon – but there was a reference to the betting.

'I've heard several rumours about Potter's predilection for the horses,' the inspector admitted. 'We suspect he had several young lads placing bets for him, and a reliable inside source, but no one has been willing to give Sergeant Brierly or Constable Lewis any details.'

'Well of course they haven't. You must send Bobby Miller. People have known him since he was in short trousers. They'll talk to him. I suggest you start with the porters at the railway.'

The inspector looked set to ask further questions, but received a sharp glance, so he simply made a note in his book instead.

'Did you search Potter's flat in Cheltenham?' she asked, remembering Lucy had mentioned it was close to the racecourse.

'The local police made the search. They didn't find much of interest.'

'No cash, perhaps, lying around?'

He flicked back through his notebook.

'None at all. Although his bank account was extremely healthy. He had over five hundred pounds to his name.'

Miss Busby took a sharp intake of breath. 'The amount Dorothy Cranford was to receive upon his demise,' she muttered.

'Well, the Crown will likely receive it now. The man had no family, and didn't leave a will.'

'Not the action of someone with damaged lungs and a shortened life expectancy,' she remarked.

He gave a wry grin. 'No. Brierly checked with the war office. His story about being gassed was fabricated.'

Miss Busby's gaze caught on the flickering flames for a moment. 'I don't suppose any letters were found in the flat?' she asked.

The inspector raised an eyebrow. 'Is there something in particular you're thinking of?'

'Mr Potter came to Lower Minton last Sunday because he was due to have dinner with Enid Montgomery, but I don't know why he went to the lake first. I wondered if someone sent him a letter to arrange a meeting, and if it had been found.'

'No such thing, I'm afraid.' The inspector's eyes slid toward her. 'And you should have—'

'I am about to explain,' she told him before he could repeat his complaints. She went on to give details of the bet Potter had placed for Enid, and the winnings she was waiting for. 'I understand there wasn't any money found on the body, but it may be worth confirming if the winnings were collected. And I should have another word with the men who pulled Potter from the lake, if I were you. They're just the sort to go through his pockets.'

'This whole business,' he muttered, as he made notes, 'could be cleared up a lot sooner if people would keep me abreast of important information.'

'So you've said. Or, indeed, if you'd sent the right people to ask the right questions in the first place.'

That caused his brows to snap together, but he didn't reply.

'I'm simply following along behind you, Inspector,' she continued. 'And picking through whatever has been missed, and Lucy is racing ahead of you, working hard to find answers first.'

'A reporter has no business interfering in a police investigation whether she's first, last, or in between.' He flicked his notebook closed and rose to his feet. 'But I take your point, Miss Busby, and I'm grateful for your diligence. I'll speak to the men who found Potter, and Bobby can go and chat to the porters.'

'That's a good idea.' Miss Busby nodded, pleased he'd taken some notice of her.

'I've sent Brierly and Lewis back to the lake today, for another search of the place, and to knock on more doors.'

'Excellent, and you might also talk to Dennis Ogden; he's the local postman.' She still thought of him as postboy, but knew it wasn't correct. 'He may have seen any letters sent to Potter from Little Minton.'

The inspector noted the name with a curt nod of acknowledgement, before putting on his coat and hat.

'I'll be in touch,' he told her, making to leave. 'And I am grateful, Miss Busby, for your assistance, but I'd rather you left things to me from now on.'

Miss Busby gave a nod, her eyes catching sight of the new leather bag hanging from the hat stand. In all the commotion of his fiery Scottish temper she'd quite forgotten.

'Thank you for the bag and kit,' she said. 'It was very kind of you, Inspector. Even if you prefer me not to use it. Are you busy this evening?' she enquired. 'Around five thirty?'

'I expect so, but it depends on—'

'Wonderful. Could you pick me up, please? I have a treat in mind, we can go to dinner at The Crown. See you later.' She closed the door on him with a smile before he could object.

She had hardly had a moment to clear away her notes and the tea things before she heard the distinctive purr of a Rolls-Royce engine. Moments later Adeline Fanshawe was on the doorstep, clad in her best winter coat with mink collar and cuffs.

'I've just seen the paper,' she explained. 'You must tell all! Come along, grab your hat and coat, I'm taking us to Lily's for a coffee and cake.'

Clutching Barnaby in the passenger seat as Adeline tackled the icy bends, Miss Busby found her mind drifting. The inspector's anger, although she'd made light of it, had upset her – and his implication that she'd harmed the investigation had knocked her con-fidence.

'You're very quiet, Isabelle. I expected to find you fizzing with excitement. Such intrigue in the paper. I assume you helped the Wesley girl with it? It smacks of your intelligence throughout.'

'Actually, Lucy did most of the work. Much to the inspector's displeasure, I'm afraid. He rather thinks us a menace.'

'Aha, he's had his toes trodden on. Good.'

'Why good?'

'Because it will buck the man up, of course.' Adeline looked over at her as if it were blindingly obvious. 'Resting on his Caledonian laurels whilst you two do all the work, then having the nerve to complain?' She clucked a disapproving tongue and shook her head.

'Eyes forward, Adeline.'

'What? Oh.'

Imminent contact with the verge avoided, Miss Busby considered her friend's words, and decided to confess her fears.

'You don't think he might have a point?'

'How so?'

'Well, if I hadn't gone to the lake and rooted about, I wouldn't have encountered the tramp. And he would still be with us.'

Adeline tutted. 'Nonsense, Isabelle, think it through.'

'I'm afraid I've done nothing but that since I identified the body,' she admitted quietly.

Adeline stopped the car with a judder of brakes.

'Oh, poor you. I hadn't thought how awful that must have been.' She laid a hand on her friend's arm and gave it a squeeze. Miss Busby felt tears threatening and Adeline sought to jolly her along. 'There he goes again, you see?' The car lurched forward as her foot thrust down on the accelerator. 'Getting you to do his dirty work for him. *He* should have found the tramp, and questioned him, *and* identified him. And you mustn't for one moment think otherwise.'

'He does seem to be bucking up a little,' Miss Busby conceded. 'But he's suggested I ought to leave things to him from now on.'

'Has he indeed! Well, we shall see about that.'

CHAPTER 14

Following a strong cup of coffee and a generous slice of lardy cake at Lily's Tea Rooms, they sat at the table feeling sufficiently fortified for plans to be set.

'Where to first?' Adeline began. 'The vicarage, or Lambert House?'

Having gleaned all that had happened since she'd left for London, Adeline was now fully armed with information and determined that she should provide assistance. Miss Busby realised she couldn't stop her friend if she tried.

'And if we time it right,' Adeline continued, 'we can go to the lake around dusk and reenact the murder.'

Miss Busby's eyes widened in alarm.

'Obviously not the actual murder,' Adeline *tsked*. 'But I've been thinking – if your tramp spotted this elderly woman at dusk, with the sun behind her, what if he was mistaken and it wasn't an elderly lady at all?'

'He did say his eyesight wasn't very good. But as all

our suspects are elderly ladies, I'm not quite sure what you'd hope to achieve?'

'Well, if nothing else we can walk off the lardy cake. Besides, can you really see one of those five women clouting Potter over the head and pushing him into a lake? No, with this news of horses and gambling my suspicions are taking another direction entirely.'

'Really?' Miss Busby sounded sceptical. 'Perhaps you could be more specific?'

Adeline huffed. 'Well, not yet I can't. But surely some young bounder from the racecourse would be a more likely suspect. If Potter was a scoundrel, he could have duped more than just his local clients.'

'I think we should call in at the vicarage first,' Miss Busby decided before Adeline got too carried away.

'Right you are. Come along.'

They motored in the direction, but as the Rolls pulled into Church Way, Miss Busby noted that there didn't appear to be any smoke rising from the chimney. 'Oh, dear. Perhaps they're out. Shall we try Letitia instead?'

Too late, Adeline had stopped the car and was already in the process of alighting. Miss Busby had little choice but to follow her through the gate and along the path with Barnaby trotting alongside her, ears pricked and tail aloft in jaunty manner.

It was a bemused and rather sleepy looking Frances Simpson who came to the door. Tall, with a long nose and shadow-rimmed eyes, she wore a shapeless grey dress too large for her thin frame and a dull knitted shawl clutched around her shoulders. There was something of the waif about her, albeit a waif grown old, and who had just woken, blinking, from a nap.

'Yes?' she asked, peering around the door.

'Good day, Miss Simpson.' Miss Busby spoke brightly. 'We are calling to see Evelyn. Is she home?'

'Oh, no…I'm afraid she's taking a walk with Harold. They've gone to…now where did she say? The lake, I believe. You'll most probably catch them, if you hurry,' she said, and began to ease the door closed.

Adeline wedged a solid boot in the frame. 'Perhaps we could talk to you, Frances. Regarding Mr Potter.'

'Oh…no, I don't think so… I'm afraid I was resting, I need to rest. And I have already spoken to the police, and so…' She wafted a thin hand, seeming to run out of words.

'Mr Potter *and* Belinda,' Miss Busby interjected, suddenly struck with an idea.

'Belinda Tasker?' The door suddenly swung open by several inches.

'Yes.' Miss Busby deftly nudged Adeline aside. 'I had a chat with her a couple of days ago and she mentioned something quite odd. Perhaps you could help?'

This did the trick and Frances opened the door fully. 'You can come in.'

They trooped in, Barnaby bringing up the rear. Frances frowned but refrained from comment.

While she disappeared into the kitchen to make tea,

Miss Busby had a chance to wander about the cluttered room. She paused at the bookshelves and noted several photos of Frances with her brother in their younger years, but only one of him with his wife.

Adeline had sat on the sofa by the smouldering fire and discovered two romantic serials on a side table. She flicked through them with a look of disdain.

'*The Hart Series* and, good gracious, *Love Story Magazine*. Not our dear vicar's, I presume?'

'Oh…you've discovered my guilty pleasure.' Frances arrived with a tea tray. 'Such lovely romantic stories, do you take them too?'

'I rarely have time to read.' Adeline told an absolute untruth.

'I enjoy a good murder mystery,' Miss Busby said, then realised the faux pas and hastily rattled on. 'How are you, Miss Simpson? You were terribly upset the last time I called.'

'Was I?' Confusion creased her pinched features, wrinkles deepening around her lips. She wavered for a moment and then plonked the tray onto the low table in front of the fire. Barnaby's button nose twitching toward the plate of dry biscuits.

'I came here to see Evelyn the day after poor Vernon Potter was found,' Miss Busby reminded her.

'Oh, I don't remember much from that day,' Frances said, her eyes taking on a glassy look. 'It was such a shock, a terrible shock…a tragedy, like the handsome hero of a book…'

Miss Busby gave her a sideways glance. 'Were the two of you close?'

A flush crept into Frances' thin cheeks. 'Yes, we were actually. He was an absolute gentleman…and his wife was deceased. No children. They'd married young, you see. Too young, really. Vernon was away at war, and she was… well, it's no matter now, of course. We were getting along so well, the two of us…' She sat down abruptly in a wing chair. 'That is to say, there was the prospect…but of course, his illness…the terrible coughing…the poor man, he suffered most dreadfully. Had we had more time…'

Adeline stifled a scoff behind her hand. The woman must be at least ten years older than Potter.

Frances was oblivious. She pulled a creased hand-kerchief from her sleeve and dabbed at her eyes. 'Alas, it was not to be. *"Love is a smoke rais'd with the fume of sighs"*, after all,' she hiccoughed between sobs.

'Oh, dear, yes, such a terrible shame,' Miss Busby muttered and helped herself to a cup of tea. Adeline took a bite of biscuit, then immediately passed it to Barnaby.

'Evelyn mustn't have crumbs on the rug,' Frances suddenly reprimanded her. 'She doesn't like crumbs, we must be tidy.'

'Please don't worry, he won't leave any crumbs,' Miss Busby assured her with a soothing tone.

'Wasn't Potter much younger—' Adeline began.

'You mentioned Belinda, dear Miss Busby.' Frances

cut across Adeline, indeed she seemed to be barely listening, her focus apparently on what she could glean from the visitors.

'Yes, I was hoping to ask Evelyn about something Belinda had said, but perhaps you could help. Belinda suggested it was Evelyn who first introduced her to Mr Potter. Was that because he'd been so helpful with your policy?'

'Not in the least.' A coldness crept across Frances' face. 'It was because she was desperate to curry favour with Vernon.'

'Oh? I rather got the impression she didn't like him,' Miss Busby replied.

'Yes, that's what she'd want you to think. But she was just as susceptible to his charms as anyone – despite being married to my dear brother.'

Miss Busby suddenly straightened up. She'd been referring to Belinda Tasker; why had Frances thought of Evelyn?

'Good lord! Was she really?' Adeline beamed. 'How wonderfully scandalous!'

Miss Busby shot her a look of rebuke.

'He would never have indulged her, of course,' Frances continued as though nothing had been said.

'But she was keen?' Adeline pressed.

'She worshipped the man.' Frances' tone was impassioned enough to have Barnaby look up in concern. 'Poor, dear Harold, try as he might, he suffers greatly from her derision and cruelty, but Vernon could do no wrong.'

'And you think Evelyn introduced him to Belinda to increase her estimation in his eyes, rather than to help the poor woman?' Miss Busby asked.

Frances nodded. 'And not just Belinda. She gave him details of several women he might sell insurance to. He saw through it, of course. He had no interest in Evelyn.' She attacked a biscuit angrily. 'Not that it stopped her fawning over him. And several times I heard her telling Harold he ought to be more like Vernon. They rowed over it on one occasion. I heard them. I don't know how Harold stands her. Vernon couldn't. He despised her.' She was almost hissing the words.

'Really? Given that she was pointing him toward various unattached and desperate women? I'd have thought Vernon would have been grateful,' Adeline stated.

Frances's cheeks reddened further, and she raised her handkerchief to her face to cover her distress, *or was it anger?* Miss Busby wondered.

'Oh dear, Frances, I do hope we haven't upset you,' she said, putting her cup down onto its saucer, then rising to her feet. 'Perhaps we should leave you to your rest.'

'No, no.' Frances was suddenly vehement. 'I can tell you more,' she insisted. 'Belinda called on Evelyn just last week. It was last Friday actually. The woman was hysterical. I was upstairs trying to sleep, but the commotion woke me and I heard *every* word.'

Miss Busby sat straight back down. 'What sort of commotion?'

'Shouting and weeping, Belinda claiming she'd been duped into taking out a policy. She said she'd never wanted it, and it was all Evelyn's fault.'

'Goodness. But she'd had the policy for some time, hadn't she? What do you think made her so upset?'

'I couldn't possibly say.' Frances dropped her voice. 'Although I have my suspicions…'

'You suspect Potter rejected Belinda's advances, causing her to regret the financial commitment,' Adeline cut in with a deft guess.

Frances leaned forward in triumph. 'That's exactly right! Vernon was so handsome and charming you couldn't possibly not fall for him, but of course his interests lay…elsewhere. He would have made that clear, of course, and the woman was livid. *"Heaven has no rage like love to hatred turned, Nor hell a fury like a woman scorned."* Shouting about his policies not even being legal, and threatening to contact the Prudential directly.'

'But she didn't?' Miss Busby prompted.

'Of course she didn't. Evelyn said that if the policies were fraudulent, Belinda would be just as guilty as anyone. She said that those concerned ought to stick together rather than making threats and throwing scenes. That soon made her hold her tongue. And besides, it wasn't fraud at all. Vernon was far too clever; he knew the shortcomings of the insurance companies. They were at fault, they were stupid, and greedy and complacent—'

'So you were never concerned about fraud yourself?' Miss Busby cut into the rising histrionics.

'No, not a bit of it. Vernon would never have put me in any sort of danger.' The vehemence grew further in her voice.

Miss Busby rose to her feet once more.

'I think we have overtired you, Miss Simpson. We should leave you to your rest.'

'Yes…but you should talk to Belinda, again,' Frances insisted. 'If I were the police, I'd look no further. And I'd be curious as to her whereabouts at the time of poor Vernon's murder, too,' she added, sotto voce. 'But you would know more than me, Miss Busby, given your preferred reading matter.'

Adeline looked askance.

'Out of interest, Miss Simpson, where were you on Sunday afternoon—'

'Adeline…' Miss Busby warned.

'Oh, no, it's perfectly alright.' Frances' tone indicated it was anything but, as she continued, 'I have nothing to hide. I was here, my brother has already vouched for me to the police.' She narrowed her eyes at Adeline, who remained unperturbed.

'But you didn't mention your concerns regarding Belinda Tasker to them?'

'Well, no…not really. As I said…' Frances muttered, 'I was awfully upset at the time…'

* * *

'I thought you said the woman was rather dopey?' Adeline remarked as they motored back along Church Way. 'She seemed pretty sharp to me.'

'I don't believe those were my *exact* words,' Miss Busby clarified, 'but yes, she was certainly sharper today than I can recall seeing her.'

'Perked up the minute you mentioned Belinda,' Adeline observed.

'She did, didn't she?'

'Have you got your notebook with you?'

'Yes, why?'

'It's lunch time, let's go back to Lily's. We can sit in the warm whilst you put your thoughts in order, and then we can attack Letitia.'

'Not literally, I hope?'

Adeline barked a laugh as they arrived back outside the tea rooms.

'How decadent, twice in one day,' Miss Busby said, waving to Maggie for a table. Once the pair were seated, lunch menus in hand, Adeline asked, 'Did you tell the inspector about Evelyn sending Potter Belinda's way?'

'Not yet, I wanted to be sure.'

'Don't let the man undermine your confidence, Isabelle. Your instincts are far keener than his where matters of Little Minton are concerned.'

Miss Busby gave her friend an appreciative smile.

'Not at all keen on the sister-in-law, is she?' Adeline returned to the matter at hand.

'No. Although I'm not sure I can blame her on that account.'

'Do you suppose she did have a thing for Potter?' Adeline peered at the menu.

'It's possible – a fantasy of sorts, perhaps. Everyone says he was handsome. And I suppose his lifestyle was more exciting than a vicar's.' Miss Busby decided she would have the soup.

'Until it got him killed.'

'There is that.'

'Terrible thing, though, envy,' Adeline continued.

'Have you decided?' Maggie appeared at the table.

'Leek and ham soup for me,' Adeline replied without hesitation. 'Isabelle?'

'I'd like the same.'

Maggie took the menus and hurried off, the tea room beginning to fill with customers.

'What did you make of Frances' implication there was some prospect on the horizon regarding her and Potter?' Adeline asked.

'It seems somewhat unlikely,' Miss Busby admitted delicately.

'I should think so,' Adeline huffed. 'Has she always lived with her brother?'

'I believe so, since they lost their parents, although I heard there was a gentleman at one time.'

'Was there? Was he mousy and dull? He must have been. Not like the fellows in those ridiculous serials she reads!'

'I never met the man. I think they were supposed to announce an engagement, but then there was some issue over money...'

'Her not having any, you mean?' Adeline was forthright, as usual.

'Possibly... She was said to be quite heartbroken at the time. And her brother was furious. Chased the man off the premises, if one is to believe what's said...'

'The vicar? I can't imagine him chasing so much as a pigeon!' Adeline was dismissive, but Miss Busby found herself wondering.

'He must have felt protective toward her,' she mused. 'I wonder, were she to be misled or used by a man again, if he would react in the same way?'

'Good lord, Isabelle, you don't think—'

'Two leek and ham,' Maggie announced, glancing over to three newcomers awaiting a table. 'And here's your rolls.'

'Thank you,' Miss Busby managed before the waitress bustled off. She set to buttering the warm, soft rolls, the enticing smell of the soup just the thing to awaken her appetite.

Adeline dipped her bread speculatively. 'It would make more sense, to have a chap in the frame. But... no...I can't see it. The vicar's a drip. Perhaps he was spritely in his youth, but now? Not a bit.'

'You're probably right.' Miss Busby sipped a spoonful of soup. 'Although I think sometimes we forget we age. I feel the same inside as I did when I was twenty, don't you?'

Adeline had a mouthful of bread roll, and gave a mute nod.

'Perhaps that's also why Frances imagined there was some form of potential romance there.'

'Well, yes.' Adeline wiped her lips with a napkin. 'But there are limits!'

The pair enjoyed their meal in companionable silence, before Adeline declared it was time for notes to be taken.

'What will you write under Frances?' she asked. 'Make note of those romance serials, they could be key!'

Miss Busby took out her notebook and pencil.

'Really, Adeline,' she commented. 'I enjoy a good murder mystery story, should I add myself to the list too?'

She turned to her "Persons of Interest" list, and briefly noted down what they'd discussed during their visit, Adeline peering over her shoulder to be sure she didn't miss anything. Looking over what she'd written, she paused for a moment to think. 'I wonder if Evelyn bullied her into the policy, simply to furnish her with the means to move out?'

'Against Frances' wishes, you mean?'

'Possibly. Perhaps Harold's too.'

'Should you put him down as a suspect?'

'No. Not yet.'

'Well, there's only Letitia to go. Come on, we ought to make a move.'

Some twenty minutes later Adeline pulled the car to a halt at the drive to Lambert House. The fancy iron gates were closed and a heavy chain locked across them, somewhat unnecessarily as it was now virtually impassable given the snow drift built up against it.

'Not much of a welcome,' Adeline observed as she gazed at the old manor house in the distance. 'Short of climbing the gate, we appear to be scuppered.'

'I think we are a little long in the tooth for climbing gates,' Miss Busby agreed, and then remembered the small wooden gate she'd seen when first visiting the lake with Barnaby. 'Can we park further toward the lake? I have an idea.'

Adeline made a mountainous task of turning the large motor car around.

'I've known Letitia for an age,' she said over the thump and crunch of tyres mounting the verge. 'Although I haven't seen her to talk to in an awfully long time. She's never been the same since her husband died.'

'How did you meet?' Miss Busby asked. She only knew Letitia by reputation, and perhaps to nod to occasionally in the town. Apart from the church service for Potter, she couldn't remember the last time she'd caught sight of the woman.

'Colonel Lambert used to drink at the same club as James. He'd bring her to Ladies' Night once in a while.'

'Really? I thought she'd hardly ever left the grounds?'

'Not since he died, no. Widowhood hit her hard, like so many of us.'

Miss Busby glanced over to see a rare flash of melancholy in her friend's eyes, before she rallied.

'Always kept themselves to themselves around the town,' she went on. 'Did most of their socialising in Oxford and London. Sent Lance away to school, of course, for all the good that did. He still came back a bounder. But James would have the Colonel over to shoot a couple of times a year, and Letitia would sometimes tag along. The remote sort, fairly intelligent from what I recall.'

Adeline parked the car diagonally across the path, leaving them no distance at all to walk, which Miss Busby was rather glad about. They climbed out into the rutted snow.

'I suppose if they didn't get involved in town life as a couple, it would have been difficult for her to make friends after he died,' Miss Busby mused.

'I'm not sure Letitia was ever the type to need friends,' Adeline replied thoughtfully. 'Used to be inseparable from the boy. It must have been miserable for her when he was away at school, but he lives with her now. For all the good he's done her.'

They headed for the gate, Barnaby trotting gamely alongside.

'In what respect?' Miss Busby asked, pushing a prickly bramble aside and noting, with relief, that the wooden gate was unlocked. Interestingly, the ground had been cleared, and fresh bootprints in the snow showed it had been used sometime earlier in the day.

'He drinks,' Adeline replied as Miss Busby opened the gate. 'And is overfond of cards. Or used to be, but a leopard rarely changes its spots. Lost the majority of the family fortune at black jack, the fool.'

'Goodness,' Miss Busby exclaimed, partly at the notion of losing such a large quantity on such a ridiculous game, and partly at the trek awaiting them. The sprawling manor house had been built on a hill. It was a modest rise by most standards, but a climb nonetheless. Barnaby decided to suddenly dash off up the slope ahead of them, ears flapping and tail wagging frantically.

'Ah. Well,' Adeline said, 'at least it'll be quick going back. Come along.'

When they reached the imposing door to the house, they paused and admired the view, illuminated by the bright December sun. It was quite breathtaking, in more ways than one, the town spread across the valley, rooftops white with snow, chimneys streaming skeins of smoke, the church spire rising gracefully into the cloudless blue sky. Both women took several moments to catch their breath, before Adeline directed her attention to the grounds. 'I see she has let the garden go to pot.'

'There are only two or three of the staff in total, I believe,' Miss Busby concurred as she rang the bell and stamped chilled feet on the doorstep. There was a long wait before an undersized youth, dressed in an over-large footman's uniform, opened the door and glared out.

'Good afternoon.' Adeline took charge. 'Mrs Fanshawe and Miss Busby to see Mrs Lambert. And

Barnaby,' she added, as the dog emerged from under the bush he'd been investigating and shot through the open door.

'Mrs Lambert 'ain't seeing no one,' the scrawny youth informed them. He had cropped blond hair, dull blue eyes and flaccid lips, a most unprepossessing lad, Miss Busby decided.

Adeline drew herself up to her full height. 'She'll see us. Now do your job, young man, and let her know we're here.'

The lad sighed and made to shut the door while he, presumably, did as instructed.

'Let us in and take our coats,' Adeline objected. 'Good lord. What do they teach you nowadays?'

'You should keep your coats on, there 'ain't no fires lit down here. You can sit in there and wait if you want.' He pointed to the first doorway on the right. His green and red cuff fell over his wrist, his silver buttons were tarnished, and he wore heavy-soled boots, which looked ridiculous at the ends of his narrow-legged trousers. Adeline led the way into what was a cold and dismal parlour. She was furious and shouted after him, 'And you will light the fire when you return!'

Miss Busby shivered. There was an unmistakable air of damp to the room, and a thick layer of dust clung throughout. Barnaby ran his nose along the hearthrug, then sneezed three times in quick succession.

'I hadn't imagined it had become quite so bad,' she said softly.

'This is what happens when one shuts oneself away,' Adeline observed sharply. 'It simply won't do. Money or no money, one can at least keep the place clean.'

Neither would sit down; they stood with hand-bags in gloved hands and surveyed the limp curtains, moulding rugs, and dulled paintings on the wall.

A short while later, footsteps could be heard in the hallway, and the youth reappeared with Letitia Lambert in tow.

CHAPTER 15

'Why are you here?' the dumpy figure demanded in a high voice. 'I am not receiving. I no longer receive.'

'Nonsense, Letitia,' Adeline objected. 'I can't even recall when I last saw you, aside from the memorial service. I'm sure you recall Miss Busby, we would like to ask you some questions about Vernon Potter. Now, about that fire, young man?' She frowned at the scrawny youth.

Letitia Lambert held up a pudgy hand. Her face was fleshy and too pale from time spent indoors, her eyes small, her nose short and lips pursed. Black combs held back her white hair and a mourning necklace of jet beads was strung tightly about her fleshy neck. She wore an elaborate black dress, making the resemblance to Queen Victoria even more marked. Her antiquated style of faded splendour suited the mouldering surroundings.

'There is no need for a fire, Oliver. We will not be detained long.'

Miss Busby wondered if she was using the royal 'we'.

'Yes, Ma'am,' Oliver muttered.

'No chance of any tea then?' Adeline asked archly. 'Or some water for the dog?'

'None whatsoever.' Letitia shot a disgusted look at Barnaby, before focusing on Miss Busby, who found herself rather annoyed as Letitia's sharp little eyes moved up and down, seeming to take in every detail. 'Your friend may ask her questions, I have nothing to hide, but then you will leave.'

'Good lord, Letitia, this is really rather unnecessary,' Adeline objected, her voice rising an octave.

'I should have thought the locked gates a sufficient indication that we do not wish to be disturbed.'

Adeline flushed, then defiantly took a seat on the edge of the sofa without being asked. Miss Busby hesitated. Adeline flung out a hand and pulled her down beside her. Letitia remained standing, as Barnaby plonked himself to sit on the rug, as though waiting for a show to begin.

'Well?' Letitia prompted sharply.

Miss Busby cleared her throat. 'I understand you had a policy with Mr Potter?'

'Do you?' Letitia's reply was imperious.

'I…yes. That is to say, am I correct in thinking you did?'

'You are.' She deigned a reply.

'And…' Miss Busby was unsure how to proceed. The woman was hostile, and she knew she was on thin ice. '…How did you get along with the man, in general?'

'I didn't.' She brushed a smudge of dust from the black lace covering her substantial chest. Her actions were brusque and abrupt, as was her manner.

'Ah. That's most interesting. I understood he was quite popular with his clientele.' Miss Busby softened her tone.

'I wouldn't know. I didn't have anything to do with him. My son arranged the policy and dealt with the matter in its entirety. All that was required of me was my signature, as I have already informed the police. I think your questions are impertinent and this is none of your business.' Letitia's pudgy lips pursed in pique.

'The man is dead, Letitia,' Adeline scolded, irritated by her manner. 'We are simply trying to ascertain—'

'I repeat, it is not your business. You are merely snooping, Adeline, which I can assure you is a waste of time. I knew nothing of the man, and indeed know nothing of anything outside these four walls. And that is very much how I choose to keep it. Now if you are quite finished, perhaps you'd like to leave in the same manner you arrived.'

'Now, really—' Adeline's cheeks were almost rosy.

Miss Busby rose to her feet before Adeline could go any further. 'If you had nothing to do with Vernon Potter, why did you attend his memorial service?'

'I…' Letitia's mouth opened and closed. 'It was simply…'

Miss Busby, glad to be off the back foot, was quick to secure the advantage. 'Mrs Lambert, we do apologise for imposing on you, but as I'm sure you've heard, the insurance company has refused to settle Vernon's policies until the cause of his death is explained.'

'No, that must be a mistake. I… I have heard nothing of the sort,' Letitia stammered; she was faltering, the facade crumbling.

'I'm afraid it is not a mistake,' Miss Busby continued. 'You should have received a letter. Perhaps the weather, or indeed the gates, have caused a delay?'

'Lance collects the post. He would have mentioned…'

'That boy again, Letitia.' Adeline's tone was surprisingly gentle. 'When will you learn?'

Letitia suddenly sank into the armchair opposite. 'Lance is a good boy. He is misunderstood, he always was.'

Adeline's expression made it clear she did not agree.

'The matter of the policies has caught everyone by surprise,' Miss Busby offered, feeling a sudden sympathy for the woman. 'We're hopeful things can be resolved. All the ladies Potter sold policies to are in great need of their money, and—'

'Great need?' Letitia's expression suddenly contorted into derision, scorn spilling into her tone. 'I wouldn't be in any form of need were I simply given my due. For generations my husband's family has managed this estate. The Lamberts have brought work to this town, and it has simply washed its hands of me the moment I needed assistance.'

That took them both aback. Why would the town be expected to rally to her cause, Miss Busby wondered.

'Have you ever asked anyone for help?' Adeline protested, clearly thinking along the same lines. 'The town council, or the mayor?'

'Why should I have to ask?' Letitia blistered, fury filling her large frame. 'They have eyes. My home is falling about my ears, it is visible to the whole town. There has surely been enough gossip.' Her eyes flashed. 'Or is our current hardship entertainment for those who have envied us all these years? They forget that we have provided stability and status for decades, and now not one of them will even offer Lance employment.' She paused for breath, and her tone became somehow more vicious. 'Humphrey fought for his country. We went to India. It was a sacrifice, but we did it. And it affected our health, both of us suffered.' She appeared to be working herself into hysteria. 'And Humphrey never recovered, his heart was weakened. He did all of that and was given nothing in return, and now all I have is debt. And what other means of repaying that debt do I have? Nothing but the hope of that insurance money, and now even that, it appears, may be denied.'

Her speech could have come straight from a Victorian melodrama, and Miss Busby recalled her husband had died of a heart attack caused by an excess of port and fine food.

'Oh, for heaven's sake, Letitia.' Adeline was having none of it. 'You've led a life of luxury and ease. Nobody owes you a bean.'

'I think you've said enough—' Letitia began, but was interrupted by a commotion from the hallway.

'Mother?' An angry voice called out, and the sound of heavy boots brought the gangling figure of Lance Lambert into the room. Barnaby's hackles rose. 'Oliver said there were two women here asking about Potter.' He stopped to glare at Miss Busby and Adeline with flaming eyes. 'What do you want?' he demanded. 'My mother has spoken to the police, and that's an end to it. Now get off our property.'

'Well your manners haven't improved.' Adeline was ready for an argument.

'We really should leave...' Miss Busby tried to exit with some modicum of decorum.

Lance leaned towards them, lank brown hair falling across a petulant face, his thin lips drawn in anger. He flung an arm in the direction of the door. 'Go on, get out, you old harpies—*Ouch*! Ow, *ow*. Get your dog off me!' He yelled, suddenly grabbing at his leg and hopping about.

Barnaby had launched himself at Lance's ankle, his sharp teeth piercing the leather boot.

'Barnaby, *no*.' Miss Busby scooped the dog into her arms before Lance could lash out at him.

'Come along, Isabelle.' Adeline put her nose in the air. 'There is simply no helping some people,' she announced and marched out with their dignity largely intact.

The walk back to the lake was indeed much quicker and easier, but also far more subdued than the walk up had been. Even Barnaby had lost his bounce and he walked beside them with his ears and tail drooping.

'Nasty piece of work, that boy. Always has been, always will be,' Adeline pronounced as they approached the wooden gate.

'I don't think I could ever have envisioned such an unpleasant encounter.' Miss Busby gave a shudder. 'Or being treated quite so appallingly.'

'Nor I,' Adeline concurred. 'It's absolutely shocking, the depths to which the woman has fallen.'

'I suppose she *has* had a difficult time of it.' Miss Busby tried to feel for the woman.

'She's had it far too easy for far too long, you mean.' Adeline would not be placated.

'At least we know Evelyn didn't arrange that particular policy,' Miss Busby reasoned as she closed the wooden gate behind them. 'The awful experience wasn't a total loss in that respect.'

'They're hiding something. What else would explain their behaviour?'

'Yes, I suppose…'

Adeline wasn't actually listening. 'And how did Lance come to know Potter in the first place?'

'I'm afraid,' Miss Busby admitted, 'that may be something we ought to leave to the inspector.' She remembered his warning about the dangers of getting involved, and for the first time felt them valid. 'Barnaby was rather heroic, wasn't he?'

Adeline looked at the little dog and beamed. 'He had

Lance hopping about all over that awful room. Such a clever little doggy,' she cooed.

Barnaby's ears pricked up at the words of praise.

'Chin up, Isabelle,' Adeline continued, her tone back to its usual brightness. 'You've discovered a great deal today already, and look, the sun is just beginning to set. We couldn't have timed it better. Now, shall you be the murderer or shall I?'

It was impossible to feel sorry for yourself, Miss Busby thought, when your friend was reenacting murder with quite such gusto.

She watched from the bench as Adeline sneaked toward the bushes at the lake's edge with her scarf pulled over her head and a stray laurel branch in hand. The sun hovered just above the horizon, its long rays rendering Adeline's stout form into a black silhouette, as she raised the branch and swung it up and down upon the imaginary Potter.

Barnaby decided it was great fun, and ran to join in, taking it upon himself to try and bring the 'murderer' down. He tugged at the hem of Adeline's coat and swung from it. Fortunately she found his efforts adorable and rewarded him with the laurel branch, which he dragged proudly back to the bench.

'Well?' Adeline asked, puffing slightly as she came to sit beside Miss Busby and catch her breath.

'It *is* a little difficult to see anyone's features clearly with the sun behind you like that, but as you came out I could definitely tell you were a lady.'

'I should hope so too,' Adeline replied with aplomb. 'Although, that rather dashes my idea of it being some bounder from the racecourse. Or your notion of the vengeful vicar.'

'Speaking of whom, I wonder why they chose the lake for a walk today?'

'It's a nice spot for a stroll, Isabelle.'

'Yes, but...'

'Don't go searching for meaning in all manner of things that don't have any,' Adeline cautioned. 'If you're imagining the man scouring the lake for carelessly dropped clues, then remove them from your mind. I've no doubt he and Evelyn were simply feeding the ducks.'

'That's what everyone said Vernon Potter was doing,' Miss Busby replied dryly, then sighed. 'At least the reenactment hasn't opened up a whole ream of new potential suspects. It is quite clear that we are still looking at the same five individuals.'

Adeline pulled her scarf back into place. 'I agree, but why did the killer use the blanket?'

'She obviously didn't want to be recognised.'

'Then why kill the tramp?'

That gave Miss Busby pause for thought.

'If the woman used the blanket to hide her identity,' Adeline pressed, 'why did she feel the need to kill the tramp? In fact, why wouldn't she have taken her own shawl, or some other form of disguise, were she intent on murder? Finding a blanket on the ground seems awfully fortuitous. What would she have done otherwise?'

'Perhaps the tramp saw more than he let on. Or perhaps she simply worried that he may have. I doubt she would have expected to see anyone else up at the lake – it was cold on Sunday, with an icy wind if I recall, and with darkness just around the corner. Oh, Adeline, I don't know,' she sighed, 'perhaps when someone has killed once, it doesn't seem so very hard to kill again.' Her shoulders slumped a tad. 'It's all so very horrid, at heart.'

'You're growing maudlin again, Isabelle. Time to get you home.'

* * *

They returned just as the stout figure of Nurse Delaney was striding up the lane toward Lavender Cottage.

'Miss Busby! I was just coming to give you the news.' The nurse had wrapped a heavy wool cape around her shoulders.

'Oh, Lord, not bad, I hope?' Miss Busby paused at her front door.

'Not at all, she's coming on a treat.'

'Would you like to come in?' Miss Busby offered, letting Barnaby into the cottage and stamping the snow from her boots. Adeline stopped beside her.

'I won't, thank you,' Nurse Delaney replied, her round cheeks red from the cold. 'I'll have to get back for Joe's tea. I wanted to tell you that they've moved Mary to the respite home in Stow-on-the-Wold.'

'A respite home?' Adeline sounded worried.

Miss Busby was aghast. 'Oh, but she'll hate that; she was always terribly independent.'

'We shall see how she settles, but she's more concerned about her dog.'

'Please assure her that Barnaby can stay with me for as long as she needs.'

'Excellent. That will stop her fretting. And if you wish to pay a visit, the hours are two til five weekdays, and noon til four on weekends. But no-one is to stay long, she'll need her rest,' the nurse told her and then turned on booted heel and strode off, banging the garden gate behind her.

Relieved at the news, Miss Busby divested herself of hat and coat, then went to feed Pud and Barnaby in the kitchen. Pud looked to be utterly put out, it was extraordinary how cats were quite capable of showing their feelings. She gave him an extra helping while Barnaby wasn't looking.

Adeline had made hot cocoa and brought two steaming mugs to place beside the freshly stoked fire.

'I simply cannot get over Letitia,' Miss Busby mused, making room for Pudding on her lap. 'Is she unwell, do you think?'

'She seemed perfectly well to me. And clearly nothing has dented her appetite.'

'I meant in her head.'

'No, there's something far worse going on there, mark my words.'

'Such as?'

'Well, that's more your area, isn't it? But I'd start with Lance. Shall I pass your bag?'

'Please.' Thus armed, Miss Busby balanced her notebook on her lap and made the final heading under her "Persons of Interest" list, updating her notes with all they'd learned from their uncomfortable visit to Lambert House.

'Letitia would have the most to gain from Potter's death,' Adeline suggested. 'The woman clearly can't bear the financial straits she's found herself in.'

'Hmm.' Miss Busby paused to sip cocoa. 'I wonder why Lance didn't tell her about the letter from the insurance company. He must have received one.' She clasped her cup in both hands. 'Perhaps he didn't want to worry her.'

'Good lord, Isabelle. Your tendency to look for the best in people is as irritating as it is laudable. There'll be a far more sinister reason behind it. And he set up the policy, don't forget. He'll have had his eye on the payout one way or another. You can't add him as a suspect, I suppose?' She sighed. 'Perhaps he dressed in his mother's frock and donned a shawl?' Her expression was hopeful.

'What would Potter have thought if Lance had approached him dressed in a frock?' Miss Busby replied tartly. 'And I doubt it would have fooled the tramp. But

I shall mention Lance's ill temper to the inspector. In fact,' she glanced up at the clock over the mantel, 'I really ought to freshen myself up, he'll be arriving any moment.'

'In that case, I shall leave you to it,' Adeline said, getting to her feet and ruffling Barnaby's ears en route to the door. 'Shall we meet tomorrow so you can tell me what he says?'

Miss Busby toyed with the idea of inviting Adeline along. She had a habit of asking difficult questions without a second thought, but the inspector was the fiery type and she wanted to tread carefully with him. Lucy wasn't kindly disposed toward the inspector either, and one more woman added to the mix might be more than he could tolerate.

'Yes, let us do that. I'll see you in the morning.'

CHAPTER 16

'I thought you might appreciate a good hot meal after a long day.' Miss Busby had been pleased to find the inspector with a smile on his face. He'd picked her up and was now guiding the car through the dark, snowy lanes.

'Aye, you were right. I never say no to game pie. Especially if there's pheasant involved.'

Mention of pheasant brought Little Minton's notorious poachers to mind. 'How did your interview with Ron and Stan go?'

'You were right, again. After some close questioning, the pair admitted to taking £20 from Potter's waistcoat pocket, along with the ticketed receipt in Enid Montgomery's name.'

Miss Busby tried not to appear smug, because it really wasn't ladylike.

'I interviewed Mrs Montgomery again at her home, she confirmed that the bet was hers,' he went on.

'And have you given her the winnings?'

'I'm afraid it's not quite that simple.' He slowed as they turned a corner.

'Well it ought to be. The two devils in question are behind bars, I take it?'

'They are,' the inspector confirmed as the warm yellow glow of the gas lamps of Little Minton came into view, cosy and welcoming against the surrounding blackness.

'I knew the pair were nefarious,' she continued, 'but I wouldn't have imagined them capable of murder.' She was filled with sudden dismay. 'To kill just for money…' She muttered. They hadn't even been on her suspects list and now the excitement and purpose of the last few days would come to a close. The discussions, outings, and shared theories. The renewed vigour she'd discovered…

The inspector pulled the car to the side of the road opposite The Crown: Little Minton's largest, and most genteel, public house.

'They didn't kill him. Both men have alibis for the time of Potter's death,' he said, turning off the engine. 'They were in the Dog & Duck all Sunday afternoon and evening with at least ten witnesses between them. And the day Joe Tucker died, they were working as beaters on an estate near Cirencester.'

Miss Busby felt a guilty pang of relief as she climbed the three stone steps to the door of the pub. Built of the familiar, honey-coloured Cotswold stone, The Crown boasted bright lanterns hanging above the painted sign, the front door hung with a huge festive garland in fresh greenery and red ribbons.

The hosts, Mr and Mrs Harbottle, were a formidable pair originally from the north east, and held no truck with troublemakers or mess makers alike. It was the sort of establishment where you made sure to wipe your feet thoroughly before entering.

'In that case, why are you detaining Ron and Stan?' she asked as the inspector held the door for her. The smell of venison and pastry swept around her nostrils; she sighed in anticipation.

'As a lesson to thieves.' His voice turned cold. 'But I'll let them go tomorrow with a suitable fine. Once they knew they were found out, they became cooperative, and we've had some valuable information from them.'

'A little late, perhaps. And more to save their own skins than anything, I'd imagine.'

Divested of their coats, they selected a quiet corner where they could talk without being overheard. Cushions were placed on wooden chairs, cloths covered the tables, and there were even rugs on the floorboards.

'I also spoke to Belinda Tasker again this afternoon,' he said. 'Her alibi for the time of Potter's murder is not quite so easy to verify.'

'No one saw her at the graveyard?' Miss Busby asked, having already feared this to be the case.

'I'm afraid not. But she's not alone in that. Other than the vicar and Miss Simpson, none of them have alibis to speak of. I've set Constable Lewis on it, and he's also gathering information on Joe Tucker's movements the day he died.'

'What about Enid? She has staff at home, they must have known where she was.'

'It was their afternoon off, they went to the moving picture show and she was at home on her own.' McKay leaned back in his chair.

'Did Belinda mention Evelyn Simpson?' Miss Busby continued.

'Several times, and not kindly.'

Not wanting to land the grieving florist in any more trouble, Miss Busby decided it best not to mention the woman's visit to the vicarage, and the allegations she'd made.

'Shall I order?' the inspector asked with a keen glance at the menu chalked up over the polished oak bar. 'Two plates of game pie and mash?'

'Please, and perhaps a small dry sherry while we wait?'

He returned with a dainty glass for her and a pint for himself. Miss Busby told him about Evelyn Simpson's role in selecting Potter's clients. 'All but Letitia Lambert,' she said. 'Her son, Lance, arranged the policy.'

He took a long drink of his beer. 'Constable Miller made enquiries about Lance today. In conjunction with some of the porters who were placing regular bets for Potter. Several of them mentioned Lance being an acquaintance of Potter's from the racing stables in Chipping Norton. Apparently he worked there from time to time.'

'Potter?'

'No, Lance.'

'Really? His mother is under the impression no one would employ him locally.'

'You've spoken to Letitia?' He frowned.

Miss Busby took a sip of sherry. 'I was walking Barnaby with Adeline, and we found ourselves in the vicinity.'

Curiosity won over disapproval. 'And what did she say?'

'Nothing of relevance. She was unnecessarily hostile towards us.' Miss Busby sighed. 'And Lambert House is in a dreadful state. Then Lance arrived and was most unpleasant. Barnaby bit him.'

He grinned at that.

The door opened and a familiar figure walked in. The inspector had his back to the room and hadn't seen the new arrival. Lucy took her coat off and hung it up, she was wearing her smart red jacket and brown skirt.

'It *is* useful, isn't it,' Miss Busby began, 'sharing information like this?'

'Aye. As you've already mentioned.'

She shot him a bright smile, then raised a hand in the air.

The inspector turned in his seat, only to glare at the approaching young reporter. Who, in turn, looked annoyed at the ambush.

'A dry sherry for Miss Wesley, perhaps?' Miss Busby suggested.

'No, thank you. I never drink when I'm working.' Lucy's tone was terse as she hovered by the table.

Miss Busby wondered if she might ask for another for herself. 'Please do sit down, Lucy. It's just an informal chat.'

'I never 'chat' with reporters,' the inspector growled.

Miss Busby engaged her schoolmarm tone. 'Then you may go and order another game pie and a lemonade while Lucy and I do so.'

McKay stomped to the bar with bad grace.

'I thought I was coming to discuss the latest news with you.' Lucy was clearly unimpressed.

'You are. And to have dinner.'

'You didn't mention *he* would be here,' Lucy objected.

'I knew you'd been trying to pin him down, and thought I would assist.'

'Well, he doesn't look awfully pleased about it.'

'He's like that at first. Take no notice.'

The inspector returned, placed a glass of lemonade in front of Lucy, shot another glare at Miss Busby, then sat down, furrowed lines between his dark brows. 'The pies will be a while. Mrs Harbottle is apparently, "up to her eyes in it".'

'She always is on a Saturday.' Miss Busby remained determinedly bright in the face of her bristling companions. 'Now, Miss Wesley has been to visit Potter's insurance companies – what news?'

Lucy glared at McKay. 'I don't remember getting an ounce of news from the police.'

'Nor should you,' he retorted. 'It's not our job to write your stories for you.'

'Nor is it ours to solve your crimes,' she riposted.

Miss Busby shot each of them a stern look in turn. 'The inspector and I have been through this, Lucy. We each have information to share. If you are both feeling blockheaded about it, I shall be the first to begin.' Neither of them said a word, so she proceeded to tell them about her visit to Frances, and the notion of her being enamoured of Mr Potter.

'He *was* handsome,' Lucy said, digging into her bag. 'I have a photograph. It was in the newspaper archives from a charity dinner he attended.' She passed it to Miss Busby, and then took out her notebook and pencil.

'Oh, yes, he was rather striking,' she agreed, surprised at the pleasantness of the man's features – it didn't sit with her vision of him as a villain. He had dark eyes, and dark hair greying at the temples, a straight nose and lips curving into a disarming smile. There was something mischievous in his expression, as though adventure were in the air, with the possibility of laughter and romance.

'Do you suspect romance to be the angle, rather than money?' Lucy was asking.

Not to be outdone, the inspector pulled his own notebook from his pocket and flicked it open. 'There is nothing romantic about murder,' he declared.

'I was addressing Miss Busby.' She offered him a sharp smile that went nowhere near her eyes.

Miss Busby passed the photograph back. 'I do think matters of the heart may have come into things,' she admitted. 'Although all of the ladies involved are older than Potter.'

'And Evelyn Simpson is married to the vicar,' the inspector added. 'I think the whole notion to be firmly in the realm of female fancy.'

'And what would you suggest from the realm of male fancy?' Lucy shot back.

'Money, of course,' McKay retorted.

'How incredibly simplistic,' Lucy remarked.

'The truth usually is.'

Miss Busby watched the pair as if she were at a tennis match.

'And which elderly lady do you believe murdered Potter for money?' Lucy demanded.

'None of them,' the inspector declared, lifting his pint to his lips.

Miss Busby sat a little straighter.

Lucy's eyes widened with surprise. 'Then who?'

'I am not at liberty to reveal—'

'Game pie and mash?' The indomitable figure of Mrs Harbottle appeared at the table, hefting two plates heaped with wedges of pastry oozing with chunks of dark meat, mash, buttered cabbage, and gravy.

'Ladies first,' the inspector said firmly.

'Be back with yours shortly,' Mrs Harbottle said, brushing a stray curl from her plump face. 'Seems as every soul in Little Minton is in for game pie tonight.'

'Is there pheasant in it?' the inspector asked hopefully.

'O'course there is.' She tutted and bustled away as if it were the most ridiculous question she'd ever heard.

'Perhaps you could tell Lucy what you have learned from the poachers, and Bobby,' Miss Busby suggested, then placed a fork into the thick crust, letting the delicious aroma escape. 'It will be all over town by morning; she might as well have it from the horse's mouth.'

'Perhaps I'd prefer if it wasn't all over the paper by morning,' he grumbled.

'It's too late for tomorrow's edition, Inspector,' Lucy said. 'I should have thought you'd know that.' She ate with delicate movements. 'Heavens, Miss Busby, this really is quite wonderful.'

Miss Busby nodded agreement.

The inspector grudgingly told Lucy about the men who found Potter's body and the winnings they stole.

'If they found Potter in the lake, how was the £20 in his pocket still dry?' Lucy asked, putting down her fork and reaching for her notebook.

'It wasn't. They dried the notes by the fire.'

'Well, the heart of the matter can't have been money then, can it?' Lucy fixed dark eyes on her adversary.

'What?' McKay frowned.

'The murderer wouldn't have left such a large amount of money on the man in that case, would they?'

'I…well, the…'

'Here we are.' The inspector was granted a reprieve by the landlady bringing his food.

Miss Busby had a thought: 'Mrs Harbottle, did Vernon Potter ever come in for his dinner?'

'Him what died? No, can't say as I ever saw him about the place. Shame, as I heard he was quite the handsome charmer. Unlike Mr Harbottle...' She glanced wistfully over at the bar where her stolid looking husband was pulling pints. 'Enjoy your meals.'

'Heart... not...money.' Lucy read the words aloud as she wrote them in her notebook, before taking a triumphant forkful of mash.

'The men who found him took the money,' the inspector continued, addressing Miss Busby and doing his utmost to ignore Lucy, 'as they believed it theirs by rights. The pair put bets on for Potter, and say they had yet to be paid as promised.'

Miss Busby's head tilted as her mind whirred. 'How interesting, and the young porters at the station did the same?'

He nodded. 'Constable Miller said they made good earnings from it.'

'So Potter paid the porters, but not Ron and Stan,' she mused. 'I wonder if our poachers are telling the truth, Inspector? But then, why would he pay for bets to be placed in the first place?'

'Potter would have lost his job if he were discovered to be gambling,' Lucy said. 'Each of the companies he worked for said the same thing. It's clearly laid out in his contract. That's why he would have had people to do it for him.'

'That's true.' The inspector gave a grudging nod. 'He placed bets under Enid Montgomery's name for the same reason. She didn't object, and he saw to it that she had a little extra in with her winnings each time.'

'It must have been quite the operation,' Miss Busby observed.

'Jolly clever, too,' Lucy agreed. 'The porters can take the train along the line without paying, so it would have been easy for them to place bets in Cheltenham for Potter, which he couldn't do himself, of course, as he was too well known. When the betting shops eventually grew suspicious, the porters simply moved on to Oxford, or Cirencester. In time, they could have done the same in Reading, and so on.'

'He *was* clever, wasn't he?' Miss Busby commented. 'To outwit the insurance company on two fronts. The gambling as well as the loophole.'

'All for the money,' McKay insisted. 'That's what's at the centre of it.'

Lucy looked thoughtful for a moment. 'He was overcharging on the premiums, too.'

'Was he?' The inspector's self-satisfied expression was replaced by one of genuine curiosity.

'Yes, by quite an amount in some cases,' she replied. 'His clients should have been paying ten shillings a month, that was what he officially paid in for them, but I've heard from the ladies concerned that he charged some of them as much as a guinea.'

'That was what poor Dorothy paid.' Miss Busby's

eyes darkened with anger. 'What an awful man, stealing from decent people in that manner.'

'Letitia Lambert paid only five shillings a month,' the inspector said, consulting his notebook.

'Good grief,' Lucy exclaimed. 'She was the wealthiest of all, wasn't she?'

'Was, perhaps, although she's in dire straits now,' Miss Busby admitted. 'But she had Lance to negotiate the policy for her. I suspect he didn't let Potter get away with anything.'

'What did Potter do with all the extra money, do you think?' Lucy asked.

'Gambled it, of course.' The inspector's tone implied this obvious.

'Yes… and all the money he won from the gambling?' Lucy went on in similar tone.

'Well, that remains to be seen.' McKay remained defensive.

'You mentioned he had a substantial amount in his bank account,' Miss Busby pointed out. 'Perhaps he was saving for something.'

'Or being blackmailed,' Lucy suggested.

The inspector rolled his eyes in a most ungentlemanly manner. 'Reporters. Always thinking in tawdry headlines.'

'As opposed to the noble realities of murder, Inspector?' Lucy was quick to riposte.

'That's no reason to jump to conclusions.' He wiped his mouth with a napkin.

'Perhaps money and matters of the heart are entwined in this case,' Lucy conceded. 'There's no reason for the two to be mutually exclusive.'

Ah, a possible truce of sorts, Miss Busby thought. The two really were most alike, if too stubborn to see it.

'Lance Lambert is in this up to his eyes either way,' the inspector said. 'I'll have a chat to Constable Miller. And I think I shall go with him in place of Brierly tomorrow.'

'You might like to mention the wooden gate,' Miss Busby remembered. 'At the back of the grounds. It leads right onto the lake, and we saw it had been used recently. Prior to Adeline and myself this afternoon, I mean.'

He nodded and gave a small sigh. 'Is there anything else I should know, following your adventures with Mrs Fanshawe?'

Miss Busby dithered for a moment, then confessed, 'Only that I think it unlikely Lance is the murderer.'

'Why so?'

'Well, we had a sort of reenactment this afternoon as dusk was falling...'

The inspector raised a hand to his temples, while Lucy gave a delighted smile.

'What fun! Do tell us more,' she encouraged, while the inspector simply shook his head.

Miss Busby explained. Lucy took notes with glee. The inspector muttered about the whole thing being hardly scientific.

'But we have been of some help, haven't we?' Miss Busby said.

McKay looked at her, then sighed. 'You've both been under my feet, truth be told. I know you think you've been helpful, but you've not stopped to think this through. You've been keen to have Potter's death be declared murder, Miss Busby, and I'll not state your motive, but you must realise that having made the official declaration today has played right into the insurance company's hands. And I've been under pressure from my own bosses to do it, and I've been holding them off. There wasn't any actual evidence, and there still isn't, notwithstanding the murder of the tramp.' He looked from one woman to another as he paused for breath. Each fell silent under his gaze. 'And Miss Wesley, you might want to further your career, but I've got a duty to the dead, and the living, and it's not a game.' He finished his drink and rose to his feet. 'I'll pay for the meals on my way out,' he said and stalked off.

They remained in silence for moments more.

'That was unfair,' Lucy said, although there was no rancour in her tone.

'Perhaps we haven't given much thought to his responsibilities,' Miss Busby said quietly.

'Perhaps not,' Lucy agreed. 'But we really did want to help, and he should have taken the time to listen to us.'

'He has actually acted rather well, given the circumstances,' Miss Busby said as they lingered over their drinks.

'No he hasn't,' Lucy replied, then conceded. 'Well, I suppose he has, although he didn't need to be quite so bad tempered about it.'

Miss Busby sighed in defeat and finished her drink.

Lucy did the same. The pair sat in somewhat morose silence as the inspector's remarks took root.

Then Miss Busby had an idea.

'He was kind enough to buy me a rather nice new notebook,' she said, pulling the item from her bag. 'I'd quite like to transfer my thoughts regarding each suspect into it, now that I've spoken to everyone involved. Perhaps we could do it together, so I can be sure I haven't missed anything.'

Lucy brightened. 'That's a good idea, who shall we start with?'

'Let's work through them in order,' Miss Busby said, reaching for her pencil as the pair carefully arranged their thoughts into concise note form:

1. *Dorothy Dent. Stands to lose her home (Station Master's house) upon her brother George's death. Found Potter pleasant company. Paid high premiums for a high return. In great need of the payout. Didn't seem to think she was doing anything wrong*

2. *Belinda Tasker: Struggling with florist's shop and no assistance. Regrets taking out the policy and fears being caught in a fraud. Not at all fond of the man. Even less fond of Evelyn Simpson, whom she holds responsible. Knew perfectly well she was doing wrong.*

3. *Enid Montgomery: Lives somewhat above her means at The Grange, but took out the policy solely to benefit her staff, whom she regards as family. May have found something of a kindred spirit in Potter, if reluctant to admit it. Shared his penchant for the horses. Knew she was doing wrong but suffered no qualms.*

4. *Frances Simpson: Resides at vicarage with brother, not keen on sister-in-law. Adored Potter & harboured apparent thoughts of more than just a financial relationship. Believes Evelyn was also so inclined, and resents her for it. Doesn't appear desperate for money, seeming quite comfortable with her brother. Possibly badgered into the policy by sister-in-law eager for her to move out. Remains convinced she did nothing wrong.*

5. *Letitia Lambert: Living in the now dilapidated and damp Lambert House. Son Lance arranged the policy with Potter. Mother & son both so defensive and hostile little more to be gleaned. Rear gate to the grounds offers easy access to the lake, and has been recently used.*

'Well…' Miss Busby remarked. 'There you have it.'

'They're an interesting bunch, aren't they?' Lucy said, scanning the finished notes. 'All quite different, really, even though they are perhaps all in the same boat.'

'Financial hardship doesn't discriminate,' Miss Busby sighed. 'Although perhaps Frances…'

'I expect she feels trapped,' Lucy suggested, reading her entry again. 'If she's purely reliant on her brother, and he's somewhat at the mercy of his wife…'

'Yes, I suppose you're right,' Miss Busby agreed. 'It must be quite difficult.'

The two sat in silent contemplation for several moments, before Lucy asked if Miss Busby was ready to be taken home.

CHAPTER 17

Miss Busby awoke to find Pudding curled up to one side of her on the bed, Barnaby on the other. The pair put her in mind of the inspector and Lucy: determinedly antagonistic on the exterior, but with great potential to get along when they forgot themselves for a moment.

Pud stretched, looked over at Barnaby, then gave him a swift clout around the ear with a sheathed paw.

Laughing, Miss Busby gave the bemused dog an extra cuddle.

Having chivvied the pair out into the snow bound garden, she lit the kitchen range and put water on to boil for tea. Opening the living room curtains, she was greeted by the sight of a stout Christmas tree tramping up her front path in heavy boots.

'Good morning, Dennis.'

'How did yer know it was me Miss?' His voice was muffled behind the branches as he set the tree, and her Christmas wreath – which had been hidden by its bulk – beside the front door.

'An educated guess.' It was far too early for Bill from the market to be out with deliveries, and the chap had a knack for getting others to do his work for him.

Dennis took a moment to catch his breath, then fixed the wreath to the front door for her. Miss Busby smiled to see it instantly brighten the outside of the cottage.

'It's very pretty,' she remarked.

'Very prickly an' all,' Dennis muttered, rubbing his hands.

'Belinda really does do a wonderful job,' Miss Busby went on, ignoring him. 'Does your mother have her wreath yet?'

'Dunno Miss.'

'Well, is there one on your front door, Dennis?' She managed to keep most of the exasperation from her tone.

'Don't think so, Miss.'

'You must tell her to see Mrs Tasker in Little Minton, then. She would appreciate the custom, I'm sure.'

Dennis muttered something noncommittal in response, before grasping the tree once more and shuffling sideways through the door. When it was finally standing straight and tall in the corner of the living room, and Barnaby had been given strict instructions as to indoor trees not being at all like outdoor trees, Miss Busby had an idea.

'Have you had breakfast, Dennis?'

'Yes, Miss. Mum did kippers. But I wouldn't say no 'ter summat more.'

Setting him the task of chivvying the fire and sweeping up the pine needles he'd shed on the way in, she made tea and toast for them both.

'We can sit in here,' she called from the kitchen, pulling out the chairs at the little table opposite the range. She knew Dennis was a devil for crumbs.

'Thanks, Miss!' He sat down and layered on butter and jam with gusto. Miss Busby was rather more frugal, having somewhat overdone the treats the previous day.

'Do you know the young footman from Lambert House?' she asked. She hadn't known the lad; he certainly hadn't been one of her charges, but Dennis' role as postman meant he knew just about everyone.

'Oliver?' He laughed. 'He's no footman, Miss. A chancer, more like. Only got the job because Master Lance Lambert owes him over a game of cards. Wishes he hadn't now, mind.' He took a substantial bite of toast and a gulp of tea.

'In what respect?'

Dennis chewed vigorously before replying, 'Ain't been paid in weeks, he says.'

'Then why does he stay?' Miss Busby passed him a napkin.

'Says Master Lambert will see him right when his mum gets her money.'

'The two are acquainted?' Miss Busby arched a disbelieving brow. She couldn't picture the angry young man she'd encountered the previous day being one to fraternise with the hired help.

Dennis shrugged, reaching for a second slice of toast. 'Not really, but that's who he won the job from. No one else would employ him. He's a right idiot. Wears that uniform to the Dog and Duck. Thinks he looks the bee's knees.'

Miss Busby leaned forward, so intrigued she forgot to chide Dennis for patronising that particular establishment.

'Why on earth would anyone bet a job?'

'When Master Lambert runs out of money for cards, he bets anything else he can, Oliver says. Jobs ain't easy to come by just now, 'specially with lodgings included.'

Miss Busby found herself momentarily marvelling at all that went on beneath the surface of their little towns. And wondering where a youth like Oliver found the funds to gamble away on cards in the first place. It was, she decided, perhaps best not to ask.

'Oliver does jobs up at the racing stables in Chipping Norton sometimes,' Dennis went on, as if reading her mind. 'He's scrawny, see, there ain't nothing to him, so he works the horses sometimes for the jockeys. That's where he knows Master Lambert from.'

'What does Lance Lambert do at the stables?'

'He's supposed to muck out and clean the tack but acts like it's beneath him, Oliver says. Stands around talking to the jockeys most of the time, telling anyone who'll listen he woulda been one himself, if he weren't born so tall. Well, anyone could say that, couldn't they? Maybe I wouldn't a' been a postman if my dad was shorter!'

Standing to pour more tea, Miss Busby's mind bubbled along with the water on the stove. 'Do you remember seeing a letter from anyone in Little Minton, recently, addressed to Mr Potter in Cheltenham?'

Dennis' eyes widened in surprise. 'Bobby Miller asked me that same question!'

'And what was the answer?' she asked, preparing a sliver of toast for Barnaby, who'd been incredibly restrained until now.

'Nope, not that I could think of.' Dennis shook his head.

'Oh, that's a shame.' She supposed postmen wouldn't necessarily recall details like that, particularly during the Christmas card rush. 'More toast?'

Dennis looked longingly at the jam. 'I would, Miss, but I've got three more trees in the van…'

'Something to take with you, then. And I wonder if you might do me a small favour…'

Having seen Dennis off with a packet of jam sandwiches and a swiftly penned note addressed to the inspector, with instructions that it must be delivered to the station post-haste, Miss Busby set to work on the Christmas tree.

When Adeline arrived in the Rolls a short time later, she stopped in the entrance to admire her friend's handiwork.

'It looks utterly beautiful, Isabelle.'

'Cheery, isn't it?' Miss Busby wrestled a length of silver tinsel from Pud's paws, and draped it around the middle branches. 'Could you help me with the star? Barnaby, *leave.*'

A soggy wooden soldier dropped to the rug, his sword chewed clean off.

'No one will notice,' Adeline proclaimed gaily, hanging the soldier towards the rear of the tree before giving the dog a pat on the head. 'Hand me the star and I shall do the honours.'

'Thank you.' The benefits, Miss Busby thought, of having a taller friend. 'It's just the candles now.' She lifted Pud from the box of decorations, and they wedged them into brass holders with clips attached to secure the pretty white candles in place on the branches.

'Shall we light them?' Miss Busby asked. 'We ought to wait until it's dark, but I'm rather keen to see how they look.'

Adeline glanced at the clock over the mantel. 'We haven't time. We should be off if we're to catch Evelyn.'

'Should we?'

'Yes. The Sunday service will be finishing soon.'

'Oh… right. Very well.' Miss Busby had no recollection of such plans being laid.

Adeline *tsked*. 'You *do* still want to talk to the woman, don't you? I had the idea on my way over.'

'Of course I do.' She fetched her coat and bag from the stand, called Barnaby, then scooped Pud into her arms.

'Isabelle, you are not bringing the cat, surely?'

'I can't leave him here with the tree. It's the novelty

of it. He'll eat half the tinsel. Besides, he's no trouble. He can stay in the car.'

'Just so as long as he doesn't scratch my leather uphol-stery,' Adeline muttered as she started the engine. 'We can visit Mary Fellows once we've seen the Simpson woman. I haven't been to Stow in an age.'

Miss Busby recounted events discussed at The Crown the previous evening, as well as all that Dennis had told her about the footman, Oliver, and Lance Lambert. Actually she omitted the inspector's admo-nition about her and Lucy's meddling. She was feeling rather contrite on the matter and would prefer not to have her friend weigh in with a well meant diatribe.

'I was convinced the answer lay in matters of the heart, but now I'm not so sure,' Miss Busby confessed. 'There's clearly something untoward going on at the racing stables, and Potter may well have been at the heart of it.'

'It might be prudent not to dig into his gambling too much,' Adeline suggested. 'If it was against the terms of his contract, it could void the policies. The insurance companies will take any opportunity to save themselves the funds.'

'Oh, Lord, you're right.' Miss Busby sighed. 'It's all such a minefield.'

'Chin up, Isabelle. "*Faint heart never won fair lady.*" And one of our fair ladies must be possessed of a fierce heart indeed, if they are our killer.'

Miss Busby didn't find this remotely cheering.

The stirring sound of *Jerusalem* poured from the church as they walked up the path. Miss Busby glanced back to give the two furry faces at the window a stern look, as if to remind the pair to behave themselves, before following Adeline into the chilly church and taking a seat at the back.

As the hymn ended, the vicar began reading the parish notices in his customary dull monotone, while Adeline's eager eyes flicked over the congregation. 'Frances is at the front in the middle,' she whispered.

Miss Busby nodded.

'Evelyn's in the row behind.'

A small woman in front of them turned and glared from beneath a large hat.

Adeline remained unperturbed. 'No sign of Letitia,' she observed. 'Although that's to be expected.'

'Belinda is here,' Miss Busby said softly. 'Although I don't see Dorothy.'

'Nor Enid,' Adeline confirmed.

'No. From recollection, Enid rather fell out with God some time ago I'm afraid.'

'She came to the memorial service,' Adeline reminded her.

'She didn't fall out with Potter.'

Harold Simpson's droning came to a halt, before he requested the assembled, 'Go in peace, to love and serve the Lord.'

'Come on.' Adeline was up and out like a greyhound racing from the traps. Miss Busby offered a consolatory

smile to the hat lady, and followed at a more appropriate pace.

'Shouldn't we wait for Evelyn?' she asked.

'In a moment. Let's see who else we can corner first.
'Ah! Good morning Mrs Tasker!'

Belinda shot a startled look at Adeline, before notic-
ing Miss Busby beside her. Her expression turned cold
and she hurried away as if she hadn't heard.

'Well! How rude!' Adeline exclaimed.

'Yes,' Miss Busby agreed quietly. 'I was going to ask
if she could make up a bouquet for Mary. I wonder
what—'

'Miss Busby. A word?' Evelyn was watching from
beside the small side door to the vestry, her own expression not dissimilar to the florist's.

'Good morning, Mrs Simpson. Yes, of course.'

They followed her inside as Harold trudged out to
bid his flock farewell.

'What is this I hear about you preying on Frances?'
she demanded. 'I rose above the matter of you sending
that newspaper reporter to snoop around at the vicarage – Harold and I had the good sense not to talk to
the woman – but this really is a step too far.'

Miss Busby flushed pink.

'Preying?' Adeline scoffed. 'We most certainly did
nothing of the sort.'

'We had been hoping to talk to you,' Miss Busby rallied, before Adeline's indignation could cause further
affront. 'Miss Simpson informed us you were not at

home, but kindly invited us in. I can assure you there was no "preying" involved.'

'Prying, then,' Evelyn snapped. 'My sister-in-law is not quite all there, as well you know. Whatever she told you should have been taken with a large pinch of salt, rather than reported to the authorities.'

'Ah. You had a visit this morning?' Miss Busby hadn't expected the inspector to follow up so swiftly. He must be taking her seriously at last.

'At a most unsocial hour, yes. And he said Vernon's death is now declared murder, so I suppose the insurance won't pay out now.' Her eyes flashed angrily. Two wooden chairs sat empty in the cramped room, a scarred table next to them, a few hooks on the peeling whitewashed wall; it felt cold and unloved somehow.

'Frances said Belinda Tasker visited you in a dreadful state regarding Potter prior to his murder,' Adeline pressed, seeming genuinely curious rather than confrontational, although it could often be hard to tell the difference.

'That is quite frankly none of your business.' Evelyn directed a sharp look at Miss Busby. 'I should have expected better of you.'

'Mrs Simpson,' Miss Busby tried an explanation, 'there has been a misunderstanding. No harm was intended, I assure you. We were simply trying to ensure Frances receives the payment she is due. I am fortunate to have the ear of the inspector, and was merely concerned with ensuring he had all the facts.'

'Well, it is a fact, Miss Busby, that he has already spoken to each of us – several times. You need not concern yourself further.' Evelyn crossed her arms over her chest. 'Frances is utterly distraught over the whole matter, whilst Belinda is quite convinced you are attempting to pin either fraud, murder, or both upon her.'

'That would explain the frosty reception,' Adeline observed.

Miss Busby sighed. 'I will explain things to her.'

'Perhaps it would be prudent,' Evelyn went on in clipped tones, 'to talk to one's neighbours directly in future.'

'We're not neighbours,' Adeline pointed out.

'I meant all of us locals,' Evelyn snapped.

Miss Busby gave a tight-lipped smile. 'Of course. And the inspector is quite convinced there was nothing untoward between Frances and Vernon Potter, so do please put her mind at ease.'

Evelyn's eyes widened, then she banged the vestry door closed before hissing, 'Well *of course* there was nothing untoward between them! Frances is thoroughly insipid. Vernon would never have been remotely interested in her.'

Miss Busby arched an eyebrow. 'I seem to remember you saying you found the man shallow.'

'Well, yes, I did.' The wind suddenly dropped from Evelyn's sails. 'And he was, he had no scruples, and no…heart.'

'You didn't think Potter a catch, then?' Adeline asked.

Evelyn's cheeks flushed fuchsia. 'What a preposterous question. I am a married woman.'

'Indeed you are,' Adeline said wryly. 'And to a vicar.'

'Goodness, time is getting on!' Miss Busby jumped in before matters could sour further. 'I'm so glad we could clarify the situation, Evelyn. We are on your side, after all. Vernon Potter's underhand dealings must not be permitted to get in the way of the Little Minton Ladies receiving their due.' She stepped towards the door. 'I'm quite sure his murderer will be apprehended soon, and we shall all be able to return to normal.'

'I should hope so.' Evelyn grudgingly opened the door and the pair made their way out.

'Good Lord,' Adeline exclaimed as they made their way into town. 'She's almost as cuckoo for the man as her sister-in-law!'

'Adeline, really,' Miss Busby cautioned.

'Well, she is! The pair of them were clearly besotted, and each adamant the other wasn't good enough for him. An insurance salesman, of all people!'

CHAPTER 18

'Could you stop the car here?' Miss Busby asked as Lily's Tea Rooms came into view. 'I'd like to take some pastries for Mary.'

'Good idea. See if they have any Battenberg, would you? I do enjoy a slice on a winter's evening.'

Returning to the Rolls to drop off a paper bag emitting a deliciously sweet and marzipan aroma, Miss Busby was about to dash across to the florist when Adeline announced she would come too. 'In case the woman is hostile.'

Miss Busby sighed. There'd been too much hostility of late, and she worried over her part in it all.

The tinkle of the shop bell brought Belinda Tasker from the back, and Miss Busby pre-empted further iciness by holding both hands up in supplication before repeating what she'd told Evelyn.

'You could have come to me.' Belinda looked more hurt now than angry. 'I would have explained. As it is, I had to explain it to that inspector. I worked myself into a panic over the implications of the policy, that's all. Anyone with a conscience would have done the same.'

'Of course,' Miss Busby soothed. 'It's perfectly understandable.'

Adeline was gazing about at the drooping flowers and dull painted walls with a frown on her face.

'Perhaps you could tell *that* to your inspector, then,' Belinda said wearily. 'He seems only able to understand alibis and sightings.'

'Sightings?' Adeline came to join them.

'Yes, apparently I was "seen" near the lake on Sunday, although he wouldn't tell me by whom. Whoever it was is lying. And unfortunately, there were no "sightings" of me by my daughter's grave, so now he thinks *me* the liar.'

Miss Busby wondered at this. The inspector hadn't mentioned a sighting, nor had Frances, Evelyn, or Letitia. Perhaps he'd spoken to Frances this morning before Belinda... however, the spinster *had* seemed particularly antagonistic toward the florist...

'Oh, I shouldn't worry about that,' Adeline insisted. 'No one has an alibi, as I understand it. You're all in the same boat.'

'Evelyn and Frances do,' Belinda corrected her morosely. 'They have both vouched for each other.'

'Have they really?' Adeline countered. 'I thought it was her brother—'

'The inspector will get to the bottom of it all,' Miss

Busby interrupted, not wanting Adeline to blurt out any more sensitive information. 'Belinda, you must try not to worry. Now, we are on our way to see Mary Fellows at the nursing home, and I would like to take her some flowers. What would you suggest?'

Some short time later Miss Busby carried the large bouquet to the car and settled beneath the blooms as Adeline handed her the cakes. Both animals in the back raised noses to sniff the air, but remained curled up on the tartan rug covering the leather seat.

'Should we let them out for a quick run about, do you think?' Miss Busby asked.

'Will the cat come back?' Adeline's expression was doubtful.

'If there's a bit of custard slice involved, he will be certain to.'

'Let's do it up at the nursing home, then. They'll have more chance to explore.'

The sun glistened from the blanketing snow lying across the surrounding fields and trees as they drove towards Stow-on-the-Wold. Every turn of the road brought a series of arresting views; from magnificent mature woodland to softly undulating hills, to rugged farms, broad water meadows, trickling brooks and tree-lined lakes. A truly glorious corner of old England.

'We really are fortunate, aren't we,' Adeline said, 'to live somewhere so beautiful.'

'Yes. But whoever would have imagined it could be quite so deadly?' Miss Busby said, then sighed. She'd been struck by the notion of a lad as young as Oliver gambling, and somehow found it almost as distressing as the two murders. Perhaps that was the trouble, she mused: in a place so picturesque, no one wanted to look at what lay beneath. She glanced down at the snow roses in Mary's bouquet, pretty enough, lacking the thorns of true roses, but also lacking their singular beauty. She wondered if the most remarkable beauty and the sharpest thorns must always come as a pair.

'Well, now you're getting maudlin.' Adeline shook her head and settled her foot a little heavier on the accelerator. 'Where is this place – Hill House, did you say it was called?'

'Yes, although we may be a little early. Slow down as we pass through the high street Adeline, then look for hills.'

The small town was busy with families out browsing the shops, all dressed in winter togs of thick coats, hats, mittens and knitted scarves. A tall Christmas tree had been placed in the square and decorated with red painted pine cones and ribbons. The local choir had gathered around to sing carols and shake buckets in the hope of donations. A crocodile of smartly uniformed school boys cheered as the Rolls Royce sailed sedately by.

Adeline continued along the narrowing road as the shops and bustle faded behind them, and turned to Miss Busby. 'Should we have asked someone, do you think?'

Peering around the bouquet, she replied, 'Eyes forward, Adeline. I don't think there's any need.' She pointed at a large green painted sign proclaiming "Hill House Convalescent Home."

'Ah, yes, there it is!'

Stretching out before them was a long, elegant driveway leading up a steep incline to a building that looked part schoolhouse, part cottage hospital.

In sharp contrast to Lambert House, the grounds surrounding the home were well-kept, the drive cleared of snow, and electric lights glowing in many of the windows.

'It looks really rather nice,' Miss Busby said, feeling the lightness of relief. Mary adored her little garden, and would no doubt feel at home surrounded by grounds such as these. Tubs of snowdrops brightened the doorstep, and wisteria climbed around the front door, hinting at colourful wonders to come with the spring.

'It's very new,' Adeline said, parking the car askew, one tyre mounting a snowy flowerbed. 'James used to rail about some of them being awful, but this looks delightful. Mary certainly picked the right time to require help.'

'I suppose she did, in a way. Although we haven't quite picked the right time to visit.'

With a flash of gold, Adeline checked her watch. 'We're only a few minutes short. Let's release the animals and catch up with your notes while we wait.'

Barnaby jumped eagerly from the car and pottered through the snow to investigate a privet hedge. Pud preferred the cleared driveway, and after a long stretch and a quick sniff about, sauntered to the front steps and settled on the doormat in a patch of sunshine, his ginger coat radiant in the light.

Miss Busby took her newly updated leather notebook and pencil from her bag, and considered what to add. 'The sighting of Belinda near the lake on Sunday is the most surprising, and perhaps the most concerning,' she said.

'The vicar's wife clearly being enamoured of Potter is more surprising, I should say,' Adeline countered. 'And equally concerning!'

'Adeline, really. The man was charming, everyone says as much.'

'Yes, but Evelyn didn't, did she? Not when you first spoke to her.'

Miss Busby thought back. Adeline was quite correct. 'No, she didn't. The reverse, in fact.'

'Make a note!' Adeline pressed.

Miss Busby obliged, but followed up with, 'Both Simpson women were far too old for the man. Did he encourage it?'

'I suppose he may have done.'

'Lucy showed me a photograph of Potter.'

'Really?' Adeline had been staring out of the windscreen, but turned to look at her. 'And what did you make of it?'

'I can understand why they fell for him, he had an air of devilment about him,' she remarked, then added. 'But in a nice way.'

'Devilment?' Adeline was less than impressed.

'Excitement, adventure – you know the sort.'

Adeline harrumphed in a most unladylike manner. 'I have always preferred the steady and dependable type myself,' she replied tartly.

Miss Busby knew that wasn't true, but refrained from saying so. 'What if one of the trio from the vicarage attempted to drop the florist in hot water by making up a sighting of the woman?'

'The inspector can tell us who reported seeing her.'

'I do feel for poor Belinda, though,' Miss Busby continued. 'She has lost so much.'

'We all bear losses, Isabelle.'

'Yes, but all our circumstances are different. And there was something Belinda said earlier, what was it… in regard to her concern over the policy… "Anyone with a conscience would have done the same…"'

Adeline pondered this for a moment, her gaze on something beyond the silver lady mounted on the long bonnet. 'And as she was the only one who panicked… you suspect she's the only one with a conscience.'

'I wouldn't put it quite like that, but it does occur to me that her reaction marks her out from the others.' Miss Busby paused with pencil in hand.

'I'm quite sure Dorothy Cranford has a conscience,' Adeline conceded.

'Well, of course she does.' Miss Busby nodded. 'But I'm not sure she realised the implications when she took out the policy.'

'You mean she didn't want to consider them. Dorothy is more than sharp enough where it comes to what she wants.' Adeline was caustic.

'As is Enid Montgomery,' Miss Busby said.

'And she indulged and encouraged the man's gambling. Do you find her without conscience, Isabelle?'

'You are putting words into my mouth, Adeline.'

'Not at all, I'm whittling down our suspects and I think you may be onto something.'

'Well, I don't think Enid is without conscience.' Miss Busby stated. 'She is simply not the type to panic.'

'But morally, in terms of knowing the policy wasn't quite…honest, shall we say. Do you find her conscience lacking?' Adeline persisted.

Miss Busby paused, before deciding, 'No. Because the policy wasn't to benefit herself. It was to provide a pension for her dependents.'

'So she says,' Adeline said tartly. 'What about Frances? She knew the policy was decidedly off, in terms of clever loopholes and the like, and she will be the beneficiary of the spoils. Does that leave her without conscience?'

Miss Busby felt like one of her former charges faced with a difficult maths problem.

'No…' she considered. 'The policy will benefit her, and her brother and sister-in-law, who currently bear the burden of her care.'

'Which doesn't seem to worry her.'

'True,' Miss Busby agreed. 'And there's the vicar…'

'There is.' Adeline nodded. 'Because he sounded Potter out and decided he was perfectly acceptable.'

'Yes,' Miss Busby said darkly. 'Although we now know it really wasn't acceptable, at least not for a vicar.'

'I never liked him,' Adeline remarked. 'So very dull.'

Miss Busby sighed, not being able to think of any words of refute.

'Which leaves us with Letitia.' Adeline's eyes shone with mischief. 'Are you able to find a conscience at work there?'

'Yes.' Miss Busby surprised herself. 'In the form of Lance. She wishes to provide for her son.'

'But it was Lance who arranged the policy, not Letitia.' Adeline sat back with an air of triumph. 'And purely to benefit himself. Therefore…'

'…Lance is the least likely to be in possession of a conscience, and therefore our most likely suspect.' Miss Busby brought the conclusion.

'Well done!'

'It's a fascinating way of looking at the problem, but you're forgetting our stooped lady in the shawl,' Miss Busby reminded her friend.

Adeline deflated. 'Ah, yes, there is that.'

'I know,' Miss Busby sighed. 'Just when you think you're getting somewhere.'

'Stooped, though.' Adeline thought for a moment. 'None of our ladies are particularly tall. But Lance is. What if a wig, and perhaps some skill with makeup, were applied?'

'We've already been through this, Adeline,' Miss Busby cautioned, then put away her notebook. She looked around for Barnaby who was nowhere to be seen, but after giving the bag of pastries a shake, he soon appeared from around the side of the building.

'Good boy.' She broke off a piece of custard slice to give him. Pud was slightly harder to encourage, and had to be fetched from his sunny spot by Adeline, but he enjoyed his treat all the same.

'Should we try and smuggle Barnaby in to see his mistress?' Miss Busby suggested.

'Isabelle, it's a medical facility. The dog is a walking mass of germs.'

Miss Busby's heart tugged a little as she shut the car door on his little face, his bright brown eyes dulling to disappointment. 'I shall give her your best,' she assured him.

A cheerful nurse in pristine white uniform and stiffly starched cap greeted them at the front desk. She promised to find a vase for the flowers, but informed them that Mary would not be permitted the pastries. 'She's on a specific diet, to help her recovery.'

'More for us, then,' Adeline reasoned, tucking them into her handbag.

They were led along a corridor, freshly painted in primrose yellow with polished wooden floors, to a bright, airy room where a number of ladies were reading, playing cards, or dozing peacefully. They were all wrapped in comfortable dressing gowns with blankets tucked around their legs. The room was very warm, heated by large cast iron radiators and winter sunshine. Mary Fellows was in a cushioned armchair by the French windows, alternately gazing out at the snowy grounds and glancing down at the newspaper in her lap.

Her eyes lit up when she saw Miss Busby. 'Isabelle, and Adeline! How very kind of you to come! Is Barnaby with you?' She peered behind them eagerly.

Miss Busby shot Adeline a glare. 'He's in the car. Perhaps you might feel up to a short walk later?'

Her thin face fell. 'I'm afraid I am not allowed outside. The cold puts a strain on my heart, they tell me.'

'Does it really? Not to worry, I have an idea,' Adeline announced, then left abruptly.

Miss Busby took a seat beside Mary to tell her the latest goings-on, but the paper in her lap was the *Oxford News*, and she realised that Lucy's article had beaten her to it.

'She writes very well, doesn't she?' Mary remarked. 'There's something to be said for lady journalists. They notice a lot more detail than the gentlemen.'

Miss Busby nodded 'They also notice things new police inspectors fail to see...' She was about to add more but Adeline suddenly appeared outside the window clutching Barnaby in her arms.

'Oh, there's my boy!' Mary pushed away the blanket from her knees and tottered unsteadily to the window. The moment Barnaby caught sight of her he yipped in delight, his stubby tail wagging furiously, and Miss Busby found herself quite overcome.

When Adeline returned, without the dog, Mary told them her plans for the day – lunch, followed by a nap, then bridge, supper and a programme on the wireless. Adeline remarked that it all sounded rather jolly, and Mary admitted it was much better than she'd imagined.

'I do enjoy the company actually, but I miss my books,' she said, her voice frail, but sounding happy. 'I wonder, Isabelle, were you to come again, if you would bring some books? Most of the ladies here are avid readers of the romance serials, but I'm afraid they are not my cup of tea at all.'

'Frances ought to put her name down for a place here,' Adeline said, somewhat unkindly.

'Frances Simpson?' Mary asked.

'The very same!' Adeline gleefully related the events of yesterday with some caustic comments of her own.

'My word, so she was keen on the insurance chap. Well that's another suitor gone in strange circumstances,' Mary remarked with a smile. 'I don't believe the first one was ever found.'

Miss Busby shot up straight in her chair.

'What do you mean, 'wasn't ever found'?' Adeline asked.

'The gentleman she was engaged to some years ago,' Mary said, as a hand bell sounded nearby. 'He wasn't found. It was as though he'd disappeared from the face of the earth and nobody has heard a word of him since. Now, I'm afraid you must excuse me, that's the luncheon bell. Thank you so much for coming, and Isabelle, you are a dear for looking after Barnaby. He's had such a hard time of it. Did I tell you that I found him tied to a lamppost?'

'I think you may have done...' Miss Busby began.

'Loathes men, you know. Well, I expect he has cause. It would have been a man who left him, of course. No heart whatsoever, some of them.'

'Come along, Mrs Fellows.' A nurse appeared to help Mary to the dining room. 'You're in the first sitting, mustn't let good food go cold,' she explained to the visitors.

'No, quite, but Mary, how exactly did—'

'Do come again, won't you Isabelle?' Mary called as she made her way out of the room on the nurse's arm.

'Yes, I shall, and soon!' Miss Busby replied, intrigued and bemused in equal measure.

'Good Lord,' said Adeline as they returned to the car. 'Has Frances killed *two* of them? Three, if you include the tramp.'

Miss Busby spent the journey back to Bloxford convincing both herself and Adeline that Frances Simpson was not a habitual killer of suitors, be they imagined or real. 'It's perfectly logical for the man to disappear. He wouldn't have wanted to show his face after breaking the vicar's sister's heart.'

'Well, there must have been more to it than that – Mary certainly appeared to imply a scandal of some sort.'

'You see scandal everywhere, Adeline.'

'I most certainly do not!' she countered, then added, 'Although it is rather fun when one finds it.'

'Will you stay for lunch?' Miss Busby asked as Adeline brought the Rolls to a halt outside Lavender Cottage.

'What are we having?'

'There's some soup I can heat.'

'Lovely.'

Adeline lit the Christmas tree candles, which did a good job of keeping Pud away from the tinsel, while Miss Busby warmed a pot of chicken soup she'd made previously. After giving scraps to Barnaby and Pud in the kitchen, she carried two steaming bowls and two thick slices of bread and butter through to the table in the living room. They ate in the cosy glow from the candle lights on the tree.

'We need to find out more about this disappearing chap,' Adeline said.

'It will probably be nothing.' Miss Busby sat back. 'But we can ask her when we next visit.'

'Isn't there anyone else who would know?'

'Well, there's Frances of course, but it would probably upset her even further.'

'I don't mind asking her.' Adeline shrugged.

'No, I suppose you wouldn't.'

'Perhaps Dorothy Cranford has pulled off an absolute masterstroke in being the least likely suspect,' Adeline went on, unperturbed.

'Not Enid?' Miss Busby asked with a smile.

'No. All that financial palaver with her husband. It would be too obvious.'

Miss Busby shook her head good-naturedly. 'I think that's probably enough detecting for you for one day.'

'You may be right,' Adeline said, getting to her feet. 'I shall head home, Dolly is going to set my hair for me.'

Miss Busby was well acquainted with Dolly, Adeline's kindhearted maid. 'Adeline. Hair! That's it, and your talk about wigs. Good Lord, why didn't we think of it before!'

'Isabelle, what are you talking about?' Adeline paused in the middle of pulling on her coat.

'The shawl, or blanket rather. The killer put it over her head because it was windy last Sunday,' Miss Busby was almost fizzing with excitement.

'Oh how clever of you, Isabelle.' Adeline's eyes gleamed. 'And we know who wears a wig.'

'Yes, we do, don't we?' Miss Busby said, and then felt a little sad, because she liked the woman and hadn't wanted it to be her at all.

'Come along.' Adeline buttoned her coat up. 'We will strike while the iron is hot. We still have those pastries. Well, most of them…' She brushed crumbs from her blouse. 'It wouldn't do to arrive empty-handed.'

They shut both animals in the kitchen, along with a dish each of chicken, while they headed off in the Rolls.

CHAPTER 19

'Battenberg, how kind! It was Patrick's favourite.' Dorothy smiled as she took the proffered bag and ushered them into the cottage. 'I shall make tea.'

'Please don't trouble yourself on our account,' Miss Busby said, noting that Dorothy looked tired and a little pale. 'We are on our way into town and just thought we'd drop by with some treats en route.' She told Dorothy about Mary Fellows and her restorative diet.

'How wonderful that she's being so well looked after,' Dorothy said, with a somewhat wistful look in her eye.

'Yes, I think she's enjoying the company,' Miss Busby agreed.

Adeline looked between the two, and made a decision. 'Tea would actually be rather nice, Dorothy, if you have the time.'

'Oh, I have nothing but time, Adeline.' Dorothy smiled once again, and waved them to the small armchairs beside the fire. 'I have no plans for the day. I do enjoy a breath of fresh air after Sunday lunch, but the way my hip is these days I'm only able to take a short trip up and down the lane.'

Adeline and Miss Busby exchanged looks.

'And did you get far last Sunday afternoon, do you recall?' Miss Busby called through to the kitchen. There was a clattering of saucers, followed by a moment of silence.

'Good for the heart,' Adeline threw in brightly. 'And the digestion. James always swore by a good walk after lunch. Rain or shine.'

Dorothy came back through with the pot, and set about with the cups, not meeting either woman's eye.

'No wig today, Dorothy?' Miss Busby said softly. 'It was lovely to see you wearing it the other day. You stopped wearing it for so long after Patrick died.'

'Yes, I…well…' Dorothy's hand crept self-consciously to the thin white strands falling around her ears. 'When one is on one's own, it doesn't… That is…when there's no one to make an effort for, it hardly seems worth it. I doubt I shall bother…now that he's…' A small sob escaped her lips, and she rummaged in her pocket for a handkerchief.

'Oh, Dorothy, I didn't mean to upset you.' Miss Busby rose and guided Dorothy gently to her chair, while Adeline set to pouring the tea.

'So silly,' Dorothy managed, wiping away tears. 'He was much younger, had no interest in me, of course, but…'

'He was company,' Miss Busby said, nodding in understanding.

'Yes.' Dorothy sniffed. 'And he was so kind, and rather dashing, and when he came to visit it was as if, just for a little while, I was somebody else…living a more *exciting* life. I knew he wasn't going to live very long, of course, he made no bones about that. That awful cough of his. Oh, it's just so silly of me.'

'Not at all,' Adeline said, handing her a cup of tea and placing a hefty slice of Battenberg on a saucer by her elbow. 'Does a person good, having someone to make an effort for.'

Miss Busby shot her a glance, remembering her reaction to Frances Simpson's fondness for the man. Adeline, as ever, remained unperturbed.

'So long as you know what's real and what isn't, that's the difference,' she proclaimed.

'Anyway,' Dorothy managed, after a fortifying sip of tea, 'in answer to your question, Isabelle, I didn't get far last Sunday. That's why I didn't mention it to the inspector. I made ready to leave the cottage after lunch as usual, but the wind was beginning to get up and I didn't want my wig blown about, so I decided to stay at home. It was vanity, of course. So silly of me…' she repeated.

'Not silly at all,' Miss Busby and Adeline assured her simultaneously. They sat with her, the talk turning to the past, and what became of so-and-so, and where they are now. Feelings had been assuaged and friendships restored by the time they climbed in the Rolls and headed into town.

'Poor woman,' said Adeline. 'And she's worlds apart from that Simpson creature, before you start.'

'I wasn't going to.'

'Yes you were. Frances believed her own stories. Dorothy simply enjoyed a harmless escape each month. She knew perfectly well there was nothing in it.'

'Yes, as you said.' Miss Busby looked out of the window with a small smile. Adeline had a soft heart beneath what could be a rather blunt exterior. 'Would you mind dropping me at the station?' she asked. 'I think I ought to have a word with the inspector.'

After doing as asked, Adeline headed home and Miss Busby started up the path to the police station, where she was surprised to find an irate Lucy Wesley on the doorstep.

'Oh, Miss Busby, have you heard?' Lucy asked, turning back to the closed door to glare at it.

'Heard what?'

She looked back at Miss Busby in surprise. 'You're usually ahead of me,' she said, then explained, 'Lance Lambert has been arrested on suspicion of murder.'

'Good Lord!' Miss Busby exclaimed, her mind instantly buzzing with questions.

'And the inspector is refusing to give me any kind of statement. In fact, he became quite cross with me for asking, and threatened to arrest me for obstructing justice if I didn't leave the station.' She bristled. 'I've been as good as thrown out.'

'Ah.' Miss Busby wasn't entirely surprised, given the inspector's feelings towards reporters in general. 'Well, it's no use standing out here, you'll catch your death. Why don't you head over to Lily's Tea Rooms and warm yourself up. I need a quick word with the man myself, and I'll pop in and see you once I'm finished.'

'He won't tell you anything, you know.'

'No, I don't suppose he will, but I've a couple of things to tell him.'

'To do with Potter?' Lucy asked eagerly. 'What sort of—'

'I'll tell all over a hot cocoa at Lily's shortly,' Miss Busby said firmly, and with a polite nod, she opened the door.

McKay was by the counter, and looked up sternly at the sound of the door.

'Oh, it's you Miss Busby. I was just waiting here in case that reporter tried to get in again,' he spoke gruffly.

'If you mean Lucy, she has just left.'

'I do. I didn't think we'd ever be rid of her.'

'You only had to ask politely.'

'I asked several times. As did Miller.'

'That's right, Miss.' Bobby came through from the back and gave her a cheery smile, which died under McKay's stern gaze. 'She wouldn't take no for an answer.'

'Did you mind your manners, Bobby?'

His face turned beetroot. 'Miss, we're not at school now.'

She gave him a look. 'That's as may be, but manners are important nevertheless. When people are treated with respect, they react in kind.'

'Fetch some tea and biscuits, Miller,' the inspector ordered. 'Miss Busby, I'm glad to see you. Would you come this way? I would like a quick word.' He waved his hand in the direction of his office. He switched on the electric fire and gestured for her to take the chair nearest to it.

'Your information regarding Lance Lambert was very helpful, I wanted to thank you for your note.' He sat behind his desk, facing her.

Miss Busby nodded. 'I'm pleased to be of help, but I was most surprised to hear you've arrested Lance Lambert.'

'It was as a result of my interview with Oliver Healey at Lambert House. Once I'd explained the severity of the situation, he was a mine of information. And surprisingly eager to talk to us.'

'Oliver hasn't been paid in several weeks,' Miss Busby replied dryly.

'Hum.' McKay nodded.

Miss Busby tilted her head slightly, and waited.

'Yes, well, Oliver told me that Lance has a habit of getting to know each of the race horse's form, and selling tips based on this information. And not just from the stables at Chipping Norton where he works.'

Miss Busby arched a brow in question.

'Not being known, I'm told, for his diligence,' the

inspector explained. 'He *is* known, however, for having a network among some of the lads at other stables. And paying them for each tip.'

'Ah. How enterprising of him. And it explains Potter's remarkable luck.'

'Aye. Lance and Potter knew each other from the course at Cheltenham. They formed an alliance, which Potter apparently instigated. According to Oliver, Lance would give Potter the tips just before each race and take a percentage of the winnings in return.'

'And presumably the insurance policy, and low premiums Letitia Lambert paid, were part of the deal.'

He nodded. 'There's not a doubt in my mind.'

Bobby came in with two mugs of tea and a plate of plain biscuits.

'Thank you, Miller. Has Chief Inspector Long finished with the suspect yet?' McKay asked him.

Miss Busby simply couldn't face any more tea and left it aside. 'Who?'

'DCI Long's over from Oxford,' the inspector explained. 'He has more experience at interviewing murder suspects.'

'He wanted a crack at Lance, Miss, when we didn't get a confession,' Bobby added, earning himself a sharp look from the inspector. 'I just ducked my head in now, sir,' he continued swiftly. 'He's still not saying anything, 'cept he wants someone to contact his mother. Says he was at home with her when Potter was killed and she'll vouch for him.' He hovered for a moment before leaving, closing the door quietly behind him.

The inspector sighed and took a biscuit. 'I questioned him myself for over an hour, he wouldn't admit to anything,' he said between bites.

'But the tramp was certain it was a woman,' Miss Busby reminded him.

'But as you said yourself,' McKay sounded terse, 'the tramp admitted he was fond of a drink and his eyesight wasn't very good.'

She was about to state that the reenactment proved otherwise, but realised that she didn't actually have anything concrete to back her beliefs up. She suddenly felt on the back-foot, had all her investigating been for nothing? She tried to regroup. 'What about Oliver's statement?'

'He refused to give a written statement,' McKay replied. 'He said it will come back on him if he does.'

'Yes, it would.' She nodded. 'He would lose his job at the stables, as well as at Lambert House.'

'The latter would be no great loss,' the inspector said gruffly.

'I'm afraid it would. Were he to speak out against his employer, however nefarious, others would think twice about offering him similar employment in the future.'

'That's preposterous,' he objected.

'I'm afraid it isn't. This is a close community, we rely on each other and certain loyalties are expected, especially when one works in service.'

'Would they expect him to cover up Lance's gambling?' The inspector's voice rose in disdain. 'One rule for them, and one for those above them.'

Miss Busby sighed. 'Are you going to charge him?'

He shook his head. 'He hasn't actually done anything wrong. And the porters won't sign statements either.'

'They'd lose their jobs too, for running Potter's bets,' Miss Busby realised.

'And all to save Potter's scheme.' The inspector scowled.

Miss Busby thought for a moment, then asked, 'Why would Lance kill Potter, when his gambling habits were seemingly lining his pockets?'

'A dispute over payment, or a drunken disagreement that went too far. Gambling and drink bring out the worst in anyone, and Lance Lambert appears fond of both.'

'What about the death of the tramp?' Miss Busby turned the discussion. 'Did you receive the results of your tests on the whisky?'

He nodded. 'It's been confirmed there was a large amount of Veronal present. It's used as a sedative, but you won't wake up if you take over 50 grams of it.'

Miss Busby nodded. 'Where would Lance have obtained Veronal?'

'We haven't found that out, but he may have obtained it through his network.'

'Was any found at Lambert House?'

'No. I called the chemist and there's no prescription for Veronal to his mother, or anyone else I can find.' He leaned back in his seat.

'Hmm.' Miss Busby remained thoughtful. 'And where would the tramp have spent the intervening time, do you suppose, while he was hiding from you that day?'

'As we've already heard, he was often seen near the grounds at this time of year. He'd want to be near a source of alcohol. And Lance Lambert was certainly that.' The inspector sighed. 'There are loose ends, but Lance is guilty. I'm certain of it.'

'What about Belinda?' Miss Busby asked, hoping a change of subject might shake loose some ideas. 'She mentioned this morning someone had reported seeing her near the lake. She was very upset, and adamant it was a mistake.'

'Harold Simpson called in early this morning; he recalled seeing her at the lake on Sunday afternoon. When she claims she was visiting her daughter's grave.'

'The vicar?' Miss Busby narrowed her eyes. 'That recollection has dawned a little late in the day…'

'It has.' The inspector nodded. 'And we will follow it up.'

A commotion suddenly erupted in reception. A shrill, angry voice could be heard rising above Bobby Miller's calm protestations.

'Excuse me a moment,' the inspector said, getting up and striding out.

Miss Busby had already recognised the imperious tones of Letitia Lambert. The door had been left ajar and she could hear the woman's words quite clearly.

'How dare you detain my son without a shred of evidence. If you do not release him immediately I shall have my lawyer come and then you'll be sorry! First those awful women snooping around, and now this. It is simply intolerable.'

Miss Busby flinched. She knew Letitia didn't possess the funds for a lawyer, but suspected the threat alone would be effective. Suppressed anger in the inspector's deep voice could be heard even from this distance and she realised the confrontation would take some time to resolve.

Taking a piece of paper and a pencil from the inspector's desk, she wrote him her second note of the day, and found her way out through the door at the rear of the building.

CHAPTER 20

Lucy was the sole customer in Lily's Tea Rooms, the weather, no doubt, having an impact. She was warming herself by the fire and clutching a large mug of hot cocoa.

'That was quick,' she said. 'I thought you'd be an age. He does like to keep people waiting. He really is the most infuriating—'

'Cocoa for you as well, dear?' Maggie came over. Miss Busby smiled and nodded.

'He is only infuriating until you get to know him,' she said to Lucy.

'Well, seeing as he just threatened to arrest me, I have no desire to get to know him further, thank you.'

'Oh, dear.' Miss Busby wondered if she should abandon all hope of ever reconciling the two.

'I told him I could write a front-page piece about him finally catching the culprit and the man lost all sense of reason.'

'Ah. And you used the word "finally", did you?'

'Yes, but I said he would come off rather well – better late than never, after all. Then he unleashed a tirade about wasting police time – well, I told him, if anyone's been wasting time—'

Maggie arrived at the table with a large mug generously topped off with cream.

'Thank you,' Miss Busby said. 'That looks such a treat.'

'It is rather good,' Lucy agreed, calming somewhat. 'In fact, could I have another?'

'You can have as many as you like, dear.' Maggie smiled down at her. 'It'd be a shame to waste what's left on the stove and I doubt we'll be getting anyone else in today, it's almost four o'clock.'

'How did you know Lance had been arrested?' Miss Busby asked when they were alone again.

'I had just stopped at the garage, my car has been making a rather odd noise, when I saw the inspector go roaring by and felt the unmistakable reporter's tingle!'

'So you followed him?'

'Yes, to Lambert Hall, he was in there for an age before bringing Lance Lambert out.'

'He would have been talking to Oliver first.'

'Oliver?' Lucy reached for her notebook and held her pencil expectantly.

'The young footman at Lambert hall.' Miss Busby told her most of what she'd learned. She left out the details of Dorothy's wig, as there was no reason to share the information. In fact, she realised she'd quite forgotten to tell the inspector about it too, in all the commotion. Or was it, she wondered with a twinge of guilt, that she hadn't wanted to put her old friend in the frame.

'Well, you don't sound entirely convinced by the inspector's theory,' Lucy observed, once her notes were complete.

'I truly do not believe it could have been Lance, unpleasant though he is,' Miss Busby stated, referencing once again what the tramp had told her and how she was certain after the reenactment. 'But the inspector won't accept it, and I must admit he has a point. It is only a third-hand statement and a bit of play-acting, after all.'

'But you're positive?' Lucy asked.

'Yes, and I must say, I do find it odd that the vicar had such a sudden epiphany…'

'So who do you think he's protecting: his sister, or his wife?' Lucy asked, as her fresh cocoa arrived.

'Maggie,' Miss Busby turned to the waitress, 'do you remember the young gentleman Frances Simpson was once engaged to marry?'

'I most certainly do, he was Henry Rawlins.' The waitress didn't miss a beat. She pinched her lips in distaste. 'Oily character. Ran for the hills when he discovered her parents had left their money to her brother.'

Lucy surreptitiously picked up her pencil.

'And was Henry Rawlins local, do you recall?' Miss Busby didn't recognise the name at all.

Maggie thought for a moment. 'The family was from London. Derek used to see him on the train. He was never keen on the man, and he's always been a good judge of character. If Derek doesn't like the cut of someone's jib, they're up to no good, you mark my words.'

'And has he seen Mr Rawlins, since?' Miss Busby continued.

Maggie shook her head. 'Never showed his face again after Harold tore strips off him, I heard.'

All three women turned as the door opened and the disgruntled figure of Inspector McKay stepped inside.

'I might've known...' he muttered as he looked over at Miss Busby and Lucy.

'Afternoon, Inspector. Hot cocoa, is it?' Neither Maggie's welcoming smile nor the cheery fireplace melted the frost in his demeanour. He hesitated, then cast an eye over Lucy's drink, and relented.

'Aye, thank you Maggie.'

'Come and sit down, Inspector,' Miss Busby instructed as Maggie disappeared to the back. 'We have a new name you may wish to add to your enquiries.'

Lucy turned her head aside. Miss Busby tutted. For a moment she felt she was back in the schoolroom, dealing with two petulant young pupils. 'Inspector, perhaps you would apologise to Miss Wesley for threatening arrest? And Miss Wesley,' she went on before the inspector could object, 'perhaps you might in turn apologise to the inspector for not adhering to his earlier suggestions?'

The pair stared icily at one other, before turning as one and directing sour gazes at Miss Busby. She flushed, and cleared her throat. 'Well,' she muttered, 'if you will both behave like children, I can't help speaking to you as such.'

Lucy finally murmured something unintelligible but faintly conciliatory, and the inspector did the same in reply.

Giving both the benefit of the doubt, Miss Busby nodded, and proceeded to tell the inspector about Frances Simpson's disappearing former beau.

'I can't imagine I'd show my face again either, in his place.' The inspector shrugged. 'And as it was so long ago, I doubt it will be connected.' He glanced up at Miss Busby, before conceding, 'But, I can ask the Met to track him down, although it won't be easy in London. I appreciate your efforts, however, Miss Busby.'

'And Miss Wesley's efforts, too.'

Lucy's gaze turned in surprise, as the inspector's brow furrowed.

'She's been a wonder with her "sources", Inspector, and despite your feelings towards reporters in general, she is only in pursuit of the truth. As are we all.'

'One hot cocoa, extra cream,' Maggie announced into the ensuing silence. 'I'll be closing up once you've finished. I don't want to struggle getting home.' She crossed to the door and flipped the 'open' sign to 'closed'. 'Don't rush yourselves, mind, you'll burn your tongues!'

They sipped their drinks quietly for a moment, before the inspector said, 'We had to let Lance Lambert go.'

Miss Busby nodded. 'Not enough evidence?'

'No evidence whatsoever.' He shot a narrow glance at Lucy, who placed her hands neatly on the table, as if to show him she wouldn't be taking notes, no matter how much she may have wanted to. He continued, 'With no evidence, there is no way to secure a conviction. And without a conviction, the ladies' insurance policies won't be paid.'

'What *would* secure a conviction?' Lucy asked, resting her chin on her hand in thought.

'Fingerprints on the bottle of sedative used to kill the tramp. Or a blood-stained laurel branch under a bed. Failing that, a confession is all that's left.' He looked down at the table. 'And I was unable to provoke one from Lance Lambert.'

'So was DCI Long, presumably.' Miss Busby attempted optimism.

Lucy nodded in support. 'And there's time yet for you to break the case. We could post a reward, in the paper,' she suggested, brightening. 'For information leading to arrest. That ought to help.'

The inspector shook his head. 'We'd spend days looking for genuine responses among all those trying for the money. And besides, we have plenty of information…'

'…but no smoking gun,' Miss Busby added.

'Or laurel branch,' Lucy added.

'Or confession.' The inspector finished his drink and rose to his feet. 'May I offer you a lift home, Miss Busby?'

'Yes, thank you.' She smiled. 'Are you returning to Oxford afterwards?'

'Aye. I have to meet with the chief inspector for a further briefing.'

'Then perhaps you would be so kind as to drive Lucy home, too. Her car is making a noise, and in this weather I feel it prudent not to take risks.'

'Oh, no, I shall be absolutely fine, really,' Lucy objected.

'Nonsense,' Miss Busby told her. 'If the inspector is going that way it makes sense. You can return on the train in the morning, and have the engine noise properly investigated.'

'It's no trouble,' McKay replied and sounded as though he meant it. Perhaps Lucy's offer of a reward, however ineffective, had gone some way to showing her genuine concern.

The road back to Bloxford was difficult but passable; the inspector followed twin tracks in the snow, the headlights lighting the way as snowflakes patted against the windscreen.

'It's so pretty, even though it's awfully inconvenient,' Lucy commented. 'The perfect evening to stay in with a roaring fire and a good book.'

'Indeed,' Miss Busby agreed, glad that Barnaby had pottered about Hill House earlier and would not require a further walk today.

Lucy sighed as they slowly turned into Bloxford, where the lane grew even narrower. 'It's such a mysterious affair, though,' she said, gazing into the dark. 'Are you quite sure you don't want me to post a reward in tomorrow's paper, Inspector?'

Something flickered in Miss Busby's mind.

'Quite sure, thank you,' he replied.

The more Miss Busby thought of it, the more the flicker grew to a steady flame. By the time the inspector stopped the car outside Lavender Cottage, the flame was dancing, bright and alive with possibility. 'I wonder if the game may not be up *just* yet.'

Lucy leaned forward from the back seat. 'Miss Busby, you've had an idea!'

'Well, actually, it's something I gleaned from a mystery novel I read recently. And from your own gathering of the suspects at the memorial service, Inspector.' She gave him a nod of approval. 'I think we need to gather the suspects together and let them face each other. It's quite possible the truth will be forced out as they confront one another.'

The inspector huffed, rubbing his hands together to warm them while the car was stationary. 'And what would that achieve? Other than informing the culprit we have no evidence on them.'

'There's really nothing to lose at this juncture, is there?' Miss Busby countered his objection. 'And I have an idea as to how we could frame our knowledge… Although I need a little time to work through the details. Lucy, is there any way you could be persuaded to hold off on the front page for a day?'

'I'm not sure the editor would allow that,' Lucy confessed. 'A murder suspect arrested and released on the same day? There won't be anything in the office that could trump it.'

'You see,' the inspector muttered, 'pure self-interest, not a thought for—'

'What if the inspector were to promise an exclusive interview, with all the facts laid bare, should our experiment be successful?' Miss Busby suggested.

'Now, wait just a minute—' McKay cut in.

'And should it not be successful?' Lucy asked.

'Well, the same, I should imagine,' Miss Busby said.

'Absolutely not! The chief inspector would have my hide,' he exclaimed.

'He's hardly likely to promote you as it is,' Lucy remarked dryly.

'And there would be an advantage to having a journalist you can be sure will be most thorough and diligent in writing the story,' Miss Busby reasoned.

'Better the devil you know,' Lucy said.

Miss Busby smiled. 'Could you give us one more day, Lucy, do you think? If it becomes difficult for the inspector to be involved, I shall tell you all you need to know for an informative piece, and we can keep him safely out of the matter. Inspector, there really is nothing to lose at this point, surely?'

'I am not making any promises as regards the local

rag,' he huffed. Miss Busby put a calming hand on Lucy's arm. 'But at the same time, I'm not opposed to it. If you think we can get them all together.'

'Oh, I'm quite sure we can. If you could pick me up tomorrow morning, Inspector, I shall have all my thoughts gathered and we shall do battle!' She opened the car door and stepped out into the falling snow. 'In the meantime, do have a safe and pleasant journey back to Oxford, won't you?' And with her eyes glinting with mischief, she made her way up the path and into her cottage.

CHAPTER 21

Miss Busby feared she would struggle to rise early after such a busy day, and so was surprised to find herself awake before dawn.

She made herself tea and a boiled egg at 7 o'clock, feeling lively, bordering on spritely.

'I wonder,' she said to Pud, tickling his soft ginger ears, 'if it's perhaps more tiring sitting on one's own doing nothing of importance than it is being out and about doing a bit of everything.' Pud nudged her hand for more fuss, and purred happily. He'd prefer it if she never left the house, of course, whereas Barnaby sat at her feet, ears pricked, eagerly awaiting their next move. 'You'll have to sit this one out with Pud I'm afraid,' she said as she rose from the table. 'Come on. I'll give you each a scrambled egg to make up for it.'

After breakfast, washed and dressed in her best outfit of lavender blue tweed, she felt ready for battle. There was still an hour to wait, so she settled at her davenport desk to read through her notes one last time. Barnaby barked to warn her of the inspector's car pulling up outside and she went to greet him at the door brim full of purpose, only to find him quite the reverse.

'I'm not certain this is a good idea,' were his first words.

'Nonsense,' Miss Busby bustled, picking up her bag and telling Pud and Barnaby to stay and be good. 'We've established there is nothing to lose, and everything to gain. And besides,' she added, as he obviously remained unconvinced, 'you can simply blame an old woman's fancy if all else fails.'

'I believe I would be expected to override such fancies,' he grumbled as he followed her to the car.

'I've taught most of this village and the next,' she reminded him as she crossed the lane. 'Any one of them will tell your superiors I am not easily overridden.' Her face broke into a warm smile as she saw a familiar figure in the back of the car.

'It didn't make sense paying for the train when we were headed the same way,' McKay huffed as he got in.

Miss Busby felt suddenly quite warm inside. She'd known the pair would get along if they only stopped bickering long enough to realise.

'Good morning Miss Busby! How is your plan coming along?' Lucy asked brightly. She was wearing the tartan dress and scarf again, with her camel coat.

'Good morning indeed, Miss Wesley. I am pleased to say it is fully formed and quite ready to be implemented.'

'And where will this gathering take place?' the inspector asked, starting the car with a sigh. He really was quite hard work, Miss Busby noted, when he wasn't in control of matters.

'At the station, where I can talk you through my idea properly, and you can approve the proceedings,' she conceded.

Half an hour later, the inspector had not so much approved as grudgingly agreed. 'Although I can't see Lance Lambert confessing in front of a bunch of old women when he didn't in front of DCI Long,' he said.

'One of those "old women",' Miss Busby replied, a little tartly, 'may very well do so in his place.'

McKay shook his head, then went to shout out orders to Lewis and Brierly to fetch the suspects. Bobby Miller got to work pulling extra chairs through from the inspector's office, while Miss Busby and Lucy walked to the front door of the station.

'Such a clever idea,' Lucy whispered conspiratorially as they paused on the step. 'Getting them all together and pitting them against each other. It will be fascinating. I wish I were allowed to stay and watch.'

'I will tell you what I can, afterwards.' Miss Busby was beginning to feel a little nervous, but managed a tight smile as Lucy walked off, boots crunching through the snow.

Bobby was in the interview room, placing papers carefully around the table. Miss Busby peered at one of them to see they were the statements made by each suspect.

'It'll be a bit snug, Miss, but they should all squeeze in,' Bobby said. 'If you find your statement, that's where you should sit.'

Miss Busby soon found it and took her seat, allowing herself a moment to compose herself with several calming breaths.

Letitia Lambert's sharp tones were the first to ring out.

'I really do not see the need for such a performance. You have all the information you need from me. And to drag my poor boy into matters once again, after you wrongfully—'

'If you would follow Constable Miller,' the inspector cut in. Miss Busby imagined he'd had quite enough of the woman already. 'The sooner you take a seat, the sooner this will be over.'

Letitia's lips pursed in irritation when she saw Miss Busby. 'What is *she* doing here?' she demanded, glaring in outrage. 'Interfering again, no doubt. You really ought to find yourself a hobby.'

'Miss Busby is here for the same reason as the rest of you,' the inspector explained as the others peered nervously through the door. 'Your statements have been set out on the table, please find your own and sit down.'

It took several moments for them to shuffle in and settle. Belinda Tasker looked absolutely terrified, Letitia and Lance Lambert were visibly fuming, Frances

Simpson was sobbing into a lace handkerchief, whilst Evelyn and Harold Simpson looked almost as angry as the Lamberts. Enid Montgomery seemed faintly amused, and gave Miss Busby a nod as she sat opposite, whilst Dorothy Cranford looked confused and rather unsteady.

'Read through your statements. When you are sure you can confirm every word, and would swear as much in a court of law, sign the document again, with today's date. Then you will be free to go.'

'*Utter* nonsense,' complained Letitia, as Belinda murmured, 'I really don't see the need...they have all been signed already.'

Harold huffed something unintelligible. Enid gave Miss Busby a wink, whilst Frances continued to sniffle. Lance glared at Miss Busby across the table.

Miss Busby fixed her eyes to her own statement, made following the identification of the tramp's body.

'All finished?' the inspector asked, after papers had been ruffled and signatures made. 'There is nothing any of you would change?'

Angry 'Of course nots' and a couple of quiet 'Nos' filled the air. Letitia made to rise.

'Please remain seated, Mrs Lambert.'

'Why?'

'Because if none of you wish to make any changes, I must inform you that Vernon Potter's death remains a murder with no culprit identified, and as such, none of you will receive your payment from the insurance company.'

Letitia practically exploded, and Evelyn Simpson was predictably outraged. Belinda put her hand to her cheek, Enid frowned, and Lance Lambert pushed his chair back noisily and rose to his feet.

'This is stupid, Inspector,' he proclaimed, fists tightly clenched, although he remained trapped in the small room by the others seated either side of him. 'Just because you're unable to do your job and catch a killer, I don't see why *we* should suffer. Give my mother your superior's number, and we'll see who gets paid and who doesn't.' His eyes flashed anger.

Bobby Miller pulled open the door, alerted, no doubt, by the raised voices, and came to stand in the doorway, truncheon held ready in his hands. It was the first time Miss Busby had seen him armed, and she suddenly began to worry that this hadn't been quite her best idea after all.

'Sit down, Lambert,' McKay instructed. Where Lance had raised his voice, the inspector lowered his, and the effect was quite startling. Lance sat, eyes still burning, but with his mouth firmly shut.

'With no evidence, there is no police force in the country who could make a conviction in this case. You are all suspects– '

'How on earth am *I* a suspect?' Evelyn Simpson shrieked. 'And Harold? *We* don't have policies with that infernal man.'

'But you have both provided an alibi for someone who has,' the inspector replied coldly. 'Are you prepared to stand by that alibi in a court of law?'

Evelyn paused a moment, before hissing, 'I have already signed a statement to say as much, for goodness' sake.'

'My Lance—' Letitia began, but the inspector was ready for her.

'Took out the policy in your name, Mrs Lambert. And you have provided his alibi.'

'Well, and what about Isabelle?' she continued, glaring at her nemesis across the table.

'Miss Busby has given a statement concerning information provided by a witness to the murder.'

'If there's a witness, what are we all doing here?' Enid demanded.

'The witness was killed by the same individual who murdered Vernon Potter,' the inspector replied.

A few gasped at the word 'murdered', although they all must have known about it at this point.

'And who else might they go on to kill?' snarled Letitia. 'Given your inability to catch them? Are we all in danger now?'

'Perhaps you should ask your son,' he replied. 'Who is next on your list, Lance?'

Letitia began to splutter, but Lance only scoffed. 'You've tried to pin it on me once already. Didn't work out too well for you, did it, you useless Jock.'

'You talk with respect in here,' Bobby Miller ordered him. McKay held up a hand for quiet.

'You and Potter had quite the scheme running, didn't you, Lambert? I take it you've had your notice from the racing stables?' McKay goaded him. 'I shouldn't imagine they take kindly to insider information being passed around. You'll be hard pressed to find work now.'

'I don't need to work,' Lance replied with a sneer. 'Not now. Potter and I were saving to buy shares in our own racehorse with the money we made. I've got plenty squared away, don't you worry.'

Ah, that explains Potter's healthy bank balance, Miss Busby thought. But could Lance really have put that much aside? With Lambert House crumbling around him?

McKay watched him, but didn't respond.

Lance shrugged and lounged back in his chair, lank hair falling over his forehead. 'I'll find a new partner. And Mother and I have no need of the insurance money, Inspector. You're wasting your time trying to threaten us.'

'So you made sufficient from Potter and then killed him?' McKay accused.

'Oh!' Frances Simpson squeaked in horror. 'You are an absolute *monster*,' she shakily proclaimed in dramatic fashion, handkerchief held to her thin cheek.

Lance sneered at her. 'Why would I kill him when we were *making* a killing?'

'He was taking too big a cut, wasn't he?' the inspector accused. 'I've seen his finances.'

Lance's eyes widened for a moment, then narrowed to angry slits. 'So what?'

'The bank allowed me sight of your finances too, and it is quite clear Potter was making far more from the arrangement than you were.'

'I gave you *no* authorisation—' Letitia objected with a voice like steel. But once again the inspector was prepared. He really did have the measure of the woman, Miss Busby noted with admiration.

'I do not need authorisation where a murder enquiry is concerned, Mrs Lambert.'

'We shall see about that,' she shot back. 'Once Havers gets word of this, we shall see indeed. I will have you out of a job, Inspector.'

Miss Busby dimly recalled that Mr Havers, an officious gentleman of advanced years, used to dispense legal advice for an extortionate fee from small premises on the outskirts of Little Minton. Not having seen him around the town in many years, she'd thought him dead.

'I don't know what finances you think you've seen, Jock, but I did perfectly well out of the arrangement. And just because I'm not *sobbing* over the man, doesn't mean his death hasn't been an inconvenience.'

'And how will a new partner fit into your scheme, with no racing stables in the county likely to employ you?' McKay asked calmly.

'Oh for goodness' sake Inspector, you are *hounding*—' Letitia railed.

'It's alright, Mother.' Lance's dark eyes didn't leave the inspector's. 'Let him show his ignorance. Do you think there aren't stable hands across the country who are happy to sell tips, Inspector? Don't they teach you anything at police school? Or do Jocks not *go* to school?'

'We do, actually.' The inspector's tone was lighter than Miss Busby would have imagined. She thought he was holding his temper extremely well. 'And we learn that gambling away from the race course is illegal, so I wouldn't be quite so sure of myself if I were you.'

Enid shifted a little uncomfortably in her chair.

'Especially given the easy access to the lake from your property,' the inspector continued. 'It has not escaped our notice that the rear gate shows signs of recent use. Not to mention your grounds being known as a haunt for the tramp, Joe Tucker.'

'I can't help where I live, can I?' Lance shot back, discomfort showing in his face for the first time.

'As you can't even catch a killer right under your nose in a small town, Inspector,' Letitia flew to her son's aid, 'I shouldn't imagine there's any possibility of you proving what information was exchanged where. Gate or no gate.'

The inspector fixed on Lance, his blue eyes glinting icy grey.

'But he has admitted as much just now, hasn't he? It was obviously him!' Evelyn Simpson blurted into the silence as the two men held one another's gaze. 'He was in league with Potter, and has benefitted from his death.'

'I said I've been inconvenienced by it,' Lance snapped. 'Don't you listen, you stupid woman.'

All but Letitia and the inspector gasped in horror at the young man's rudeness.

'How *dare* you address my wife in that manner,' Harold roared, shooting to his feet and leaning menacingly over the table towards Lance.

That made everyone stare.

Miss Busby caught the inspector's eye. Was the vicar showing his true colours?

'Please sit down,' McKay told him firmly.

He didn't sit down. Red spots of anger glowed in his pallid cheeks. 'What are you waiting for? Arrest him, Inspector! My wife is quite correct,' he shouted. 'He's reprehensible!'

'Being reprehensible isn't a crime, vicar,' the inspector replied calmly.

'I thought you had *me* down as guilty, Harold.' Belinda Tasker's quiet voice cut through the tension. All eyes turned to her in surprise. 'You made up that tale about seeing me at the lake, didn't you?'

'How…how did…?' he spluttered.

'How did I know it was you? I didn't, until just now.'

'Mrs Tasker—' the inspector began.

'No, I'd like to speak, please.' Belinda straightened her shoulders. 'If he's so eager to accuse everyone else perhaps it's time he had a little of his own medicine. I know it's either you, your wife, or your sister, Harold. You're all in it together, aren't you?'

'All in *what* together?' Evelyn demanded shrilly. 'Whatever you think we're in, Belinda, I can assure you, you are in it with us.'

The inspector glanced over at Miss Busby, who gave him a slight nod. He returned it discreetly, seeming to recognise, at last, the true value of her suggestion.

CHAPTER 22

'The notion of you all being "in it together" – "it" being fraud, I believe, – was a matter you discussed between yourselves shortly before Potter's death, was it not?' McKay pressed.

Belinda flushed.

Evelyn's complexion purpled in rage. 'I see you have been telling tales of your own, Belinda,' she sneered. 'The notion of the insurance policies being fraudulent was never an issue, Inspector, despite Mrs Tasker's hysterics. My husband went over that policy to the letter, and the legalities were perfectly sound. There would have been no notion of the insurance company paying out at all if that weren't the case.' She cast a supercilious look around the room. 'But if it's fraud you're looking for, I should start with Enid Montgomery. She has some experience in that area.'

All eyes now shot toward Enid, who gave a soft chuckle. 'Really, Evelyn, is that the best you can do?' Her chuckle turned into a small, and then a harsher, cough, and she fought for a moment to regain her breath. Miss Busby shot a sharp look at the inspector.

'We have looked into the late Mr Montgomery's financial dealings, and confirmed the original findings at the time: no laws were broken.'

'She gambled, though!' Letitia Lambert piped up, seeming to get her second wind. 'Enid Montgomery was known to make bets! Why don't you arrest her for that? Or are you only concerned with seeing my son behind bars?'

'I put the odd bet on now and then to cover the premiums, Letitia,' Enid replied, her breath settling. 'I wasn't about to buy a racehorse.'

'A *share* in a horse,' Lance corrected petulantly. 'And it was Potter's idea, anyway. Thought it'd make him look a toff over in Cheltenham, and he wouldn't have to bother with the insurance game any longer. He hated it, you know, selling to you old fools!'

'He sold *you* a policy, you bounder!' the vicar shouted.

His wife hissed, 'Calm *down, Harold*.'

'Inspector, I wonder,' Miss Busby interjected, feeling the time had come to step in. 'As Vernon Potter was considered terminally ill, might his death not be attributed to that?'

The inspector looked momentarily at a loss.

'As in, he may simply have been overtaken by a fit of coughing and slipped into the lake, hitting his head as he fell,' she continued.

'Well, that wouldn't—' McKay stopped in confusion.

'Good Lord, the man wasn't remotely ill,' Enid cut in, shooting a disappointed look at Miss Busby. 'I already told you he was putting that cough on. And anyone with an ounce of sense could see he couldn't have fought at the front. He wasn't gassed.' She tutted.

'He *was* ill,' cried Frances, wringing the handkerchief between her fingers. 'How can you say he wasn't? His lungs were in a terrible state. Perhaps you exaggerate your own cough, Mrs Montgomery, to elicit sympathy after your husband *stole* from others, but you shouldn't judge my… shouldn't judge Vernon according to your own standards!'

Miss Busby's eyebrows shot up. *My* Vernon, had she been about to say?

'For goodness' sake, Frances. Do your sums. The man couldn't possibly have served.' Edith shook her head. Miss Busby shot her a supportive smile.

'Look at them!' Frances shrieked, pointing her finger. 'They're in league, those two!' She turned to the inspector, who remained impassive. 'They've obviously been talking about Vernon and his state of health, why would they do that if they weren't up to something?'

'It is human nature to be curious, Miss Simpson,' Miss Busby replied.

'Yes, Frances, do stop being quite so drippy for once. We all liked the man, after all.' Enid was matter-of-fact. 'Hard not to, really. But he played on that, and we all realised that too. Or most of us, at least.'

Lance gave a cruel laugh as Frances flushed, but she wasn't backing down.

'Oh, it's all very well, you acting so knowledgeable and superior now, Enid,' she accused, 'but Vernon was on his way to see *you* the day he died, wasn't he?'

Lance's laughter died in his throat, and he leaned forward eagerly now to listen.

'Oh, yes!' Frances went on, her voice rising as she looked around at them all, her confidence seeming to grow from the attention. 'He was going to visit *her* on that Sunday and now he's dead!' A sob trembled in her voice. Harold felt in his pockets for a clean handkerchief for his sister, but she waved it away. 'Her with her illicit past… I should look no further than Enid Montgomery. Known gambler, and now, *murderer!*'

There were sharp intakes of breath all round.

Miss Busby raised both brows at the inspector, eyes flicking from Frances to Enid. He caught on and asked softly, 'How do you know Vernon was going to visit Mrs Montgomery, Miss Simpson?'

'I…' she flustered, 'I…well, why shouldn't I know? After all, he was, wasn't he?'

'I don't recall broadcasting the fact,' Enid replied.

'Well, someone must have said, and he owed you money, didn't he?' Frances flustered.

Miss Busby's eyes fixed on her.

'And you killed poor Vernon for that money, and more, I'm quite sure of it.' Frances continued her accusations. 'That rotten husband of yours taught you—'

'That's quite enough, Miss Simpson,' the inspector cut in.

Lance began to laugh again, louder this time, and clapped his hands in delight. 'I thought I was the monster, but now it's Enid? She was Potter's favourite, you know,' he drawled. 'He always said she was worth twenty of the rest of you.'

'He would *never*!' Frances objected vehemently. 'And *she* started it, Inspector, saying poor Vernon wasn't ill. If she thought that, why did she take a policy out in the first place? Answer me that!'

Miss Busby was momentarily startled. She hadn't considered that. Then she remembered Enid's attitude to risk taking, and supposed it must all have been part and parcel of the game.

'He *was* ill.' Dorothy Cranford spoke up for the first time. 'Oh, I know he wouldn't have been fighting at the front, Enid, but the last time he visited me, when he coughed I saw flecks of…' her eyes began to water and her voice quavered '…blood…on his handkerchief afterwards.' She sniffed and looked down at her own hands. 'His cough was awful that day. Sometimes I wondered if perhaps he used the story about gas to make it all seem more heroic.' Everyone in the room was now looking intently at her. 'Well, he smoked, you see,' she explained. 'He'd talk sometimes about meals out, and so on. Cigars after dinner and the like. A lot of brandy. I always wondered if… perhaps some form of cancer…he was a little overweight, after all.'

'Overweight?' Frances screeched. 'You're one to talk! Mutton dressed as lamb, with that pathetic wig of yours. You were besotted with him,' she accused, 'but he saw you for what you were – saw right through your airs and graces. You are living off your brother's charity! *Lady* Dent, they still call you that behind your back, you know. And Vernon did too. You most likely killed him so you won't be homeless when your brother's dead and you can't scrounge off him any more!'

'Frances, really,' Enid objected, 'do make up your mind. Was it me, or was it Dorothy? Good Lord, woman, neither of us can walk more than 20 yards without needing to sit down. How you think we're capable of murder in a remote location like the lake is quite beyond me.'

'Oh, but you're *so clever* Enid, and you, *Lady Dent*, you both think yourselves so much better than the rest of us. I'm sure you could find a way. Cancer, indeed. As if you knew him better than me!'

'I have never claimed to know him better than anyone,' Dorothy replied, with what Miss Busby considered great dignity under the circumstances. 'And I was very fond of Vernon, yes. As we can all see you were, Frances.'

'Oh, you were *all* fond of him. Even I was, at the start,' Belinda broke in, her tone frustrated. 'He was nice looking, even if he could have done with skipping the odd dessert.' Frances squeaked in protest. 'But if he was ill with cancer, or something similar, why wouldn't he have said? It would have made much more sense, and saved us all so much worry.'

'How would it?' Frances' tone had risen to a near shriek. 'It wouldn't have saved *me* any worry; he was dying either way. Not one of you cared enough for the man to consider how he suffered! You all wanted him dead! You all wanted his money!'

'Our money,' Enid corrected dryly.

'This really is the most ridiculous affair, Inspector,' Lance drawled. 'Nothing but a gathering of hysterical females. His "daft old biddies", Potter called them. I demand we be allowed to leave.'

'Daft old biddies!' squealed Frances. 'He would *never*!'

'You'll demand nothing,' McKay informed Lance, ignoring Miss Simpson's histrionics

'And you'll apologise to my sister!' Harold was on his feet and roaring at Lance again.

'You're very protective towards Miss Simpson, Vicar,' the inspector remarked.

'What if I am? It's not a crime.' Harold's insipid manner was entirely gone, he was consumed with rage.

'No, but I've been wondering why you would suddenly concoct that tale about seeing Mrs Tasker at the lake on Sunday,' McKay continued.

'I can assure you I concocted nothing! It had simply slipped my mind.'

'Ah, very well, then you must have been at the lake, yourself, on Sunday, in order to have seen her.'

'I...I...'

'He saw her from the lane, Inspector,' Evelyn said, glaring at her husband. 'Good lord, it doesn't take a genius.'

'Yes, from the lane!' Harold cried out. 'Don't try and turn this around on me! *I'm* not the one without an alibi! It's Mrs Tasker who's lacking one.'

'But, Miss Simpson, I thought you said your brother was with you that Sunday afternoon?' Miss Busby questioned. 'And that you were at home?'

'I... no, I don't believe I did... I... I said Harold could vouch for me, which is really not at all the same thing. But Evelyn can tell you I was home, can't you?' Frances looked to her.

'Yes, well of course I was at the vicarage at the time,' Evelyn said, which everyone realised was deliberately ambiguous, and they immediately began asking their own questions.

As the room descended into squabbling reminiscent of the schoolyard, Miss Busby snapped instinctively, 'Quiet! Please.' That made all faces turn to her.

She looked to the inspector, who hid a smile and continued.

'You have gone to significant lengths to protect Miss Simpson before, haven't you, Vicar?' he asked into the ensuing silence. 'With regard to a former suitor.'

Frances let out a small squeal of distress, before clamping her hands over her mouth.

'This really is turning into a witch hunt. We have signed your papers, Inspector, and now we are leaving,'

Evelyn declared. 'Money or no money. Come along, Harold.' She rose and turned to her husband, who had gone a rather shocking shade of grey. 'Harold?'

He fell back into his seat. Sweat was beginning to bead on his forehead, and his hands were trembling on the tabletop.

'That was…many years ago…' he began. 'And a completely different matter.'

Frances reached out her hands to implore him, 'No, Harold, you mustn't! They'll twist it all!'

Evelyn dropped back to her seat, as the others stared at the vicar.

'Constable Miller,' the inspector said, 'collect the statements and release the others. I would like to continue speaking to the Simpsons alone.'

A gasp flew from Dorothy and Belinda. Enid grew wide-eyed, as Letitia and Lance both laughed in delight.

'Always the one you least suspect, Inspector,' Letitia crowed. 'And you never suspected a man of the cloth, did you! You had it in for my boy from the outset. You'll be hearing from Havers!'

'I'll be waiting for my apology, Jock,' Lance sneered as the others filed out. He left the room with his mother, both cock-a-hoop.

Miss Busby remained seated. Enid gave her a curious look over her shoulder, but the Simpsons had other things on their mind as the door closed on them.

'How did you know Potter had been on his way to see Enid, Miss Simpson?' the inspector asked once more.

Frances broke out into fresh, over dramatic sobs in place of answering.

'Oh, it was no secret the woman gambled with him,' Evelyn scoffed. 'Potter would talk about the others from time to time.'

Miss Busby was most surprised to see Evelyn coming to Frances' aid.

Frances, it seemed, didn't see it as such.

'Yes, and you loved talking to him, didn't you?' she accused. 'Loved your little chats with Vernon when Harold was at prayer and you thought I was asleep. Well, I wasn't! I heard you! And I know you couldn't wait to get rid of me, that's why you made Harold check the policy so carefully, to be sure I'd be out from under your feet.'

Harold shook his head silently, and even Evelyn began to pale.

'Well, the man would talk; what was I supposed to do?' she asked the inspector. 'Ignore him?'

'Why was he visiting you in the first place?' Frances shrieked. 'What business did he have with *you*?'

Miss Busby's eyes widened.

Evelyn took a moment before answering. 'None whatsoever, Frances. He came to collect your payments, but often found you so utterly insipid and inept that he preferred to deal with me.'

'Lies!' Frances shrieked, before the inspector stepped in.

'What happened to the tramp, Miss Simpson?' he demanded.

'Ask *her*,' she blurted, pointing an accusatory finger at Miss Busby, who recoiled in surprise. 'She killed him!'

Ah, I am murderer number three, or is it four? Miss Busby thought, trying not to take it personally. 'Now, just a moment, Frances—'

'If she hadn't been nosing around the lake that day, asking questions, it would never even have occurred to him!'

'Frances, that's enough,' Evelyn hissed, as the vicar moaned softly, his head in his hands.

'What would never have occurred to him, Miss Simpson?' the inspector pressed.

'To try and blackmail me!'

'Frances, no,' the vicar implored in a dull moan.

'Well, they've all got it in for me, you heard them Harold! Silly, daft Frances, jilted once – and then Vernon preferred *her* to me... "His favourite" Lance said, and he was right! Enid Montgomery! Oh, it's unbearable!'

'My sister-in-law has worked herself into hysterics, Inspector,' Evelyn shouted. 'You cannot take a word she says seriously in this state. We demand a lawyer be present before another word is spoken.'

'And get rid of the Busby woman,' the vicar said weakly. 'This has nothing to do with her.'

'It does!' Frances wailed. 'It's all her fault, all of it! That tramp would never have come to the church if it weren't for her. He wanted to hide from the police, they were searching for him after she spoke to him, making up lies…'

Miss Busby got to her feet, a horrible queasy sensation roiling in her stomach. She knew Frances was desperately clutching at straws, but the woman had unknowingly tapped into the fears that had been lurking in the back of her mind all along. She felt her knees tremble slightly, but with a Herculean effort she made one last point. 'The day I came to the vicarage with Adeline Fanshawe, Frances, you made mention of Potter's "murder".'

Frances looked up. 'So what if I did? It's what we're all here for, after all.'

'"I'd be curious as to her whereabouts at the time of poor Vernon's murder," you said,' Miss Busby went on. 'With reference to Mrs Tasker.'

'Well?' the vicar rallied. 'I'm curious too. Just because the woman sat mute until she was sure the tide was turning in her favour, then tried to pin the blame on me, I don't see—'

'It was the word "murder", you see Vicar,' Miss Busby continued. 'The police hadn't declared it at that point. So I wonder, Frances, what made you quite so sure?'

The silence that followed was heavy, before the vicar snapped, 'You don't have to answer to that woman, Frances. She is nothing more than an interfering busybody.'

'Thank you, Miss Busby,' the inspector said softly. 'That will be all.'

CHAPTER 23

'Miss Busby? You look quite discombobulated,' Maggie noted with concern as she entered the tea rooms. Lucy rose from her table in the corner and rushed to help Miss Busby to a seat.

'I'm fine, really, thank you.' Miss Busby sat a little heavily, the events of the last few days seeming to catch up with her all at once.

'I'll fetch you some tea,' Maggie said. 'And something sweet.'

'What happened?' Lucy asked as soon as the waitress was out of earshot. 'Did it work?'

The question seemed to come from far away, and Miss Busby found for a moment she wasn't quite sure how to answer.

'Oh, goodness, was it awful? I'm so sorry. What can I do?' Lucy continued.

Miss Busby lifted a hand. 'I'm fine, really. I think I just need a moment.'

Lucy ran over to hurry the tea along, and Maggie dropped four sugars in to be sure.

'Better?' they both asked, watching her take a sip.

'Yes, thank you. I'm fine, truly.'

Maggie buttered her a scone, and layered plum jam on thickly for good measure. 'Can't have anything happen to my best customer now, can I?'

Miss Busby took a small bite, and felt some of the colour return to her cheeks. 'Thank you, Maggie, you are very kind,' she said, as the waitress smiled and bustled back to the counter.

'How is your car?' she asked Lucy, after another sip of tea.

'Oh, it's nothing serious. Probably. The man from the garage was happily fiddling about under the bonnet when I left. Said he'll bring it round here when he's finished. But, Miss Busby, *what happened*? Do we have our murderer?'

'I'm afraid we do,' she replied quietly. 'It seemed all such a game, in a way, tracking her down, trapping her, but now...' She sighed, her eyes downcast.

'Her! The inspector was wrong, then? But *who*?' Lucy pressed.

'Frances Simpson.' Miss Busby's reply was flat. 'With help from her brother, I'm sure. She as good as confessed before Evelyn insisted on a lawyer. She said the tramp had come to the church the day the police were searching for him. She even said he'd tried to blackmail her.' She pushed the rest of the scone aside and looked out of the window at the passing throng; the shops adorned with festive decorations, the tree in the centre, crisp white snow abounding, all looking quite beautiful in the winter sun. 'She could hang,' Miss Busby said, her voice the merest whisper. 'Can you imagine?'

Lucy pushed the scone back towards her. 'Only if they're absolutely sure she did it. And she killed two people, remember. You mustn't feel sorry for the woman.'

'No, I suppose I mustn't. But…the loneliness… She must have been unbearably lonely to fixate on the man. It can be so overwhelming. And they all suffered from it.'

'Didn't all kill over it though, did they?'

'No.' Miss Busby gave a long, tired sigh. 'But Potter did seem to fill a gap in their lives.'

'Frances had her brother, don't forget. She can't have been *that* lonely. Oh, and that reminds me! While I was walking back from the garage, I saw a sign up at those new houses being built along the road, you know the ones? Rather small, but quite sweet?'

'Yes.' Miss Busby had a dim recollection of Evelyn being annoyed by them.

'They are to be sheltered housing for elderly residents. There's a telephone number and an address for enquiries. I took both down for you, thinking you may want to pass them on to Mary Fellows, once she's a little stronger.'

'What a lovely idea,' Miss Busby said, feeling some of the despair that had descended lift from her chest.

With the culprit found, she realised, the insurance money would now be paid to the others, and perhaps the answer to all their problems now lay within reach. She took the details from Lucy and managed the last few bites of her scone, beginning to feel much more herself.

Having heard the story told, Lucy now wanted to write it down in more formal fashion. She took her pencil and questioned Miss Busby again until she had the details in order.

Miss Busby felt it was almost a catharsis, and let out a long sigh of relief afterwards. Then they ordered a light lunch to wait for the inspector to arrive and fill in the remaining details.

It was a long wait. Lucy glanced habitually at the clock over the fireplace, thinking no doubt of tomorrow's edition.

The arrival of her red sports car drawing up outside proved a welcome distraction. The repair man, Aiden Doherty, short and stout but awash with personality, came in proclaiming at length that there was nothing at all wrong with it. 'She vibrates a little, that's all. As well she might! Lot of power, there, see – *lot* of power. Open her up, do you? You should! Do her the power of good.' He left again in a whiff of motor oil and grease.

'Shall I run you home, Miss Busby?' Lucy offered as the clock reached 3pm, neither of them able to face any more tea or sandwiches.

'Let's give it another half hour,' Miss Busby said,

eyeing the door as nervously as Lucy kept eyeing the clock.

'Cats on hot bricks, you two,' Maggie remarked, which made Miss Busby think of Pud, and then, 'Oh Lord, Barnaby!'

Lucy looked up, startled.

'I left him at home. He'll need to go out.'

'Come on,' said Lucy, seeming glad of something to do. 'I'll take you back and we'll rescue him.'

As the pair left the tea rooms and walked towards the car, they spotted the inspector advancing towards them, shoulders hunched, head down.

'Oh!' Miss Busby's hand flew to her mouth. 'Has… did she…?'

He looked around to be sure they wouldn't be overheard. 'Frances Simpson has provided a full confession to both murders. I'd rather not go into further details here.' He didn't look at all relieved, or triumphant, but rather saddened, and drawn.

'We were just leaving for Lavender Cottage, Inspector. Come with us. I'll drive you back to Oxford afterwards. You look awfully tired,' Lucy pointed out.

Looking indeed somewhat pale, the inspector nodded his thanks. 'That's kind, Miss Wesley. I'm afraid the situation has reminded me of… well, it's no matter.' He cleared his throat, and nodded curtly. 'Thank you, I should be glad of a lift.'

Miss Busby wondered what the inspector had been about to say, and it suddenly occurred to her that with all that had been going on she hadn't really learned anything about his past, other than the matter of his mother's illness. Now wasn't the time, of course, but she made a mental note all the same, as the three of them drove back to Bloxford in silence.

With Barnaby's needs met and a fresh pot of coffee brewed to revive the inspector, he told them of Frances Simpson's confession.

'There were two factors that caught her out,' he explained. 'The fact she'd known Potter was on his way to visit Enid, and the fact she'd proclaimed it a murder early on. The latter purely down to your eye for detail, Miss Busby,' he confessed.

She wasn't quite sure how she felt about that, other than slightly sick.

Lucy, suffering no such reaction, pressed for details.

He sighed, as if reluctant to divulge.

'Heroic headlines, remember?' Lucy cajoled. 'Other reporters might question how long it took you, or whose idea it was…'

He scowled at her, and Miss Busby sighed. Still a way to go between the pair of them, it seemed.

'…Whereas I shall make you the hero of the hour,' Lucy finished.

After taking a long drink of coffee, the inspector began, 'Frances was out walking around the lake on Sunday afternoon, when—'

'Why?' asked Lucy.

'What?'

'Why was she out walking in the cold and the wind on a Sunday afternoon?'

The inspector took his notebook from his pocket and flicked toward the back.

'She had taken to walking in the afternoons, believing it to be good for her figure,' he finished. 'Or that was her story. But she may have heard he was dining with Enid that night.'

'Do you think she'd taken to spying on him?' Lucy cut in.

'I prefer not to speculate.' McKay wouldn't be led into saying anything he didn't want to.

'Very well.' Lucy nodded. 'Go on.'

'She said she recognised Potter's car in the distance and walked across to flag him down as he drove into the town.'

'Why?' asked Lucy.

'For goodness' sake, because she wanted to talk to him, of course.'

'There's no need to take that tone. I'm simply being thorough.'

'You'd make a good constable,' Miss Busby quipped.

The inspector didn't seem to find the notion at all amusing.

'Potter said he couldn't stop to chat as he wanted to see a couple of the porters before he dropped in on Enid Montgomery for dinner. When she heard that confirmed, she found herself...' he checked his notes again, quoting, '...overcome with jealousy.'

Lucy nodded at Miss Busby. 'Heart, not money. I said so all along.'

Miss Busby understood for a moment why the inspector sometimes found himself exasperated with the young woman.

'She told Potter she needed to speak to him on a matter of the utmost urgency, and in private,' he continued. 'And she'd already walked around the lake, and knew it to be deserted—'

'—or thought she did,' Lucy interjected.

'Yes, I am coming to that.' He shot her a dark look, before continuing. 'She directed him to the sheltered area behind the laurels as the wind was getting up. Once they were hidden from sight she confronted him about his "other ladies" and the fact he ought to commit to her, as she claimed he'd promised.'

'Do you think he really had?' Miss Busby asked.

'I doubt it.' The inspector sighed. 'He may have given that impression, but he wasn't stupid. I imagine most of it was all in her head. She told him she wanted him to stop seeing the others, to pass the policies on to someone else.'

'But he couldn't, of course,' Miss Busby realised.

'Because his scheme would have been uncovered!' Lucy scribbled delightedly. 'It would almost make a novel, never mind a newspaper article!'

The inspector rolled his eyes. 'Potter told her about the share in the race horse, and the status it would bring, but she wasn't impressed, and only wanted him to spend whatever time he had left with her. And only her.'

'*Was* he ill, truly?' Miss Busby asked.

'I doubt we'll ever know for certain,' McKay replied gravely. 'Nothing came up on the post mortem, but we may be able to send further samples to the lab. Although there seems little point.'

'I can't imagine why Dorothy would have lied about the blood on his handkerchief.'

'Unless she was protecting his reputation,' Lucy offered.

'What was left of it,' the inspector grumbled. 'Anyway, when he wouldn't give her what she wanted, she saw red, as she put it. Said the last straw was when he wouldn't even agree to decline Mrs Montgomery's offer and dine at the vicarage instead. At that point, she spotted a laurel branch that had snapped and fallen in the wind, and swung it at him in frustration.'

Lucy gasped.

'I don't believe she meant to kill him, but he slipped on the bank and fell into the water, hitting his head on the icy ground as he went. If he hadn't been wearing such a heavy coat, he may have been able to pull himself out, despite the blows. Or if Miss Simpson had gone to fetch help…but she simply left him.'

'*That's* what will convict her,' Lucy said with frightening certainty. 'Leaving him there to drown. Such awful callousness.'

'Or perhaps just shock, and fear,' Miss Busby

tempered. 'But you haven't mentioned the blanket, Inspector, and it has been puzzling me from the outset. Why would Frances pick it up from the ground and put it over her head if she was sure the lake was deserted?'

'It occurred to her as they walked to the lake that if she had recognised Potter's car from the road, anyone passing by that way might also recognise her. And with his car parked on the path, she became concerned. When she spotted the blanket on the ground, she put it over her head like a shawl, thinking with her head covered that her identity would be protected.'

'But when the tramp saw her from much closer…'

The inspector nodded glumly. 'She said she would have wrapped the blanket around her face, but it was grubby and cold and she couldn't bear it. She couldn't be sure he'd recognised her. When he came to the church the day we were searching for him, she assumed it was to accuse her.'

Miss Busby's heart sank. 'That's why she thinks me responsible.'

'Absolute nonsense,' Lucy said swiftly. 'Murderers always blame someone else.'

The inspector nodded. 'He had seen her either way, his talking to you had nothing to do with it. Apparently she'd been praying when he slipped in. He asked for a drink, and when she refused, he made a comment that she ought to be a little kinder, "in the circumstances." Frances took it as blackmail and decided to go and fetch him one. "He wanted a drink and I gave him one alright," she said. Laced with the leftovers of one of her mother's sleeping draughts, prescribed before she died.'

'Callous to the end,' Lucy proclaimed in disgust.

'Or simply driven quite mad by unrequited love,' Miss Busby tempered sadly. 'It's such a powerful emotion, after all.'

Lucy scoffed.

'She says she panicked,' the inspector continued, 'but her actions smack of calm consideration to me, including picking up the shawl to disguise herself before she killed Potter.'

Lucy gave him a curt nod of approval.

Miss Busby sighed. 'And what of her brother's involvement?' she asked.

'She's trying to protect him, of course, but I'd stake my life on him being involved. Brierly is going to London tomorrow to speak with an officer from the Met. If there's even a hint of suspicion regarding Henry Rawlins's apparent disappearance…or a whiff of barbiturates…'

Lucy gasped.

'Her mother died before Frances became engaged to Rawlins, so the Veronal would have been available to the Simpsons even then…'

'*Three* murders!' Lucy's eyes widened.

'I would ask, Miss Wesley, that you keep that out of your report at this time.'

'But we had an agreement!'

'It may jeopardise any investigation into Rawlins, assuming he's dead, and let the vicar off the hook.' He directed a stern look at her.

'Fine. But everything else is fair game?'

'Yes. Miss Simpson has made a full, written confession with a lawyer present. You are free to print that we are holding someone local under suspicion of murdering two people, but you are aware under the law of 'sub judice' that you cannot name names.'

'I am quite aware, thank you, Inspector,' Lucy replied tartly.

He stood up. 'I must get to Oxford. I need to pass Frances' confession to my superiors.'

'Of course. I'll take you right away. Will you be alright on your own, Miss Busby?' Lucy asked.

'Oh, yes, I should think so,' she replied. 'I have Pud and Barnaby. And I'm sure the news will spread in no time. I shall expect Adeline Fanshawe on my doorstep in time for tea. Possibly before.'

'Come along, Inspector. We'll get you to the station, then I can butt heads with my editor. We may need a special edition!' She went out, looking almost radiant. 'I'll bring you a copy of the *News* tomorrow, Miss Busby,' she called over her shoulder.

McKay paused on the doorstep and cleared his throat awkwardly. 'Thank you for your assistance, Miss Busby. You have been...'

'A constant thorn?' she suggested with a wry smile.

'...invaluable,' he proclaimed, his tone sincere.

'Well, you had best be going,' she said, flushing a little pink around the ears.

'Goodbye, Miss Busby.'

'Goodbye, Inspector.'

With the door closed behind him and the car disappearing into the distance, Miss Busby looked around the cottage and gave a small sigh.

'Well, Pud?' she asked. 'What now?'

The ginger Tom sprung onto her favourite chair and stared expectantly at her.

'Ah. Perfect,' she said, settling down beside him and picking up her long-neglected novel from the small side table. As the flames crackled brightly in the hearth, and news of Frances Simpson's confession no doubt began to spread like wildfire through the area, Miss Busby directed her attention back to her favourite fictional protagonist once more, relieved that the burden of solving this particular mystery would not rest upon her shoulders.

EPILOGUE

Wednesday, December 24ᵗʰ

'It is wonderful, Isabelle, to see the place so lively again,' Adeline Fanshawe commented, resplendent in her finest frock, a dark red silk mix with a double row of shimmering fat pearls and earrings to match.

Miss Busby smiled at the sight of her living room bustling with friends. Candles burned brightly on the tree and the mantelpiece; flaming logs crackled in the grate, and Dorothy Cranford, Enid Montgomery, and Belinda Tasker each had a glass of sweet sherry in their hands and smiles upon their lips.

Mary Fellows, too, was pink-cheeked and animated, holding a tiny tot of whisky, which was her preferred tipple. She looked so much better, her hair tied neatly and wearing a thick warm frock, rather than her dressing gown. Nurse Delaney sat at her side, ostensibly keeping an eye on her as a condition of her afternoon out. The pair were deep in discussion of some mystery novel or other, a large bag of books beside Mary ready to accompany her back to Hill House later that evening. Barnaby sat at Mary's feet, but cast regular looks towards Miss Busby to be sure both of his mistresses were present.

Mary caught her smiling down at the lively little dog, so much more relaxed now than when he'd first arrived. Yesterday he'd even forgotten to bite Dennis when he'd brought the afternoon post.

'Are you *quite* sure you're happy to have him, Isabelle?' she asked. Mary had told them all upon arrival that she'd decided to apply for the new sheltered housing development in Little Minton, but although cats were permitted, dogs were not.

'Quite happy,' Miss Busby assured her once more. 'And I'll bring him to visit you often. Not that you'll be short of company there, I'm sure.'

'I'm thinking of joining you, Mary,' Dorothy said from beside the fire. 'Once the money comes through.'

'Really?' Mary asked, her eyes glinting in the candlelight. 'How wonderful!'

'Yes, I think perhaps a property developed with the older resident in mind – no more steep staircases or awkward corners – might be just the thing for my hip. And young Dennis heard from a labourer on site that there's talk of a community bus to be arranged by the owners. I should be able to visit George at the sanatorium.'

Miss Busby felt a warmth inside that she didn't believe was due to the sherry – even though she was on her second glass. 'How wonderful, Dorothy,' she said. 'I can visit you both when I bring Barnaby.'

'Room for one more?' Belinda asked shyly. All eyes turned to her. 'Only I've been thinking, the shop is getting a bit much for me now, and with the money... well, I shan't need to struggle...'

'Oh, how marvellous! We shall make quite the club! Who does that leave? Enid? What about you?' Mary asked.

'I don't think so,' Enid replied with a shake of her head. 'I have Jilly, Cook, and the boot boy to think of.'

'Well, the place can't be fully staffed yet, why don't you put in a good word for them?'

That gave Enid pause.

'And if you sold the house,' Miss Busby suggested, 'you'd have more than enough to seek out the best possible healthcare. Perhaps even take a restorative holiday somewhere warm and beneficial to the lungs?'

The others nodded eagerly. Enid seemed to waver for a moment, then said, 'One ought never make big decisions whilst drinking sherry. But I shall consider it, post-festive season,' she conceded.

'Isabelle, now, how about you? Will you join our merry band?' Mary asked.

'But she can't,' Adeline said. 'Who would have the dog?'

'Oh.' Mary looked crestfallen. Miss Busby laughed. 'I don't think it's for me, Mary. Not just yet at least. Barnaby, Pud, and I have our own little club for the moment.'

'Well, you shall be an honorary member!'

'I would like that very much.' She placed a hand over Mary's, and squeezed.

As the afternoon slipped into evening, and the sherry bottle ran dry, Miss Busby's guests began to make their various ways home with cheery goodbyes, and merry Christmas wishes, until only Adeline remained.

'Well, what a week it has been,' she said, finishing off the last of the plum pudding Miss Busby had made for the occasion. 'Whoever would have thought we had a killer at the vicarage. I still can't quite believe it.'

Miss Busby nodded solemnly. 'I suppose you never do know about people. Not really.'

'You know about *me*, I hope,' she sniffed.

'Yes, Adeline.' Miss Busby gave a wry smile. 'I know about you.'

'Good. Well. I had best be off. Now, are you sure you want to spend tomorrow with the Wesley girl? I know Jemima would love to see you, and I have room in the car.'

'Quite sure, thank you,' Miss Busby said, getting to her feet and starting to clear the plates. 'Lucy assures me I shall find a kindred spirit in her father, Richard Lannister, and was really very keen to have me stay. And it will be nice to spend Christmas with some youngsters again.'

'Are you calling me old, Isabelle?'

'No older than myself, Adeline.'

'Fair enough. Well, Merry Christmas then, and I shall see you in the New Year.'

'Merry Christmas, Adeline.'

Miss Busby was just beginning to doze by the fire later that evening when a quiet knock sounded at the door. She almost didn't answer. Lucy wasn't picking her up until morning, and she'd seen all of her friends. But curiosity got the better of her, and she rose to find Inspector McKay on her doorstep holding out a small parcel wrapped in tartan-patterned paper.

'Just a little something,' he said awkwardly.

'How kind! Would you like to come in?'

'I can't, I'm afraid.' His face was shadowed under his hat. 'I have to catch the sleeper to Edinburgh. I wanted to drop it off before I leave. I look forward to seeing you in the New Year.'

'Let's hope in somewhat cheerier circumstances,' Miss Busby said with a smile.

'Aye, let's hope indeed.' He hesitated. 'It's hardly in keeping with the season, but I thought you'd like to know that the Met have tracked down Harry Rawlins.'

'Ah? And is he still alive?'

'He is, but after he parted from Frances Simpson, he was very ill for days afterwards. He recovered, but swore he'd never go near her again. He was convinced she'd slipped something into his drink.'

'He didn't report it?'

'No.' McKay's eyes darkened. 'He's not the sort to go to the police.'

'Well, that tallies with what Maggie at the Tea Rooms said of him.' Miss Busby nodded. 'But at least he hadn't been quietly buried in the churchyard.'

McKay grinned. 'No, and I don't have to arrest the vicar just before Christmas, either.' He raised his hat. 'Have an enjoyable holiday.'

'Thank you. Travel safely, Inspector.'

He strode away into the dark and she closed the door behind him. The parcel was an unexpected surprise, she put it on the kitchen table, where Barnaby proceeded to whine at it excitedly.

'Whatever is it?' she said, watching his ears twitch and his tail wag. 'Well, let's see. No one need know we've looked early.' She peeled back a corner of the paper to reveal a tin of Crawford's Assorted Scotch Shortbread.

'Aha!' She laughed, and ruffled his ears. 'Shall we share a piece now? I won't tell if you won't...'

I do hope you enjoyed this book. This is the first in the Miss Busby series, and more are on the way.

Karen Baugh Menuhin is the author of the best selling Heathcliff Lennox murder mystery series.

If you'd like to know more, would you like to take a look at the Readers Club website? As a member of the Readers Club, you'll receive the FREE ebook and FREE audio short story, 'Heathcliff Lennox – France 1918'. There's also access to the 'World of Lennox' page, where you can view portraits of Lennox, Swift, Greggs, Foggy, Tubbs, Persi and Tommy Jenkins.

Plus you'll receive occasional newsletters with updates and free giveaways.

You can find the Heathcliff Lennox Readers Club, and more, at **karenmenuhin.com**

* * *

Here's the full Heathcliff Lennox series list. You can find each book on Amazon and all good bookstores.

Book 1: *Murder at Melrose Court*
Book 2: *The Black Cat Murders*
Book 3: *The Curse of Braeburn Castle*
Book 4: *Death in Damascus*
Book 5: *The Monks Hood Murders*
Book 6: *The Tomb of the Chatelaine*
Book 7: *The Mystery of Montague Morgan*
Book 8: *The Birdcage Murders*

Book 9: *A Wreath of Red Roses*

Book 10: *Murder at Ashton Steeple* – available for pre-order. Previewed date of publication, September 2023 (or earlier)

And there are Audible versions read by Sam Dewhurst-Phillips, who is superb, he reads all the voices, and it's just as if listening to a radio play. These can be found on Amazon, Audible and Apple Books.

A LITTLE ABOUT KAREN BAUGH MENUHIN

1920s, Cozy crime, Traditional Detectives, Downton Abbey – I love them! Along with my family, my dog and my cat.

At 60 I decided to write, I don't know why but suddenly the stories came pouring out, along with the characters. Eccentric Uncles, stalwart butlers, idiosyncratic servants, machinating Countesses, and the hapless Major Heathcliff Lennox. A whole world built itself upon the page and I just followed along...

An itinerate traveller all my life. I grew up in the military, often on RAF bases but preferring to be in the countryside when we could. I adore whodunnits.

I have two amazing sons – Jonathan and Sam Baugh, and his wife, Wendy, and five grandchildren, Charlie, Joshua, Isabella-Rose, Scarlett and Hugo.

I am married to Krov, my wonderful husband, who is a retired film maker and eldest son of the violinist, Lord Yehudi Menuhin. We live in the Cotswolds.

For more information my email address is: karenmenuhinauthor@littledogpublishing.com

Karen Baugh Menuhin is a member of The Crime Writers Association.

* * *

MORE ABOUT CO-AUTHOR ZOE MARKHAM

I'm an ex-teacher living in West Oxfordshire with my teenage son and our Jack Russell terrier. I'm fortunate enough to edit fiction for a living, and have had three Young Adult novels published. Miss Busby is my first foray into both adult fiction and the 1920s!

If you're not familiar with the Heathcliff Lennox series, here's a taster from the first book, *Murder at Melrose Court*.

CHAPTER 1

December 1920

'I must inform you, sir, that a body has been discovered on the front doorstep,' Greggs announced from the doorway.

My concentration was entirely taken up tying a Bibio. Only this morning I'd received a small box of precious seal fur for the precise purpose of creating this seemingly simple fly. The black fluff had required delicate teasing along waxed thread wound around the shaft of the hook, followed by a splash of red. I replaced the long-nosed pliers next to the screwdrivers, grips and whatnot on my workbench, and fumbled for the magnifying glass. All appeared well.

I was vaguely aware of Greggs hovering behind me and creating an annoying distraction – he knew how tricky tying off was.

'I'm busy,' I told him, eyes fixed on the vice holding the lure, scissors poised in one hand, thread held taut in the other.

'Major Lennox, sir,' Greggs persevered. 'It is rather urgent.'

I snipped, then straightened up, the fly complete, and stood back to better survey my work. 'Who is it?'

'I do not know, sir, he is in no condition to furnish a name.'

'What are you talking about, Greggs?' I looked at him sharply, wondering if he'd started early. 'Didn't you ask him?'

'The person on the doorstep is dead, sir,' he replied.

'Dead?'

'Dead, sir.' Greggs had been my personal batman and butler throughout the four years of the Great War; we both knew more than we wanted to about death, and it seemed to me that he was unlikely to be mistaken in this matter. I left the gunroom briskly and made my way through the hall. Greggs tried to reach the door first – he failed. I yanked it sharply open and walked out into the fresh winter's day. It was crisp and cold with a brisk breeze; sunshine fell upon the body of a large fat man lying on his back across the worn stone flags of my portico.

Greggs was right; the man looked very dead. 'Did you check?' I asked.

'No, sir – back's been playing up.' Greggs motioned vaguely behind him.

'Your paunch is more of an impediment than your spine, Greggs.'

'As you say, sir.'

'Well, best have a look – just in case...'